Mills & Boon
Best Seller Romance

A chance to read and collect some of the best-loved novels from Mills & Boon—the world's largest publisher of romantic fiction.

Every month, four titles by favourite Mills & Boon authors will be re-published in the *Best Seller Romance* series.

A list of other titles in the *Best Seller Romance* series can be found at the end of this book.

Elizabeth Hunter

THE TREE OF IDLENESS

MILLS & BOON LIMITED
LONDON · TORONTO

First published 1973
Australian copyright 1982
Philippine copyright 1982
This edition 1982

© Elizabeth Hunter 1973

ISBN 0 263 73776 4

Set in Linotype Baskerville 10pt. solid
02-0282

*Made and printed in Great Britain by
Richard Clay (The Chaucer Press) Ltd,
Bungay, Suffolk*

CHAPTER ONE

THEY were a quarter of an hour late in landing. Caroline Fielding glanced impatiently at her neat gold watch and ruefully tried to shift into a more comfortable position. A quarter of an hour was not a long time, but anything seemed excessive after the long, four-hour flight from London. Yet when she thought how quick it was now compared to even a few years ago when she had made the journey several times a year to spend the school holidays with her aunt ... Her own parents had seldom been in England in those days and she had welcomed the chance to stay with her aunt rather than go to one of the many holiday homes her father had hopefully found for her. It had been an early lesson that money, even when amply provided, did not necessarily mean either comfort or happiness.

And now Aunt Hilda was ill and had asked in turn that Caroline should help her. It had not been the most convenient moment to answer the summons. Another week in London, Caroline thought, and Jeffrey Carson would surely have asked her to marry him. Another week—it didn't bear thinking about! She was no nearer knowing what she wanted now than she had been months ago. They were a habit with one another, she thought. They went to the same places, did the same things, and were suitably matched in every way. It was only now and then that she hungered for another, half-forgotten excitement that had had nothing to do with Jeffrey at all.

The sun struck hot as they left the plane. Caroline watched her fellow passengers struggle across the concrete apron, laden down with their possessions, and followed at a more sober pace, well pleased that for once she was uncluttered, having only her handbag and her coat to carry. The immigration formalities completed, she wandered out to the front of the airport building, wondering if her aunt would have thought to send anyone to meet her. She half hoped it would be Philip Klearchos. It had been years since she had seen him. She remembered, smiling, how he had always been her aunt's favourite, despite the fact that he had been her husband's nephew and no blood relation of hers at all. But then her aunt had fallen in love with the whole island of Cyprus when she had fallen for the handsome, black-haired Greek Cypriot who had become her husband. She had embraced her new life with both hands, spoke both Greek and Turkish, and had tried to instil the same enthusiasm for the place into her niece. Caroline had not resisted very hard, but another life had always been waiting for her, a life built around her roving parents and their interests, a life which had recently become much more real to her now that her father had retired from his drilling for oil and Jeffrey Carson had arrived on the scene.

'Miss Fielding?'

Caroline started and turned, surprised to see a complete stranger addressing her. 'I am Miss Fielding,' she agreed tentatively.

'Kyria Klearchos asked that your car should be delivered to the airport. I have it outside. There is only the formality of signing certain papers and writing out the cheque for the car. You have your international driving licence with you?'

Bewildered, Caroline nodded. 'But I shan't need a car of my own here!' she protested.

'Madame, your aunt, ordered it to be brought to you here,' the salesman reproved her. 'She was unable to see me personally, but her nephew came on her behalf to choose and test the car. There is no mistake, *kyria.*'

That sounded like Philip! 'I expected him to come and meet me,' Caroline said aloud, unable to hide entirely her disappointment that he had not come.

'But with your own car you can take the Geunyeli

6

road to Kyrenia. If he had come, you would have had to go round the long way or wait for the United Nations convoy. I am sure that is why he hasn't come himself.'

Caroline accepted the explanation with a slight shrug. She had forgotten that the United Nations was still policing the island, holding the so-called Green Line between the two communities. When she had visited Cyprus as a child, it had been before the troubles that had blown up again after Independence. She remembered the people as welcoming, dignified, and tremendously friendly to a child such as herself. She couldn't help feeling that the tension she had read about in the papers must sit oddly on Cypriot shoulders, be they Greek or Turk.

'Where do I sign?' she asked casually. He pointed to the places on the transfer papers for the car, checked her driving licence, and accepted the cheque she wrote out for him. Caroline was not frightened by the cost of the car, but she allowed herself a momentary annoyance with her aunt for not consulting her first before spending her money. How could her aunt know that her niece was as wealthy now, thanks to her father, as she had been well-heeled as a child?

But when she saw the car she realised that she had no cause for complaint. It was the sort of car she had always dreamed of owning, though when she saw the name Gallant written on the dashboard, she was not aware that she had ever heard the name before.

'It is a Japanese car, Miss Fielding. It has all the usual fittings: a radio, seat-belts, heater, everything! You are pleased with it?'

Caroline gave him a smile which turned into a grin. 'Yes, I'm pleased,' she admitted. 'Thank you for bringing it to the airport for me.'

'I was glad to oblige Kyria Klearchos,' the man replied. He sketched a salute and shut the door on her, stepping back smartly as she let in the clutch and drove away from the airport as smoothly as if she had been driving the car all her life.

The road was just as she had remembered it. A shepherd led his flock of sheep and goats over the hills beside the road, waving his hand in greeting as the car passed by. A couple of Turkish farmers, dressed in the baggy trousers that both communities like to affect, gossiped as they sat at one of the tables put out in front of one of the numerous cafés that lined the route. On either side the barren hills rose and fell for as far as she could see, to change rapidly as she came within sight of the Kyrenia range of mountains and passed through the checkpoint where a Turkish policeman stood on guard, and ran down the last mile or so into Kyrenia.

She did not go into the town as she had first thought of doing, but turned off immediately on to the road that led to the village of Bellapais, where her aunt had lived ever since her marriage to Michael Klearchos just after the war. A great deal of building was going on, but otherwise it was just as Caroline recalled it when she thought back to the holidays she had spent there.

The village stood high above the valley on a fertile slope, and was dominated by the ancient abbey that had fallen into ruin, but which was still used as the church which served the surrounding community. The narrow streets were full of people and donkeys who moved lazily aside at her approach, glancing without interest at the slim, fair girl at the wheel of the car. It was strange not to be recognised, but that was the penalty of growing up. She had been a schoolgirl when she had last pushed her way through these very streets.

Her aunt's villa had not changed either. It stood, leaning out over the village, its windows closely shuttered. It was built in the old style, rendered and painted a startling white, with carved wooden doors, and bamboo ceilings patterned in squares of wood for coolness. The car had to creep up a concrete ramp to park in the garage that had been dug out beneath the house. Another car was already in the garage, which surprised Caroline.

She couldn't remember that her aunt had ever driven anywhere.

There was a babble of voices inside the house as she pushed open the door and walked into the hall. The wooden furniture, consisting mainly of wooden chests and scrubbed wooden dressers, bore a coating of dust that never would have been there in the old days. Caroline felt a sudden coldness around her heart. Could her aunt be really ill? Too ill, for instance, to leave her own room?

'*Aunt Hilda!*'

'In here, my dear! Come in, come in!'

Caroline hesitated in the doorway of her aunt's bedroom. At first sight it was full of people, more than half of them dressed in black, and all of them women, but as she blinked in the gloomy atmosphere in which her aunt chose to live, she saw that in reality there were only five women gathered there and that all of them were looking accusingly at her.

Caroline tiptoed across the room and dropped a hasty kiss on her aunt's cheek. 'Hello, Aunt Hilda. I'm sorry you're not well,' she began.

'I am dying,' her aunt returned simply.

Caroline was appalled. 'Surely not!'

Aunt Hilda laughed softly. 'It is not so very bad, my dear. Life has meant very little to me since Michael died. It has been a very lonely time for me.'

Caroline flushed. 'I *would* have come——'

'Of course you would have come! You have come! Now that I have sent for you!'

'I wanted to,' Caroline claimed. 'But Father retired this year, and before that——'

'It doesn't matter,' her aunt cut her off. 'You are here now. I am grateful to you, Caroline. I wanted someone of my own just now. It isn't fair to leave it all to Philip to look after an ailing old woman.'

Caroline pulled herself together with difficulty. 'I thought Philip might meet me?' she said coolly.

'Why? I arranged for you to have a car. Wasn't it

there, waiting for you?'

'Yes, yes, it was.' But it hadn't been the same as having Philip meet her, Caroline thought. The last time she had been here, she and Philip had done everything together, and she had wanted to see him again for that if for no other reason.

'Well then?'

Caroline met her aunt's piercing glance and summoned up a smile. 'I've no complaints, though I could have done with a cheaper car for the time I'm here. I could even have hired.'

'Are you wishing me into an early grave?'

Caroline knew that she was being teased, but she was not quite comfortable with her aunt as yet. 'Of course not!' she disclaimed.

'Good. I told Philip to pick you out a car you wouldn't be ashamed to be seen driving, so you can blame him if it's too grand for you! Though I imagine you can still afford the best?'

Caroline bit her lip. 'I suppose so.' She gave her aunt a concerned look, but it was too dark to see how she was looking. She *sounded* as sprightly as ever! 'Wouldn't you like me to open the shutters?' she suggested.

'Not until my friends have gone,' Aunt Hilda rapped out. 'They have been extraordinarily kind to me these last few days. I don't know what I would have done without them.' She waited expectantly while Caroline searched her memory for the few odd words of Greek with which she could add her own thanks to her aunt's. Surprisingly, for it had been a long time since she had said anything in that language, the words came tripping to her tongue and the three older women, looking like so many crows about the bed, thawed into wide smiles and a flood of recollections about her own exploits as a child that made them all laugh. One of the two younger girls, who both wore colours, came out of her corner, smoothing her skirt down over her hips.

'You don't remember me, do you?' she said to Caroline. 'No, don't apologise, you hardly knew me in the old days. It was only after you had gone that Philip and I became friendly. I'm Ileana Zavallis.'

Caroline muttered a greeting, disliking the other girl on sight. Despite the dim light, there was no mistaking the sulky look about the mouth, or the languorous sweep of her eyes, half-hiding the insolent expression with which she looked at any other woman, or the too hot look of flattery she undoubtedly cast at any man who came within range.

'Ileana comes and sees me often,' Aunt Hilda put in.

Caroline was surprised. She would not have thought that the other girl was the type to give up her time for an old woman to whom she was not even related.

'Kyria Hilda makes coming here a joy to me,' the girl responded, dropping her eyes in apparent shyness.

Caroline met her aunt's malicious gaze. 'It's kind of you nevertheless,' she said politely. 'I hope you'll still come now I am here?'

Insolent eyes looked her up and down, the sulky mouth turned down at the corners. 'I shall come, yes. I shall come to see the Kyria—and Philip too!'

'Philip?' The name was out before Caroline could prevent it.

'He is living here now,' her aunt told her.

'*Here?* But what about his parents?'

Ileana tossed her hair back behind her shoulders. 'His parents died a couple of years ago. Didn't you know?'

Caroline shook her head. 'What happened?'

'I thought everybody knew! I was quite sure that your aunt would have told *you*,' Ileana marvelled. 'I suppose you weren't interested?'

Caroline swallowed down her anger and turned to her aunt. 'Why didn't you tell me, Aunt Hilda?'

'I thought it would be soon enough to tell you when you came out to see me,' her aunt retorted. Caroline's own anger died at the tartness in her voice. She *should* have come to Cyprus earlier; she would have done if she hadn't become so involved with Jeffrey.

'I see,' she said. 'Will you tell me what happened now?'

'They were drowned. They took the yacht out together, leaving the man they usually took with them behind, because they wanted to get in a quick sail before dusk. A storm blew up, very suddenly, as Mediterranean storms so often do. They ran for shelter, but they never made it. They were found, of course, and are buried with the rest of the family, but Philip hated being on his own, so he moved in here with me.'

Caroline was very conscious of her aunt's own sadness at the tragedy that had been summed up in those few words. When, just after the war, Hilda Fielding had been posted to Cyprus, she had been quite simply furious. She had gone into the Services as her bit towards the war effort, but she had not enjoyed any of her two years in uniform and, once the war ended, she saw no reason why she should continue to wear it. But in Cyprus she had met Michael and Constantine Klearchos. Within weeks she had been married to Michael and had never come back to England again. Constantine's wife, Amalia, had become her best friend on the island and, when Michael had died, if it had not been for her brother-in-law and his wife Hilda would have completely broken down. To have lost them too was a burden that must have done much to make her so ill now, Caroline thought, and wished again that she had known and that she had come out sooner to her aunt.

'I see,' she said again. 'I wish I had known.'

Aunt Hilda sniffed. 'I think Philip was expecting to hear from you. When he didn't, he said people only lost touch with old friends when they wanted to and that you probably didn't intend coming back to Cyprus.'

'Oh, it wasn't that!' Caroline blinked, horribly aware that she was close to tears. 'It wasn't that! I've thought about the holidays I spent here a lot, and I

12

always meant to come back. But it didn't work out that way——'

'I know,' Aunt Hilda said wearily. 'You've already explained. My brother retired and you felt obliged to live at home for a while.'

Caroline nodded uncomfortably. She really couldn't tell her aunt about Jeffrey—not with all these other people present. Besides, she didn't think Aunt Hilda was going to understand just what Jeffrey meant to her. He was very different from anyone in the Klearchos family. He was gentle and not at all arrogant—more, he was quite prepared that she should take the lead in their relationship. Most of all, he was very different from Philip who had never allowed her a say in anything from the first moment she had met him.

Ileana looked pleased with herself. 'I see Philip often,' she announced with pride. Her eyes met Caroline's, daring the English girl to object to this arrangement. She might just as well have said, 'You've had your chance with him and you didn't choose to take it, so it's my turn now!' Caroline wondered why she didn't. Her aunt would have cheered her on in her present mood.

'Philip has always done exactly as he likes,' she said aloud.

Ileana smiled slowly. 'He is a man. A man expects to be looked up to here in Cyprus.'

Caroline flushed, aware of her aunt's malicious amusement. It was almost as though they had already met Jeffrey and found him wanting, though for the life of her she couldn't see that there was anything particularly admirable in a man who thought himself innately superior to every female around him, as Philip did, and as his uncle and father had done before him.

'In England——' she began.

Her aunt made a caustic sound. 'A day never dawns that I don't thank God I was born a woman,' she said slyly. 'And for Michael, who made me realise that I

13

was a woman—his woman. He made all my other ambitions irrelevant. What greater happiness can one ask?'

Ileana looked impatient. 'Most women want children——'

Caroline glared at her. 'But not to be married for the sake of the future generation,' she put in smoothly, glad to see the surprised reaction of the other girl.

'There is no danger of that with Philip!' Ileana retorted.

'Of course not,' Caroline agreed. 'But he is the only Klearchos left, isn't he? And I'm sure Aunt Hilda nags him to death about it. She always did!'

Her aunt chuckled. '*Caroline!* No one nags Philip twice about anything! A nudge in the right direction is as much as one can hope for. Don't put ideas into Ileana's head, my dear.'

Caroline started. She cast a look at Aunt Hilda's face, but it was impossible to tell what her relative was thinking. 'You look tired, Aunt,' she murmured. 'Wouldn't you like to rest for a while?'

'I do nothing else! But there, I suppose I must. But tell them to go gently, Caro. They don't understand that there is something in the English nature that makes us sometimes want to be alone, and they are very kind to me in their own way—especially Ileana!'

The women had already noticed the fatigue on the Englishwoman's face, however, and were gathering their possessions together with a flurry of their black skirts.

'Come, Ileana! Kyria Klearchos will wish to speak privately with her niece!'

Ileana rose from her perch on the foot of the bed with a flounce and dropped a kiss on Aunt Hilda's cheek. 'If you need me, I shall be glad to come any time,' she said. '*Any time!* I promised Philip I would.'

'Very kind of you, my dear,' Aunt Hilda murmured.

'It's no more than I ought to do,' Ileana assured her earnestly. 'I feel like an honorary niece of yours, even

14

though we are not related, and I'll still be here when Caroline has to go back to England.'

Aunt Hilda frowned. 'She's only just got here!'

'But she'll have to go home some time!' Ileana protested.

'*Why?*' Aunt Hilda turned a frightened glance on her niece. 'My brother has his wife. Why do you have to go back?'

Caroline hesitated. 'I can't stay here for ever,' she managed, her throat dry. 'I have my own life—in England——'

'I see,' said her aunt. 'How long can you spare me?'

'Oh, it isn't like that!' Caroline pleaded. 'Only I promised Jeffrey——'

'Jeffrey?' Aunt Hilda's eyes blazed angrily. 'Who is Jeffrey?'

'Just someone I know.'

'A man?'

Caroline laughed rather wildly. 'Well, of course a man! His name is Jeffrey—Jeffrey Carson.'

'Are you going to marry this man?'

Caroline licked her lips. 'I don't know. He—he hasn't asked me yet——'

'What has that got to do with anything? Do you *want* to marry him?'

'I—I think so!'

'And I think not! Goodness me, I never thought to hear you shilly-shallying like this over any man. At least you'll be able to make up your mind while you're here! You'd better invite him out here to visit you and see how he stands up to a different environment. *Don't know!* It sounds a pretty wishy-washy relationship to me!'

Caroline wished violently that Ileana would go and not stand there, staring at her as though she were some kind of freak.

'I don't want to live with someone who'll think it's his right to order me about just because I'm his wife! Jeffrey is a very gentle person. He respects me and I respect him!'

Her aunt merely looked amused. 'Respect never made a good husband yet, not the kind of respect you mean, Caro *i anepsiá mou*. Never mind, I should like to meet this young man of yours just the same. Do your parents approve of him?'

'They think he is—suitable,' Caroline agreed more cheerfully. If Aunt Hilda liked her well enough to call her niece in Greek then she could not be as cross with her as she had supposed.

'Rich?'

'Suitable,' Caroline maintained.

'You prefer this man to *Philip*?' Ileana burst out. 'I am very glad, of course, but he must be a remarkable person. Perhaps he has heard of the size of your *prika*!'

Caroline tried to explain that the endless discussions about the bride's dowry that preceded every marriage in Cyprus were virtually unknown in England. 'Besides, I have very little of my own,' she added.

Ileana looked at her in disbelief. She would have liked to discuss it further, but the other women were waiting for her to take her leave with them. Caroline ushered her into the hall and walked with her to the front door, thanking all the ladies for their visit, firmly shutting the door after them.

When she went back into her aunt's bedroom, she found Aunt Hilda struggling to get out of bed and ran to help her.

'Aunt Hilda, why didn't you write before? If I'd known you were as bad as this I would have come no matter what Jeffrey and my father said! You know that! Why didn't you send for me before?'

'Philip wouldn't hear of it.'

'It hasn't anything to do with him! What changed your mind?'

Her aunt swayed on her feet. 'I thought it might be too late if I didn't. It's time Philip married and, when he does, he wants to live in this house. Most of the Klearchos lands belonged to Michael, my husband, as

16

the older brother, and it's right that Philip should have them. Michael and I always intended that you should live in Cyprus in the end. We never thought of your settling down in England somehow. It would all have been so *right* for you to have followed my example. Michael would have seen that you were amply provided for, but now I suppose Philip will look elsewhere. Ileana has an extensive dowry, I believe.'

Caroline stared at her aunt. 'Do you mean that Uncle Michael thought I might marry Philip? That he would have *bribed* Philip to marry me? Why, we were only children when I was last here!'

'That's the way marriages are often arranged out here. Michael was very sad when we couldn't have children together. He thought the Klearchos–Fielding mixture was a very good one. It was natural that he had hopes of you and Philip and did all he could to make the match as attractive as possible.'

'I think it's outrageous!' Caroline stormed. It *was* outrageous! Yet somehow she couldn't find it as shocking as she should. She could imagine Uncle Michael scheming to bring about a second marriage between the two families, and he would make the lure as attractive as he could to get his own way——! 'What was he going to use for bait?' she demanded, her suspicions thoroughly aroused.

'The Klearchos inheritance. It means a great deal to Philip——'

Caroline blinked. 'What was I to get out of it?'

Her aunt gave her a surprised look. 'A husband. What else?'

'Then it was all meant for Philip?'

'Of course. Naturally everything you owned would become his if he were to marry you. Don't think about it, darling, if it upsets you. We didn't know anything about this Jeffrey of yours then. It makes things rather awkward, but not impossible!'

'If I marry Jeffrey my money will be my own, and— and *everything else?*'

'I daresay, if that's important to you. Caroline, would you mind if I had a little sleep now? Why don't you go and take a look round the village? It's changed quite a lot since you were last here.'

'Has it?' Caroline gave her an uncertain look. 'How ill are you, Aunt Hilda?'

'Not ill enough that you can't go out and enjoy yourself every now and again, but bad enough to be glad to have you here.'

Still Caroline hesitated, but her aunt showed no sign of telling her anything more. 'Get along with you, dear! You must be thirsty and the girl is out visiting her future mother-in-law, so I can't offer you anything here. Why don't you go the new café in the village and have a coffee there?'

'All right,' Caroline agreed indifferently. 'What is it called?'

'The Tree of Idleness. What else?'

Caroline laughed, 'I thought that was where all the men sat when they sat under the tree by the old café?'

'I expect that was what gave them the idea. It's very pleasant there on *both* sides of the road, but women are more welcome in the Tree of Idleness, especially when they're on their own.'

Caroline settled her aunt back into bed, her spirits lifting as she thought about the village of Bellapais as she had known it. It would be fun to have a look round and talk to the donkeys and the odd person she recognised in the street. It made Jeffrey and her life in England seem very far away.

The village was not as much changed as she had first thought. The abbey was just as she remembered it, romantic, golden, and quite unlike the more common squat, domed Byzantine churches of Cyprus. It was a Frankish Gothic construction, much of it now in ruins, with only the church still in use and converted to the Greek Orthodox rite. Beside the abbey was the square that she remembered, where she had sat as a child, on the ground because Philip had always taken the only

18

chair, and had stared out across the valley to the sea. It was there that she had first thought the trees around the abbey had looked like a child's licked paintbrushes and had been laughed at by Philip for her pains. It had been there that the boy who had been no more than a pleasant companion for the holidays had turned into something more, something that she hadn't known how to handle, when he had ducked his head and kissed her on the cheek, telling her that she was pretty enough to eat. Philip had had an eye for the girls even then, but she had been a shy, gauche teenager not yet come to such things, and she had taken to her heels and run as fast as she could away from him. No one had ever known, though, how for years she had clung to the memory of that casual caress.

The new café, with its shops full of souvenirs for the tourists who flocked to the village, took up a large part of that square now. The name, written in English, showed who most of the customers were and a group of English young people were already seated at one of the tables, busily writing their postcards home.

Caroline chose a seat at the other end of the verandah, where she could look her fill at the abbey and remember the peace that she had always known in Cyprus, a peace that was threatened this time by her aunt's illness and meeting Philip again. She ordered herself a coffee from the waiter and sat back in her chair with a sigh. Philip would be a man now, not that it mattered to her. But she knew a nervous knocking of her heart as she thought of seeing him again. She put a hand up, shading her eyes from the glare of the sun. A step on the ground behind her made her half turn to see if her chair was in someone's way, but she was too late to move. A man's hand was placed on the back of her chair and a dark head came between her and the sun and kissed her full on the lips with an expertise that made her gasp.

'So,' said Philip—a Philip who was almost unrecognisable now that he had reached his full stature and had filled out accordingly. 'So, the poor little rich girl finally came! *Kalos orisate*—welcome back, Caroline Fielding!'

Caroline clenched her fists, shocked by a momentary, physical fear that danced through her veins at his touch.

'*Epharisto poli, kyrie*,' she murmured formally, and wondered why he laughed.

'Lord?' he mocked her. 'It used to be Philip in the old days!'

She blushed. He had given her no title, but then that was like him. He had not changed at all! 'Philip,' she amended, and turned away, not daring to look at him again.

CHAPTER TWO

'You haven't changed as much as I thought when I saw you from the abbey,' he said, his eyes bright with laughter. 'You have designed a very sophisticated shell for yourself. I approve!' He looked her over, noting with interest how she looked away, pretending she had not noticed, and the way the colour rose in a tide up her cheeks. 'You've grown up a bit,' he added. 'Last time I kissed you, you ran away!'

'Did I?' She shrugged her shoulders to show him that she couldn't remember the incident. It was a justifiable deceit, she thought. Anything was better than that he should know how long it had lingered in her memory, or how disturbing she had found the re-peat performance today. 'I expect you gave me cause to distrust you. You were always ordering me about in those days!'

'And now you've come back for more?'

She shook her head. 'Not I! Besides, I'm told you have other interests these days!'

He shrugged, not caring what she thought. 'Tell me about yourself,' he invited her. He sat down in the chair opposite her, effectively blocking out her view of the valley, and put his head on one side, watching her closely. 'What made you suddenly put duty above in-clination and come and see your aunt?'

'She wrote to me——' Caroline broke off. Why should she explain herself to him? His opinion couldn't possibly matter to her!

'Why didn't you come before?'

'My parents came back to settle in England,' she said simply. 'It was the first time for years that we could be a family together—not that it's any of your business!'

Philip frowned. 'I heard your father had retired. A bit young, isn't he?'

21

'One does retire early in the oil business. Did you expect him to stay in the Persian Gulf until he was sixty-five?'

'I hadn't thought about it,' he admitted. 'It's hard to imagine you having another life away from here. All right, Caroline Fielding, I acquit you of callously neglecting your aunt, but I still want to hear your answer to another charge——' She gave him a quick, startled look, her eyes wide— 'Why didn't you write when my parents were drowned?'

She looked away. It was ridiculous to suppose that he might have been hurt by her silence, so it was probably no more than a residue of anger at her neglect that had made him sound so stern and unyielding.

'I didn't know,' she said. She wriggled uncomfortably under his harsh gaze. That was one thing she had not remembered, how he could hand out a look like the Avenging Angel himself, a look which had always reduced her to pulp and made her stupidly anxious to please him. 'No one told me, Philip, until my aunt mentioned it just now. I'm very sorry. It must have been terrible——' She lapsed into silence, nervously picking at her fingers. 'I'm sorry,' she said again.

He must have been out in the sun a great deal to have a tan like that. It suited him. His black hair had always curled in a violent disorder, and his heavy-lidded dark eyes had always reminded her of the eyes of the saints who stared out at one from the mosaics in the ancient Byzantine churches, but as a boy he had always been rather pale. Perhaps it was because he had still been studying at the Pancyprian Gymnasium in Nicosia in those days. He had not had such strong-looking, wide shoulders in those days either, but his hands were still the same, hands that could give comfort as easily as they could coerce a reluctant shoolgirl into climbing higher, walking further, and diving deeper than she had really wanted to.

She looked up and was dismayed to discover that he had been studying her all the while she had been looking at him. She thought she had changed far less than he had. She was much the same shape as she had been then, and she wore her hair in much the same way, and her eyes were still the same shade of green.

'You could have written and told me yourself,' she went on unhappily. 'You knew how fond I was of your parents—especially Amalia.'

'I thought I knew,' he answered. 'I thought perhaps that now you have emerged from the chrysalis of adolescence you might have gone on to other interests?'

'Like what?' she demanded. 'I'm just the same now——'

'If you believe that, you'll believe anything!' he said dryly. 'What do you do to your hair to keep those yellow streaks in it?'

'N-nothing. It grows like that.'

'Hmm.' His lips twisted thoughtfully. 'I suppose the whole of you just grew like that?'

'I—I don't know what you mean!'

He looked hard at her. 'I'm not complaining. You make a very pleasant picture sitting there in the sun; beautiful, rich, and looking as though you have never soiled your hands with anything as mundane as work. But I'm sure a lot of men like you that way and have told you so, no?'

Caroline blushed, strangely reluctant to tell him about Jeffrey. 'At least I'm not mercenary enough to—to——'

'*Yes?*'

'N-nothing. I'd forgotten you were a Cypriot and that therefore things are different for you—in that way. I mean, that you wouldn't see anything—anything wrong in it!' she concluded.

'Wrong in what?'

'In marrying a girl for what she can bring you,' she said bluntly.

He raised his eyebrows. 'Aunt Hilda has been talking, I see! Are you expecting me to marry you for the Klearchos inheritance?'

'Of course not!' She looked down her nose at him, wondering what it would be like if someone like Philip—Philip himself!—should kiss her as a man kisses the woman he loves.

'There's no of course about it!' he retorted. 'Mind you, I'm making no promises. A pretty little butterfly is not my idea of a wife! I don't approve of playing in the shallows, when the whole depths of the ocean are out there waiting for me. It may be fun for a while, but it wouldn't last!'

Caroline found herself smiling. 'I remember,' she said. 'You almost drowned me last time I went swimming with you. *And* you made me thank you for rescuing me!'

'I like a woman to be well-mannered,' he said, somewhat smugly, she thought. 'That's why it made me so angry when you didn't write!'

'You could have written yourself,' she murmured. How could he put all the blame on her? It wasn't fair! But then when had Philip ever been fair? 'What do you want me to do? Go down on my knees and say I'm sorry?'

'You could try it,' he drawled. 'I'd say it was a long time before you put yourself out for anyone else's feelings. Tell me about this boy-friend of yours?'

Her eyes met his with a flash of anger. 'How do you know about him?' she demanded.

'There's always a boy-friend when a girl is as pretty as you are. Why don't you want to talk about him? I suppose he lets you walk all over him and you wish he'd stand up for himself more. Poor Caroline! You never did like a weak hand on the reins. Where did you find him? Or did your father find him for you?'

Caroline tensed indignantly. 'I can find my own friends! He's very nice! As a mattter of fact Aunt Hilda has suggested that I should invite him out here so you may meet him and then you can judge for yourself!'

His eyebrows rose. 'I already know what I think

about him.' His eyes showed open mockery. 'It's what you think that's interesting.' He smiled slowly. 'How do you find your aunt?' he asked, changing tack with a disconcerting thoroughness.

Caroline shivered. 'Does she get up at all?' she countered. 'She won't tell me what's wrong with her, but she looks awful. I wish she'd told me she was ill before. She must have known I'd come!'

'To do what?'

Caroline paled. 'To nurse her, of course. I'm not completely heartless! I'm—I'm very fond of her.' Unshed tears burned the back of her throat. 'I never thought you'd be like this!' she complained. 'I always thought you liked me.'

'Liked you? I'd need notice of that question. Liking isn't the first word that comes to mind when I think of you.'

'Then you *don't* like me!'

The mockery left his eyes to be replaced by another expression she liked even less. She was suddenly, heart-shakingly aware of her own femininity.

'I didn't say that,' he murmured. He took a long look at her mouth and smiled reflectively. 'Why do you want me to like you?'

She might have known he would make her feel a fool. 'I—I thought you did, that's all,' she said. 'It doesn't matter, though. I don't care!'

Philip leaned forward across the table, his face very near to hers. 'No?' His lips met hers and he put a hand behind her head to make sure she did not escape him. 'Try a little honesty for a change, my dear!'

'I don't know what you mean!' she declared. The feel of his mouth against hers had evoked a delight within her that she had never known with Jeffrey. Supposing Philip should guess how she felt? That would be a humiliation not to be borne!

'Then why don't you admit that you care very much what I think of you?' he said quietly.

'You're an old friend——'

'What has that got to do with it?'

Caroline opened her eyes wide. 'H-hasn't it?' she stammered.

'Not as far as I'm concerned!' He patted her hand and smiled kindly at her. 'At least I've found out what I wanted to know, Caroline.'

'Oh?' The single, frigid syllable made him laugh.

He looked mockingly at her. 'You're not yet a woman, whatever this boy-friend of yours has been telling you, and that is just as well for you!'

She licked her lips, swallowing the lump that had gathered in her throat. 'I don't know what you're talking about! I'm not sixteen now! That was a long time ago! You can't say I'm not a woman when I'm twenty-two!'

'A maiden; a callow, green girl with no experience of life——'

'I'm not! Anyone would think you were the first man to ever kiss me!' she told him.

'I was!'

She put a hand to her mouth, wishing that she had not crossed swords with him over anything as trivial and as embarrassing to her as the memory of that first, fleeting caress. 'But not the last!'

Philip stood up lazily. 'I daresay I shall be that too.' He looked down at her, suddenly impatient. 'My dear girl, you don't know what you're talking about. I doubt if any man has kissed you, really kissed you, in your whole life! If you stay around for long enough, and stay looking as pretty as you do now, I may take your education in hand and give you a taste of what being a woman can mean before you turn your back on the whole venture with this boy-friend of yours. But at the moment, you still have to convince me that there is anything there to rescue——'

'Oh!' she gasped. 'I'd forgotten how arrogantly conceited you are, Philip Klearchos! I hate you!'

'I doubt it. Any more than you hated me when you

26

were sixteen and my father used to tease you by calling you Kyria Philip Klearcho*thoo*! The woman of Philip Klearchos, in case you have forgotten all your Greek! *Yinéka mou! My* woman! Ah, you do remember! Then don't pretend to me that you don't!' He put a coin under his coffee cup and sketched a farewell salute in her direction. 'I'll see you up at the house,' he said. 'Don't be long, as someone has to get us a meal tonight if you want to eat. *Adio!*'

Caroline sat on in a stunned silence. There was so much that she had forgotten, she thought ruefully. She had certainly forgotten how women in the Greek language take their husband's or father's name in the genitive case, making her Caroline of Fielding, Caroline belonging to Fielding, or, worse still, Caroline belonging to Philip Klearchos, as his father had used to call her. No wonder most Greek women preferred to be known by their Christian names!

Naturally it had not taken Philip long to remind her. Her face burned at some of the other things he had had to say to her. Yet he had been quite right, she did care what he thought of her, she always had. It was that which had made it such a bitterly disappointing encounter. She had been eager to see him again, to bask in the warmth of his approval that she had come out to visit her aunt, and he hadn't approved of her at all. More, he had let her know that he despised her as being *callow*, a word she would never have applied to herself or anyone else, and had confused her, and kissed her, and had made her feel more of a woman than she ever had, even if he didn't consider her one.

He was living in her aunt's house now. She couldn't stay under the same roof with him. She could not! Her heart pounded within her. Supposing he were to make good his threat of adding to her education? He was quite capable of it and her defences already needed a strategic overhaul after their first short meeting. But she couldn't desert Aunt Hilda as soon as she had come either. It was a fine fix, and she'd only arrived that day!

Caroline stood up, pushing her chair back as she did so. It made her feel crosser still to find that Philip had left sufficient money to pay for her coffee with his, without asking her, and without giving her the opportunity of thanking him. She supposed she would have to find the opportunity that evening, and that annoyed her more than ever. She didn't want to have to thank him for anything! She didn't want to acknowledge his presence even, let alone be gracious to him.

She was still brooding over the problem he had presented her with when she let herself in the door of her aunt's villa. Her shoes were rubber-soled and so she had made no sound as she came up to the door and pushed it open. She and Aunt Hilda stared at each other in mutual surprise.

'Oh, darling, you're up!' Caroline said with real pleasure.

Her aunt, however, looked anything but pleased. 'I'm not bed-ridden yet, if that's what you mean!' she snapped.

'But that's wonderful!' Caroline put an affectionate hand on her aunt's shoulder. 'You look marvellous, now that I can see you in the light——'

'My looks flatter me! I may not be going to die right away, but I'm far from well, as Philip will tell you. I need to have someone with me, to see to things for me, or I wouldn't have sent for you!'

'I was glad to come,' Caroline said awkwardly.

Aunt Hilda was silent for a long moment. It was impossible to tell what she was thinking, and after a while Caroline didn't try. She stood there, quietly waiting for the older woman to make up her mind about the niece she had done so much for as a child.

'I should have written to you before,' Aunt Hilda said at last. 'Never mind, my dear, it isn't too late for us to pick up from where we were when you were last my guest in Cyprus, is it? It won't be quite the same, of course, for Philip and Ileana—but then you have this Jeffrey, haven't you? So you won't mind what Philip does these days. You know, my dear, if I were you I'd write to that young man of yours and get him out here quickly. You'll feel much better about things when you have him with you, I'm sure.'

'All right,' Caroline agreed, 'I'll write to him to-night.'

'Good.' Her aunt yawned with relish, looking for all the world like a cat who has managed to find a supply of stolen cream and can't quite believe her luck. 'Help me back to bed before you do so, will you? I've been up far too long!'

'O arravoniastikos mou then theli na ergazome pia!'

'I'm sorry, what did you say?' Caroline said in the same language, coming reluctantly out of a pleasant day-dream of what it would be like to go swimming again with Philip.

'I said my fiancé doesn't want me to work any longer,' Maria repeated. 'He didn't want me to work outside the house at all, but the Kyria was ill and needed someone, so I came. But now you are here to do the work for her and for the master, so my fiancé says I must return home.'

Caroline sighed. Her efforts at getting the evening meal the day before had not been particularly success-ful. Aunt Hilda had gamely made the most of the toughened morsel of meat she had been offered. Phil-ip's comments had been deliberately unkind and hurt-ful.

'It's just as well you're rich and beautiful,' he had said, 'because no one is going to marry you for your cooking!'

She had taken due note of the word 'beautiful', it had given her the necessary courage to defend herself. 'I've never cooked on anything like that monster in the kitchen before!' she had protested.

'It's a bad workman who blames his tools!'

'Go and look at it!' she had commanded. 'If I had

my way it would be out tomorrow and something more possible put in——'

'But you won't get your way in this house as easily as that!' he had retorted.

'It's *my* aunt's house!' she had snapped at him.

He had raised his eyebrows. 'Then I should suggest it to her. But I think you ought to know that Uncle Michael had that stove put in for her as a wedding present, and *she* has always managed to produce quite adequate meals on it.'

'Quite adequate' was a misnomer, as Caroline very well remembered. Her aunt had always been a superb cook, but then she had been properly taught by her mother before her, whereas Caroline herself had seldom been called upon to cook anything more difficult than a boiled egg.

'Oh,' she had said, feeling inadequate. 'I didn't know.'

'No,' he had agreed dryly. 'Nor did you make any effort to find out. It's a good thing you can afford to pay for help, isn't it?'

Caroline had allowed his assessment of her to upset her for the rest of the evening. It might have had something to do with sleeping in a strange bed, though that had never bothered her before; it might, and this was more likely, have been the food that she had forced down her throat sooner than admit that it was inedible; but, whatever it was, she had hardly slept at all, going over and over every word that Philip had said to her. What she couldn't understand was why he seemed to resent the fact that she had a great deal of money and had never had to work for her living. It didn't mean that she had never known hard work, nor that she had no sympathy with those who had no money behind them and had only their own endeavours to support them. Could it be because he thought that every woman should be dependent on the man she married and she never need be that? No, that she couldn't believe. Philip had never resented her possessions in the past.

And now Maria's fiancé didn't wish her to work in the Klearchos household any longer, and she had no idea what to do about it. She looked in dismay at the Cypriot girl, with her strong, broad back and the heavy-hipped legs that told of centuries of hard work on the land.

'*O kyrios*, the master, won't be pleased if you go without any notice,' Caroline said.

'*O kyrios* will understand.' The girl smiled a slow, secret smile. '*O kyrios* understands very well. He will say nothing about my going. He knows that it is not wise to keep a man waiting—already George stops and speaks to the other girls of the village although he is promised to me! *O kyrios* himself has given me money so that we can be married quickly, and that is what I want to do!'

'Very well then,' Caroline agreed. 'I'll tell my aunt.'

Maria nodded quickly. 'Kyria Hilda has been kind to me. I should not like her to be angry.' She gave Caroline an uncertain look. 'You will tell her that the master has agreed to my going?'

Damn Philip! What had the servants to do with him? Caroline sighed again. 'Yes, I'll tell her. But, Maria, surely you have a friend, or know of *someone* who wants to earn some money in the village. With my aunt being so ill——'

'Kyria Hilda knows all that has to be done in a house!'

'But she's too ill to do it!'

Maria frowned, turning Caroline's words slowly over in her mind. 'Kyria Hilda is unwell?'

Caroline made a desperate sound. 'You *know* she is!'

Maria frowned the more fiercely. 'But the Kyria Hilda is not alone,' she pointed out, her face brightening. 'You are here with her! You, who are her niece, her own flesh and blood! She has no need of others now!'

'No,' Caroline said weakly. 'Then you don't know of

31

anyone——?'

Maria shook her head. 'It is not the time of year. The vines need attention now. There is much to do on the land.' She shrugged her strong shoulders. 'If the women did not do the work now, it would be left to the men and they would be fit for nothing else!' She laughed slyly. 'You would not like it if the master was to wear himself out doing your work, would you?'

Caroline was too astonished to reply at once. 'But Philip wouldn't——' she began.

Maria nodded her head sagely. 'He is the kindest of men!' she enthused. 'It is natural that he should amuse himself while you have been in England, but other men would not have waited so many years. You owe him much, Kyria Caroline. You must be glad to be here to serve him now!'

Caroline's eye kindled, her sense of humour rapidly deserting her. 'Philip has nothing to do with my coming to Cyprus!' she denied flatly.

Maria merely smiled. Looking at her, Caroline felt her temper flare within her and turned away hastily before she threw something at that disbelieving, well satisfied face. It would be a relief, she told herself, not to have Maria round the house, watching her, thinking of her as some kind of mouse that Philip was waiting to pounce on—when he had punished her a little for being away so long. Why, it was intolerable! She lifted her chin in a belligerent gesture and spoke very clearly in case the girl should have any excuse for not understanding her Greek.

'The master and I were children together, Maria. I am like a sister to him. I plan to marry someone in England, and he has his eye on another girl here in Cyprus. I think you must have misunderstood the situation!'

But Maria went on smiling. Then she giggled. 'You think the master will want to marry Kyria Ileana?' She shook her head, scarcely able to speak for laughter. 'Never! Why should he marry such as she?'

32

The colour flooded into Caroline's face. 'I don't know. *But he is!*' Her voice shook despite her and she was further alarmed by the look of sympathy in Maria's eyes.

'Don't distress yourself, *kyria*,' the girl said gently. 'I will believe that *o kyrios* means to marry another girl only when I see his ring on her finger—properly blessed in church!'

'But *I* don't want to marry him!' Caroline protested, knowing that her words were falling on deaf ears. 'I'm practically engaged——'

Maria stifled another giggle. 'Your aunt is calling you!' she interrupted, going off into peals of laughter. 'She will maybe believe you that you wish to marry another man! Oh, *kyria*, you are so funny! Of course you will stay here now that you have come!'

This time Caroline could hear her aunt calling too and stood up with relief, almost running to the door to answer her. Aunt Hilda was sitting up in bed, looking decidedly cross.

'Where have you been, Caroline?'

'Talking to Maria. Her fiancé wants her to work in his fields and give up working here. I was trying to persuade her to stay a little longer.'

Her aunt twitched her bedjacket up over her shoulders. 'Whatever for?' she demanded irritably.

'She's quite a good cook.'

Aunt Hilda's mouth relaxed into a malicious smile. 'My dear! Your standards are not very high!'

Caroline gave her a desperate look. 'What do you want?' she countered, hoping to divert her aunt away from that particular subject.

'Some coffee, if it wouldn't be too much trouble? I thought you might like to bring yours in here too and we can decide on a plan of campaign——'

'What about?'

'Good heavens, don't look like that, child! About how we're going to manage the house, what else?'

Caroline bit her lip. 'I've written to Jeffrey,' she said

abruptly. 'I've told him he'll be welcome to stay here. But I won't have Philip laughing at him——'

Aunt Hilda veiled her eyes thoughtfully. 'Of course not! But why should he? Is he a very laughable young man?'

Caroline conjured up a picture of Jeffrey in her mind. There was nothing in the least amusing about his features that she could see. He was fair, like herself, with a thin, sharp chin, and a shy smile that made most women go out of their way to make him comfortable and look after his needs. Caroline had done just that herself. She had even started knitting him a sweater when he had told her that he liked to see women knitting, instead of doing nothing as she preferred to do when looking at television. The sweater had never been finished—it probably never would be now!—but she would like to see Philip inspiring her to embark on such a task, which proved as nothing else could how much in love with Jeffrey she was!

'He's a very—pleasant person,' she said uncertainly.

'How nice!' said Aunt Hilda.

Caroline smiled defensively. 'He *is* nice,' she insisted. 'Much nicer than Philip!'

'I daresay,' her aunt remarked dryly. 'Are you going to make the coffee, dear?'

'*Yes!*'

Caroline came back a few minutes later with a tray in her hands, her colour still high from their earlier exchange. She looked at her aunt thoughtfully, wondering if she should embark on some sort of apology for her behaviour or whether it would be better to say nothing.

'I don't know what we are going to do without Maria,' she said. 'I've—I've never kept house before.'

'You can learn,' her aunt said comfortably. 'It's something everyone should know even if they never have to put that knowledge into use, don't you think?'

'But Philip——'

Her aunt's eyes twinkled up at her. 'Philip will stop

teasing you as soon as he sees you are serious about it! Besides, I expect you'll make quite a good job of it when you put your mind to it. I'll help you all I can.'

Caroline considered the matter. 'It's the cooking——' she said slowly.

'It's much easier than it looks. Get Maria to explain the stove to you before she goes. It's idiosyncratic, I know, but it works when coaxed. The trick is to get the pressure right before you start.' She took a sip of coffee and gave a small sigh of pleasure. 'At least you know how to make coffee, my dear!'

Caroline drank her own coffee with a rising sense of panic. She couldn't do it! She would make a crashing fool of herself and Philip would make one of his remarks, destroying what confidence she had left, and she would hate herself and him even more than she did already!

'I can't!' she exclaimed. 'And what's more I won't!'

'Nonsense,' her aunt retorted. 'Any fool can cook if she can read a cookery book and keep her head.' She looked at her niece in acute irritation as Caroline jumped to her feet and started towards the door. 'Where are you going now?' she complained.

Caroline took a deep breath, her mouth set in a mutinous line that meant business. 'I'm going in to Kyrenia to buy a cookery book before I change my mind! Is there anything I can get you?'

Aunt Hilda put a hand to her brow and pushed back her hair. 'Not a thing,' she said.

CHAPTER THREE

CAROLINE looked round the mess in the kitchen with a guilty smile. It wouldn't take long to restore order, but she couldn't help feeling that better cooks than she would not have countenanced the muddle in the first place. In this Philip agreed with her. He appeared in the doorway and whistled softly under his breath. Caroline whirled round to face him.

'If you can do better you're welcome to try!' she shot at him.

'It would be difficult to do much worse! What are you trying to do?'

Tears stung at the back of her eyes at his tone. 'I'm getting dinner,' she said, gritting her teeth. 'What does it look like?'

He smiled slowly. 'It will take you a long time unless you get some kind of system into your cooking. What are we having?'

She didn't want to tell him that. She knew as well as he did that their menus of the last few days had been remarkably similar in content.

'If you want anything special——' she began.

'I do.'

'Oh.' She thought about that for a moment. 'What?'

'Lamb Kleftiko,' he said with all his usual decision. 'It's time we had something with some taste to it instead of that pap you've been serving up.'

'But I don't know how to do it!'

He raised his eyebrows. 'It isn't difficult!'

Caroline shook with anger. How many more people were to tell her that any woman worthy of the name could run a house with one hand tied behind her back, and that cooking came naturally to any female no matter how stupid. She simply didn't believe them! *She* couldn't do it!

'If it's so easy why don't you do it yourself?' she rounded on him.

'All right, I will. But I'm not going to do anything until there's room to put something down. I wouldn't have believed that you could make such a mess—you don't anywhere else!'

Caroline untied the strings of her apron and threw the garment on top of the pile of vegetables, meat, and dishes on the table. 'I've had enough! You can feed me for a change!'

'Not in this pigsty I won't!'

Caroline hesitated and was lost. She had made the mess, so it was only fair that she should clear it up— only she couldn't help wishing that other people's sense of justice would sometimes match hers! What was she doing trying to cook anything in this kitchen in the first place? She glowered across the table at Philip longing to have the courage to walk out the door and leave him to it, but not quite daring to actually do it.

'It's only surface dirt,' she explained. 'You see, everything one cooks seems to need just about everything around, and if one stops to put anything away, the saucepan boils over, or the meat burns, or *something*!' She sighed heavily. 'I'm no good at it!'

'You haven't tried,' he retorted.

'*What?*'

'Now, now, don't lose your temper——!'

'Then don't make *stupid* remarks! How d'you suppose you've eaten at all these last few days?'

He shrugged, a superior smile tugging at the corners of his mouth. 'Largely because Aunt Hilda had rallied round to help you. But that can't go on, as you very well know. The idea is for you to help her, not the other way round.'

Caroline flushed. 'All we have to do is replace Maria and then neither of us would have to do it! What's wrong with that?'

'It's just the bone-selfish solution you would come up with!' he observed.

37

'I don't see why,' she said evenly. She picked up a pile of clean bowls and buried her head in a cupboard, ostensibly putting them away. 'What's wrong with having someone to do the work?'

'Somebody has to pay her wages.'

She turned round and faced him, her eyes spitting with anger. 'If that's the only objection, I'll pay the wages myself!'

'Not in your aunt's house, you won't! And she can't afford to employ another girl at this moment. She's had an expensive time recently, what with medical bills and that sort of thing. Surely it isn't much to ask for you to do this for her?'

'She didn't mind paying for Maria——'

'I paid Maria's wages.'

Caroline picked up another pile of saucepans and retreated back into the cupboard, her mind in a whirl. Her aunt had never been rich, but she always had more than enough money to live on. What had happened since Michael Klearchos' death to change her circumstances so drastically? She came back into the kitchen, frowning at the sight of Philip with his hands in his pockets, propping himself up against the wall.

'Why hasn't Aunt Hilda got enough money?' she asked abruptly.

'Haven't you asked her? I thought you knew all about the family finances. Hasn't it occurred to you that your aunt is a proud person and doesn't like to ask for charity from either one of us?'

'But that's ridiculous!'

'You said it, honey!'

Caroline winced. 'I shouldn't have any share in it anyway,' she burst out.

'I'm not arguing about that either!'

'Then why was it done that way?'

Philip's lips twisted into a bitter smile. 'Don't you really know?' he taunted her. She shook her head. 'Well, I don't think it's much of a secret,' he drawled. 'I imagine she and Michael both thought to make you a more attractive proposition in the marriage market, but I want a little more than a dressed-up inheritance for a wife. You wouldn't do for me at all!'

'Nobody's asked you, sir, she said!'

'Not in words perhaps, but I can feel it simmering away underneath. You'll have to make it very clear that you want to have nothing to do with me if you don't want to be pushed into my arms. Having this young man of yours to stay should help. When is he coming?'

Caroline took a deep breath. She suspected that Philip knew as well as she did that Jeffrey was arriving that evening. It had been one of the reasons why she had started thinking about cooking the dinner so early. Jeffrey would be surprised to find her in the kitchen, but he would be even more surprised if the meal she offered him was of a lower standard than the kind to which he was accustomed. Any difficulties in its preparation wasn't the sort of thing that he would be interested in hearing about. In his well-ordered life meals had always appeared at properly regulated intervals, and they always would or he would know the reason why and make other arrangements, Which would be fine, only she didn't see Jeffrey getting the better of Philip in an out-and-out clash over her cooking methods, and she had a strong suspicion that she would be the one who would get hurt.

She glanced across the kitchen at Philip, reflecting that he had already managed to hurt her. She didn't want to marry him any more than he wanted to marry her, but there are ways and ways of saying these things. It seemed to her that he had deliberately chosen the one way that he knew would hurt her. He had looked at her as a woman and had found her wanting.

'I'm going to fetch him from the airport at six o'clock.' She hesitated. 'Philip, you will be nice to him, won't you?'

His eyes filled with familiar contempt. 'Are you telling me that he's going to care what I think?'

'He might,' she admitted. 'All men haven't got your impregnable conceit!'

'True,' he agreed. 'Tell me some more about this swain of yours. He seems a nice, obedient type.'

'He's nice,' she said grudgingly. 'I wouldn't say he was particularly obedient——'

'He obeyed your summons to come to Cyprus quickly enough!'

'Oh, that!' said Caroline. 'It happened to come at a good time for him, when he wanted to take a holiday anyway. Besides, he was missing me.' She coloured and averted her face from Philip's hard gaze. 'He never knows what to do with himself when I'm not there,' she added. 'He gets bored easily.'

'He must do,' Philip agreed with malice. 'Doesn't he know any other girls?'

Caroline's temper erupted again. 'Of course he does! But he happens to be honourable as well as nice. He's as faithful to me as I—as I am to him!'

'No wonder he bores you stiff,' Philip commented.

'He does not!'

Philip nodded his head thoughtfully. 'Anyone with a temper like yours would be bored stiff with such a passionless romance. If I wasn't otherwise involved, I'd be tempted to make my point by showing you what it's like to be treated as a woman rather than a porcelain doll, but you wouldn't thank me for it, would you? Perhaps you're better off as a sleeping beauty——'

Caroline lifted her hand to slap him, restraining herself only at the very last moment. 'You don't know anything about Jeffrey!'

'I know enough! Slap away, Caroline, and I will kiss you! Why don't you try it?'

She very nearly did! She faced him over the table, her eyes blazing. 'Because I don't want you to kiss me! I don't want to have anything to do with you! Why can't you leave me alone?'

'Are you sure it's not because you think it's vulgar to go round slapping people?'

God give her patience, but he was asking for trouble! 'What if I do?'

He laughed out loud. 'You used to have the courage of your convictions, my dear. What made you the spiritless, wan creature you are now? If that's what Jeffrey has done to you, the sooner you send him packing the better!'

'It's none of your business!'

'Now that's a poor answer,' he jeered. 'Poor Caroline! You don't want me to meet him, do you? You're afraid he won't stand up to being compared with another man you know well, aren't you? Well, don't think that I'm going to help you out. I'm not going to pretend you're a fragile beauty who'd wilt if she tripped over a fact of life. I've known you too long for that! You may be lucky, Jeffrey may like the real you better than you think.'

'Jeffrey knows the real me!' she claimed fiercely.

Philip laughed again. 'Does he? Does he know that you resort to tears when you can't get your own way? That you're afraid in thunderstorms? Or that you'll risk your life rescuing a foolish dog and will expect him to do the same? Does he even know that the quickest way to make you lose your temper is to pull your hair?'

Caroline shook her head in silence. 'That was when I was sixteen,' she said. 'It's different now.'

'How different?' he mocked. He reached out suddenly and grasped a strand of her hair, giving it a quick tug before she had time to defend herself. In an instant, Caroline was yelling retribution and her flailing fists contacted first his broad shoulder as the only part of him she could reach, and then, more satisfyingly, his face. He caught her hands in his and clipped them behind her back, staring down at her, his eyes very black and unreadable. Caroline tried to wriggle free, but his hands only tightened on hers, bruising her fingers.

'I hate you!' she stormed at him, trying not to cry.

41

She kicked out at his shins, hoping to bring her full weight down on his sandalled feet, but once again he was before her, lifting her bodily off the ground and wedging her tightly between his chest and his strong arms.

'I knew you'd cry about it,' he said stolidly. 'You don't have to. All you have to do is admit you were wrong and I'll let you go!'

'I won't! *Never!*'

His eyes shone with a light that scared her. 'Never?' he mocked her.

She pulled at her hands in his. She had not been as angry as she was now for a long, long time. But then she hadn't had Philip to torment her into losing her temper. 'Philip, please let me go!' She veiled her eyes with her lashes and forced herself not to struggle against him. *That*, she remembered, had never worked, for he had always been by far the stronger physically. Just sometimes, though, he had given way if she had asked him nicely. 'Philip, please!'

'Not until you admit——'

'I won't!'

'No?' He bent his head. 'Dear Caroline, would you like me to kiss you now?'

'*No!*'

But she was too late. His lips took possession of hers as easily as if she had wanted it that way and hadn't tried to turn her head away from him. He lowered her feet to the floor and let go her hands, pulling her close within the circle of his arms. And she didn't struggle at all. She was too surprised to do anything except to hope vaguely that he wouldn't let her go. His lips were warm and firm against hers and it was—wonderful! She wouldn't mind if he never let her go! But then this was Philip and he didn't mean any of it. He was only showing her how lucky Ileana, was, no more than that!

'Philip,' she said when she could, 'I'll admit anything!'

'Anything?'

The colour rose in her cheeks and she hid her face from him, clutching at his shirt beneath her fingers. 'I haven't changed,' she whispered. 'I hate people pulling my hair, and I'm still afraid in thunderstorms.'

'And you're not on kissing terms with Jeffrey?'

She blinked as a feeling closely allied to panic assailed her stomach. 'I'm thinking of marrying him. I'm awfully fond of him.' Her voice broke and she swallowed hard. 'He—he thinks I'm beautiful!'

'And that makes him special?'

She felt suddenly shy and a little ridiculous. 'To me it does. *He* doesn't make me do things I don't want to do and—and he doesn't lecture me all the time!'

'And I do?'

She nodded. 'And anyway, you don't want to have anything to do with me—you said so. And he does! He *wants* to marry me. He'd do anything for me!' she asserted firmly, not at all sure that Philip would believe such a claim, or even if he did would find anything admirable in it.

Philip released her and stood away from her. 'What would you do for him?' he countered.

She stared at him for a long moment in silence, trying to repress the feeling of rebellion that was being born despite her somewhere in the depths of her being. She didn't want to have to do anything for Jeffrey! She didn't want to see him every day for the next goodness knows how long! And most of all, she didn't want to be his wife!

'I don't know how to make Lamb Kleftiko,' she said, breaking the silence and changing the subject in one desperate throw. It was, after all, what he had said he wanted to eat.

'It's easy enough. I'll show you if you like. We'll need the *kleftiko* pot and some bits of lamb——'

'What *kleftiko* pot?'

He grinned at her puzzled face. 'It's that earthenware pot over there. "*Kleftiko*" comes from the Greek

43

word to steal. It's a way of cooking much favoured by Greek brigands. They bury the pot in the earth with a fire underneath it and leave the meat to cook very slowly. Shepherds use the same method sometimes. Someone else's lamb is apt to taste sweeter than one culled from one's own flock!'

Caroline tried not to giggle. 'But that's dishonest!'

'Oh, very!' he drawled. 'That's what makes it attractive!' He took the covered earthenware pot from her and put it in the sink to soak. 'It's better to leave it in water overnight,' he told her. 'The pot is porous, you see. But I daresay this will do.' He opened the refrigerator and took out some pieces of lamb, sprinkling them lavishly with salt and pepper. 'It has to be browned in a frying pan. Think you can do that?'

Caroline nodded. She rather enjoyed the responsibility of putting the heavy iron frying-pan on to heat and watching the lamb slowly brown, at the same time giving off a pungent odour of hot meat that one seldom got from the differently fed lamb at home in England.

'What do I do now?' she asked when the meat was done.

'Put it in the pot,' he ordered, smiling at the look of fierce concentration on her face. He watched her transfer the lumps of meat into the wet pot and then himself added a little oregano, a kind of wild marjoram, lemon juice, and white wine. 'That's it!' he said. 'Put it in the oven at a low heat and you won't have to think of it again for another four hours. Not very difficult, is it?'

'Is that really all?' she demanded, looking round the practically untouched kitchen.

'There are the vegetables to do, but you can do those later on. Okay?'

She turned back to the sink, knowing that she would have to thank him and yet reluctant to do so. It was unfair that he should be right so often and at her expense.

44

'How do you know how to cook?' she asked instead, unaware that her inward struggle was plainly reflected on her face.

'It's easier to learn a few basic dishes than have to rely on other people,' he answered. 'I expect Ileana would oblige, but if you ask a woman to cook for you it's apt to give them other ideas. I'll be glad to give you some more lessons any time you say the word, if that's what you're leading up to!'

'Thank you,' she said gruffly.

'Ouch!' he said. 'Never mind, love, Jeffrey is coming to pour balm on your bruised pride and tell you he loves you, even if you are rather useless!' His smile deepened into pure mockery. 'I suppose it is you he loves and not your expectations?'

Caroline stuck out her tongue at him. 'He doesn't know I have any,' she maintained stoutly.

'No? He knows you have money in the bank, presumably?'

'No more than any of the other girls he knows!' Caroline protested.

'My word, what exalted circles he lives in! Aren't your poor Cyprus relations going to come as a shock to him?'

'He's not a snob!' Caroline retorted. She bit her lip, hating the implication that she might be ashamed of Aunt Hilda, when she wasn't and never would be. 'He'll love Aunt Hilda, and he doesn't have to have much to do with you, does he?'

But Philip only drawled, 'I should ask him, if I were you, if he'd still want to marry you if you hadn't a penny in the world.'

'I don't have to,' Caroline said. 'He isn't like you! One can't buy someone like Jeffrey.'

Philip blinked at her. 'Why don't you try to buy me?' he suggested.

She shrugged her shoulders. 'You're more interested in Ileana.'

'I see,' he said. 'You give in far too easily, my timid

45

one. I'm sorely tempted by the size of your bank balance *and* by the Klearchos inheritance. I might be persuaded to take you along with them—if you ask me nicely!'

'Well, I won't! I don't want you any more than you want me!' She showed her teeth in a not very successful attempt at a smile. 'Jeffrey is worth ten of you——'

'Financially speaking, I daresay, but when it comes to marriage, *yinéka mou*, you'll want a man in your bed, not a looking-glass to tell you how pretty you are!' He put out a hand and touched her cheek, running a finger along the line of her jaw. 'You don't need to be told that!' he added.

Caroline winced away from him as if his touch burned her. 'I must go and meet him.'

'Already? Can't you wait?'

She stamped her foot at him because she knew she only wanted to get away from him and the strange excitement he induced in her. 'No, I can't!' she said violently. 'He loves me and I love him!'

Philip tapped her lightly on the chin. 'That in your teeth, my dear. At the moment you love only yourself, but I have hopes of you. However, go and meet the poor man, if you must, and I'll strive to be polite to him while he's here.'

Caroline recovered herself with difficulty. 'That's big of you!' she muttered with heavy sarcasm, then she wished she hadn't, because the only visible effect on Philip was that his smile grew wider and the mockery in his eyes grew deeper. She felt herself blushing and was horribly aware of him, of the feel of him, and of the way he had held her, and even more of the way he had kissed her. She hadn't liked the sensation of helplessness he had induced in her, but she longed to know if he had felt that same feeling of wild excitement and the same curiosity as to what would happen if he were to kiss her again. She swallowed and looked up at him with a shy smile. 'Thank you for the cookery lesson.'

'My pleasure,' he drawled. 'I shouldn't want Jeffrey

to think badly of you!'

Caroline drove to Nicosia at breakneck speed. For part of the way she had the road almost to herself, but then she came up against one of the United Nations Convoys taking a long train of cars through the Turkish district, so she turned back and went through Kyrenia, going the long way round to the airport. The rapid changes in the scenery had always fascinated her and never more so than now, despite the turmoil of her emotions and her frustrated anger with Philip.

He had always won every serious argument between them. At sixteen, she had rather admired his high-handed attitude towards her. She had made quite a hero of him in her imagination and had longed for his approval more than anything else in her whole life. But such an attitude would be ridiculous in anyone six years later. She was grown up now, and he had no right to treat her as though she were still sixteen and in need of his care and guidance!

She turned her mind resolutely to considering Jeffrey Carson. He was a much nicer person than Philip! Besides, her father liked him, and her father had never had anything good to say about the young Philip Klearchos. 'Too Greek by half,' had been his considered verdict, adding in the same cold tones: 'There never was a truer saying than that one should beware the Greeks when they come bearing gifts. Don't be taken in by him, my dear!'

Actually Philip had never given her anything except a few bruises and a great deal of unsolicited advice, but Caroline had listened to her father and she had been suspicious of Philip's motives towards her ever since. And that reminded her that she now had something to be suspicious about. Why had he kissed her? And why, oh, why had he suggested that he might be persuaded, if she offered sufficient in the way of material inducement, to marry her, when he quite obviously didn't even like her very much?

47

Tears stung her eyes and she had to blink rapidly in order to be able to see where she was going. He had been teasing her, she thought, but his teasing had not been kind. It would have served him right if she had pretended to take him seriously and had offered him terms, but one could never be sure that Philip wouldn't have found some other way of taking the wind out of her sails.

Approached from this angle, the airport had the look of a military encampment, but the impression was soon dispersed as she turned in through the gate and parked close to the terminal building. She was far too early for Jeffrey's plane, so she sat in the car to wait for his arrival, amusing herself by thinking of all the things they would do together in the next few days. How good it was that he was coming! Seeing Cyprus with him would overlay her earlier impressions of the island which were full of memories of Philip: Philip chasing her; Philip explaining the old legends of the Greek gods; Philip buying her ice-cream; and sometimes the young Philip's features, just as if the years between had never been to dull her memory of exactly how he had looked. Yes, Jeffrey's coming would be good for her! She needed him here far more than she had ever needed him in London.

The aeroplane came skimming in over the horizon, clearing some dusty trees and lowering its undercarriage, just as the water-birds do, breaking their speed against the surface tension of a lake. Caroline watched the silver plane disappear into the distance, a mixture of dust and fumes streaming out behind it, and got leisurely out of the car to make her way towards the terminal building. She knew from experience that it would still be some time before the plane would turn and taxi across the runway before finally nestling into its allotted place on the tarmac. It would be longer still before the passengers would be released from the crowded cabin to filter their way slowly through Immigration Control, before they were allowed to collect

48

their luggage, and greet the people who were awaiting their arrival.

Caroline forced herself to walk slowly down the main hall of the building, her cardigan swinging free from her shoulders because it was not yet cool enough to put it on properly. A dozen pairs of eyes watched her progress with the dark-eyed interest of the Mediterranean male. She felt herself colouring a little, but she gave no other sign that she had noticed their attention. Indeed, she lifted her chin a little and gave them back look for look, rather enjoying the exchange. It made her feel completely female, and that was a good feeling. Philip—— But she would *not* think about Philip any more! Only it was funny to think that he, too, could make her feel all woman with a casual look, whereas Jeffrey treated her as an equal, and as a friend, and protested often that he loved her, and yet didn't make her feel particularly desirable at all.

She frowned, staring up at the place where she expected Jeffrey to appear, and then found to her surprise that she was frowning at him. She smiled too quickly and with a lavishness that she hoped would cover up her lack of eagerness, and waved to him to hurry on down to her. His face looked pink against the dark tan of the local men and small beads of sweat told that he was feeling the sudden difference in temperature between London and Cyprus. He hesitated at the foot of the stairs, put his briefcase from one hand into the other, and kissed her punctiliously on the cheek.

'Good to see you!' he murmured.

'Oh, Jeffrey! Is that the best you can do?' she reproached him.

His face grew pinker still. 'It's a bit public for my better efforts,' he excused himself. 'I hadn't realised Cyprus is so far away. I was beginning to wonder if I'd ever get here!'

'Far away from what?' she retorted. She wished she had said something soft and welcoming, but the desire

49

to needle him got the better of her. 'It's quite near to heaps of places—Turkey, Syria——'

'I daresay, but it isn't near to home and London. You've always spoken of it as though it were somewhere in Surrey, not in the thick of the Middle East. I wasn't expecting it to be foreign at all. Look at all those signs! I can't even read them, let alone understand what they mean!'

'They're in Greek,' she said. 'I can't see what you're complaining about, Jeffrey, as they're in English too especially for you——'

'That's something, I suppose,' he admitted grudgingly. 'I feel a fool when people don't understand English.' An uncomfortable thought struck him and his briefcase changed hands again. 'I say, I suppose all your people understand English all right?'

Caroline gave him a bland look. 'Of course.' Oh dear, she thought, Philip will make mincemeat of him, and it's all my own fault for bringing him here! 'Aunt Hilda is as English as you are,' she added comfortingly. Perhaps she could warn Aunt Hilda not to lapse into quaint bits of Greek while he was here, only, if she did, she could well imagine that her aunt would delight in confusing him, and then she would feel worse than ever!

'Jeffrey, you will try to like them, won't you?' she pleaded with him, her eyes wide with the dismay she was feeling.

He patted her kindly on the shoulder, blinking into the harsh evening light. 'Good heavens, yes!' he exclaimed. 'I pride myself that I can get along with anyone for a couple of weeks or so. I shan't let this Greek fellow, Klearchos, get a rise out of me! Though, between ourselves, my dear, I shan't be sorry when I have you safely back in London. I'm told that no woman is safe with these chaps and you're looking very attractive in that dress you've got on. Very attractive!'

But Caroline only sighed and hurried him across the road to where she had parked the car.

CHAPTER FOUR

AUNT HILDA said she was going to get up for dinner. 'I want to see this Jeffrey of yours,' she told Caroline. Her sharp eyes took in her niece's strained face and she added with a little nod of her head, 'Everyone arrives from England looking pale, especially at this time of the year. He'll look better to you when he's had a bit of time to acquire a tan.'

Caroline sniffed. 'There's nothing wrong with Jeffrey! He looks fine to me!'

'Then what are you looking so missish about?'

Caroline opened her eyes wide. 'Me?' she protested. 'Is this some kind of conspiracy to make me wish I hadn't invited him out here?'

Aunt Hilda gave her a speaking look. 'Whom would I conspire with from my bed?' she demanded crossly. 'You know I've been too ill to do anything much——'

'And that's another thing,' Caroline went on, pressing home her advantage while the opportunity presented itself. 'What made you ill? I wish you'd tell me all about it, aunt. I had a letter from Daddy asking what was the matter with you. What am I to tell him?'

'That it isn't any of his business,' her aunt suggested with a wide smile. 'He wouldn't be interested in the details—and don't pretend to me he would be!'

'But *I'm* interested!'

'Yes, dear, I know you are, and I love you for it, but there really isn't a lot I can tell you. I suppose it was the shock of losing Michael, and then the other two being drowned, coupled with the fact that my heart has been playing up for a few years now.'

'You never said anything!'

Her aunt smiled. 'You didn't ask.'

Caroline flushed. She was bitterly aware that she had hardly written to her aunt at all this last year.

Cyprus had seemed so far away and she had been much more interested in her father's arrival in England. It had been exciting, for her father was only just fifty, which was ridiculously young to retire, and there had been all the business of buying a house and re-designing the garden in the way her mother had wanted it. There hadn't been time for anything else—except Jeffrey.

'That didn't mean I didn't want to know!' she said painfully.

'Well, now you do know, so you can stop looking so anxious and help me put some clothes on. I have a long yellow thing in the wardrobe, I think I'll wear that. It will cover up what I have on underneath, but doesn't look too much like a dressing-gown. What are you going to wear, Caroline?'

Caroline shook her head. 'I don't know. I haven't thought about it. Aunt Hilda, do you think you ought to get up?'

'Of course I should! It isn't every day that a pleasant young man comes to stay with me! What are you giving us to eat?'

Caroline buried her head in the wardrobe and took out the yellow dress her aunt wanted to wear. 'Lamb Kleftiko.'

Aunt Hilda's laugh made her look round. 'Did you know that is Philip's favourite dish?' the older woman asked.

'He cooked it!' Caroline said, daring her aunt to make anything of it.

'Good!' that lady responded cheerfully. 'I'm getting hungrier by the minute and, if Philip had anything to do with it, at least we'll have something we can eat!' She smiled at her niece's crestfallen face. 'You're coming on splendidly as a cook, but we do seem to have had rather a lot of bacon and eggs these last few days.'

Caroline held out the dress, dropping it neatly over her aunt's head. 'I'll tell Philip that you're pleased he's taken a hand——'

'Aren't you?'

Caroline could only deplore such a direct question. The colour flooded into her face and the more she tried to look cool, calm, and collected, the more she blushed and the more miserably self-conscious she felt. Her aunt watched her in the looking-glass with a fascinated interest.

'Caroline,' she said at last, 'have you been fighting with Philip?'

'Of course not!'

'Then what's the matter?'

'*Nothing!*'

'Nothing? Well, if you say so, my dear. But Philip has always been fond of you and it would be too bad if you were to disappoint him now!'

Caroline faltered in her step, almost tripping over her aunt's long skirt. '*I* disappoint *him*? How could I? He thinks I'm an incompetent idiot! And anyway, what about his disappointing me? I thought at least he'd treat me like an adult, but he's exactly the same as he always was, bossing me about and finding fault with everything I do! As for being *fond* of me, he wouldn't care if he never saw me again. In fact, I think he'd like it that way!'

'So that's what's wrong!' Aunt Hilda surmised.

'No, it isn't!' Caroline retorted, goaded into further indiscretions. 'I don't care what he does either! If he wants to marry Ileana, that's quite all right with me. I have Jeffrey——'

Her aunt's astonished gaze brought her to a crashing halt. 'I didn't mean to shout,' she said awkwardly, 'but he's been doing his best to niggle me all day!'

'It looks as though he succeeded!' Aunt Hilda remarked dryly. 'It certainly takes me back to have the two of you spitting at each other. Michael used to say you were like two volatile chemicals, but that when you came together you would stabilise into something as necessary as common table salt. What makes you think he wants to marry Ileana?'

Caroline preferred not to say. She shrugged her shoulders. 'Something he said. It doesn't matter. You shouldn't pay any attention to me; it was only that I'd forgotten how irritating he could be.' She was silent for a long moment, then she burst out: 'Aunt Hilda, I've got to learn how to cook properly!'

Her aunt began to cream her face. 'All right,' she said, 'we'll have a few lessons starting tomorrow, if you can fit it in with whatever you are going to do with Jeffrey.'

Caroline gave her an uncertain look. 'But you aren't well enough——' she began.

'I'm quite well enough for that!' Aunt Hilda declared. 'Are these lessons to be a secret between ourselves?'

Caroline nodded, fiddling with her fingers. 'I don't want Philip to know,' she explained. 'He'd only be unpleasant about it and I couldn't bear that, not with Jeffrey here.'

Her aunt said nothing, but Caroline couldn't help noticing the almost comic pleasure in her eyes before she looked away and murmured something about it being time for Caroline to get herself ready for dinner. She watched her niece leave the room with a barely restrained grin and hugged herself with glee, dancing a cheerful jig in the middle of her bedroom floor.

Jeffrey was taller than Philip. Seeing them standing side by side on the verandah, Caroline hesitated an instant before calling attention to herself. She had never thought of Jeffrey as being particularly tall, but then he was so thin that his added inches didn't count as much as they should. Philip, shorter by half a head, had a breadth of shoulder that more than made up for the difference. Indeed, he was not shorter in the body at all, it was in the legs. Jeffrey had the long legs of so many northerners: Philip had the stubby strength of the Mediterranean male, very sure of himself, and never doubting for a moment his powers to attract the

54

opposite sex. There was no doubt as to which she preferred. She felt more at home with Jeffrey and that was
very precious to her. Philip was like an irritating burr
that she could very well do without!

They turned in unison and smiled at her. Jeffrey
pulled another chair forward and beckoned her into
it.

'Kyrie Klearchos——'

'*Kyrios* Klearchos,' Caroline corrected him automat-
ically.

'Oh?' said Jeffrey. 'I thought one addressed people
as Kyrie?'

'One does,' Caroline said, frowning. 'You weren't
addressing him. You were referring to him, which is
different.'

Philip grinned. 'Since when have you been such a
pedant?' he teased her.

'I'm not!' she denied. 'Only one may as well *try* to
get these things right!'

'I'll remember that next time——'

Caroline jumped to her feet, irritated beyond en-
durance. 'Will you have a drink, Jeffrey?'

'I have one.' He looked at her with pained surprise.
'Where are you going now, Caro? I've hardly seen you
at all so far this evening.'

'I'm just going to look at the dinner,' she answered,
avoiding Philip's mocking lift to his eyebrows. 'My
aunt is going to join us,' she added to further justify
her departure.

'That's another thing,' Jeffrey said. 'I thought your
aunt was too ill to leave her bed, but she was out in
the garden just now. At least, I suppose it was her? She
looked a bit like you from the back—older of course,
but a similar shape.'

Caroline was as astonished as he. 'Aunt Hilda?'

'Why not?' Philip drawled. 'She's been feeling a bit
better these last few days since you came. I think she
was lonely before.'

'You were here!' Caroline said sharply.

Jeffrey looked from one to the other of them. 'Loneliness is hardly an excuse for disrupting other people's arrangements. Caroline is only her niece, not a close relative, like a daughter. She has her own life to lead.'

'Oh, shut up, Jeffrey!'

He was hurt. 'You know how inconvenient it was for you to come out here just now. Your father was still raging about it when I saw him yesterday——'

'I know,' Caroline said. 'But I had to come. Aunt Hilda means a great deal to me. You wouldn't understand!' She was very much aware of Philip's interest and she resented it. What she did had nothing to do with him and she didn't care any longer what he thought of her! She lifted her chin and smiled at them both, daring them to say any more. 'I'll call you as soon as dinner is ready.'

It gave Caroline a poignant pleasure to see her aunt take her rightful place at the top of the table. She looked at Aunt Hilda closely and thought how different she looked from the drawn, pale creature she had been on the day Caroline had arrived. In fact she looked as well as Caroline had ever seen her, with a fine glow to her skin and her eyes as bright as they had been when her husband had been alive and had sat in the chair opposite her that was now occupied by Philip. She began to wonder if her aunt had ever been ill at all. Had it been a ruse to bring her running to Cyprus? She thought it quite likely, but what she couldn't understand was *why*. Her aunt had only had to say that she wanted to see her and she would have come at once, no matter what objections her father had raised.

'I hope you're going to do some sightseeing while you're here,' Aunt Hilda was saying to Jeffrey. 'Philip has a love for the place that makes him a very good guide——'

'Oh, but,' Jeffrey began uncomfortably. 'I was rather hoping that Caroline would show me round.'

'Well, of course! She won't want to be left behind, will you, dear?' Aunt Hilda turned warm, liquid eyes on to her niece. 'But as a guide she leaves a great deal to be desired! I don't suppose she could even tell you who Aphrodite was!'

'Aphrodite?' Jeffrey repeated. 'What has she to do with anything?'

'She has everything to do with Cyprus,' Caroline supplied. 'To begin with she was born at Paphos and this made the island hers in a special way. According to the legend, and everybody believes it here in Cyprus, Ares, the god of war, was jealous of Adonis who was Aphrodite's lover, so he transformed himself into a wild boar and slew Adonis with his tusks when Adonis was out hunting. Aphrodite ran to her lover, trying to help him, and tore her feet on some thorns and the drops of her blood turned the white roses red—there had never been any red roses before—and the blood of the dying Adonis turned the flowers of the field, the anemones and the poppies, scarlet. It's a pretty story, don't you think?'

Jeffrey smiled at her with a rare charm. 'Do you remember when I gave you some red roses?'

Caroline nodded, trying not to blush. 'You see what a lot we have to thank Aphrodite for!' she joked.

Jeffrey didn't answer. He pulled at his collar as if it were too tight for him, a gesture which had never failed to irritate her.

'You must go to Paphos,' Aunt Hilda chimed in, 'and see where she was born for yourself. If you go next Sunday, Philip can drive you. He knows the road better than Caroline does.'

Caroline licked her lips. She longed to see Paphos again in Philip's company. 'Will you, Philip?'

'If you like,' he agreed.

Jeffrey tugged at his collar again. 'I'd rather go somewhere else,' he said. 'Isn't there somewhere we can go by ourselves?'

Caroline bent her head, hoping that someone else would answer him. To her surprise it was Philip who broke the silence. 'Well, Caroline?'

'I'd prefer to go with you!' she burst out. 'What I mean is——' She stopped, took a deep breath and hurried on in a wave of embarrassment: 'I suppose we could go to Larnaca tomorrow. There's a church at Kiti called the Church of Panagia Angeloktistos. It means it was built by angels,' she added. 'It has a very fine mosaic in the apse. And—and we could go on to the Tekke of Umm Haram. It's beautiful there! In all Cyprus, it's one of my favourite places.'

'Built by angels!' Jeffrey scoffed. 'You do talk a lot of rubbish, darling. Still, if that's what you want to do, at least we can be alone there.'

Caroline stirred uncomfortably. Her eyes went to her aunt, silently seeking her permission. Aunt Hilda would not like her to be alone with any man and might well cavil at her niece putting herself in a position where people might talk about her. They might know that English girls had more freedom than any Cypriot girl would dream of wanting, but they would expect the niece of Kyria Hilda Klearchos to know better, to be more like one of themselves.

'May I—may I go, Aunt?'

Aunt Hilda inclined her head slowly. 'You'd better ask Philip, dear. He's the master of the house, not I!'

Caroline blenched, her mouth closing in a firm line. She would not ask him! She would never ask him! Never, never, *never*!'

'You may go,' Philip drawled. 'You can give my regards to Umm Haram. It's a long time since I've been able to visit her.'

Jeffrey frowned. 'Should I know who this Umm Haram is?' he enquired.

'She was the Prophet Mahomet's foster-mother,' Aunt Hilda explained, looking pleased with herself. 'She came on a holy war with her husband—women did in the early days of Islam—and fell off her mule and broke her neck. Her tomb is a very holy place to the Turks on the island.'

Jeffrey tugged at his collar and sighed. 'Oh well,' he

said, 'I don't suppose we have to go in if we don't want to. I must admit it's not my idea of a day out! I prefer an English pub and a restaurant where I can rely on getting something tolerable to eat. I'm told the food here is pretty bad?'

Caroline looked at him sweetly. 'Don't you like what you're eating?' she asked him.

His face went a shade pinker than it was naturally. 'I've no complaints about your cooking, but I'm not sure what it is. I prefer good, simple food.'

'Philip cooked it,' Caroline muttered.

'Oh!' said Jeffrey, tugging frantically at his collar. Watching him, Caroline was filled with frustration. *Nothing* was as she had planned it! She didn't dare look at Philip because she knew he was despising her, and Jeffrey too, in a way, because he was so very far from being the romantic hero she had implied that he was. Nor did she care for her aunt's impregnably polite expression that told her clearer than anything else would have done that she didn't like Jeffrey and pitied her niece for not being able to find someone better, someone whose charm would tug at her heart-strings, someone like Michael Klearchos—*someone like Philip!*

Somehow she got through the rest of the evening. It passed in an endless haze of bewildered fright. *Philip!* It couldn't be! She wouldn't allow herself to feel like that about him. She didn't even like him! He was a bully and had never allowed her her own way in anything. She couldn't possibly be falling in love with him. *And what about Jeffrey?* Caroline stared at him across the table. One thing was quite certain, she was not the tiniest bit in love with him, and she had so wanted to be! Her father liked him, he was rich and suitable, and even her mother had pointed out the advantages of living one's married life in one's own country, and her mother was an authority on that subject. She had spent most of every year in the heat of the Persian Gulf to be with her husband, but she

59

hadn't liked it one bit. She had hated being parted from her children, and most of all she had hated being parted from the soft climate of Britain and the green scenery which she loved with a passion that Caroline had never been able to share wholeheartedly, perhaps because the good times of her childhood had always been spent abroad.

When at last she had said a final good night to her aunt and had gone to her own bed, Caroline took herself to task for allowing her emotions to get out of hand in such a ridiculous manner. She would do well to consider Ileana, she told herself bitterly. *She* was the one who was going to marry Philip. She was welcome to him! He wouldn't spare her any of the humiliations that Cypriot women daily accepted as their lot in life. She would have no say in anything, but would be expected to keep his house, bear his children, and very likely work his fields as well. To be jealous of such a fate was lunatic. Why, if she married Jeffrey, or someone like him, how different her own life would be! They would employ someone to care for the children, and very likely someone in the house as well. She would have money to spend and admiration in plenty, and the only work she would be expected to do would be the occasional hour she put in on some hobby or other.

Yet she was jealous of Ileana. It was all Philip's fault! If he had never kissed her in the kitchen, she would never have known what it was like to have him touch her, or what it was like to be eaten up with this unreasonable desire to have him kiss her again.

She tried to put both men out of her mind when she at last went to bed and settled down to sleep, but the grey light of dawn was already stealing in through her window before she finally dropped off into restless oblivion, only to be woken again by a sharp rap on her door and Philips voice demanding breakfast before he went off to work.

Predictably, Aunt Hilda had overtired herself by getting up to dinner the evening before and was feeling both irritable and misunderstood when Caroline took in her breakfast to her.

'How long have you known Jeffrey?' she demanded, eyeing her niece crossly as she drew back the curtains and let the sunlight come flooding into the room.

Caroline tried to remember. 'He owns an associate company of Daddy's firm. I've known him ever since he took over there. About three years, I suppose. Why?'

Aunt Hilda hesitated. 'You don't find him—dull?' she asked.

Caroline looked astonished. 'I've never thought about it. He's nice——'

'Yes, but *nice* is such a dull word. He won't lend much colour to your married life. Are you sure you'll make him happy? You're not as conventional as your father, any more than I am, and Jeffrey strikes me as the type to be very easily shocked.' She clamped her lips together as though she had been going to say a great deal more but had changed her mind at the last moment.

Caroline actually gasped. 'I don't think my behaviour is ever *shocking*, is it? Why shouldn't I make him happy?'

'You'll ask more of him than he has to give——'

'I'm not asking anything of him!' Caroline protested.

'Aren't you?' her aunt snapped. 'My mistake! I thought you were considering marrying the man!'

Caroline coloured, but she refused to allow her aunt to needle her into saying more than she meant to about Jeffrey, or about Philip, either!

'I like Jeffrey,' she said with a smile. 'He's a very pleasant person and he's very gentle. He doesn't make impossible demands on me and want me to be something other than I am. He loves me just as I am—the pampered daughter of an over-loving father!'

Aunt Hilda looked decidedly put out. She mumbled something about Jeffrey's lack of any real interest in

Caroline if he didn't care what she did.

'I find it rather restful!' Caroline retorted.

'Now Philip would expect to be considered by his wife,' Aunt Hilda continued mendaciously.

'You mean he'd expect his wife to be a willing slave, carrying out his every order as speedily as possible!' Caroline snapped back.

'Like Michael!' Aunt Hilda remembered, smiling. 'He gave the best and he expected the best from me. Anything less would have tarnished something glorious. That's what marriage ought to be, especially for people like us. Half measures won't keep you warm at night!'

'I prefer not to discuss it,' Caroline remonstrated.

Unexpectedly, Aunt Hilda laughed. 'I'm not asking you to discuss it with me, my dear. I'm asking you to think for yourself before you accept your father's opinion that Jeffrey is the answer to all your dreams.'

'Daddy has nothing to do with it!'

Aunt Hilda sighed. 'When I told him I was going to marry Michael he made sure that I never received another penny from the family. He thought Michael would back out if I didn't bring a proper dowry with me. He could have done and nobody in Cyprus would have thought any the worse of him. It's expected here that the woman will bring her share to the marriage, and I had nothing except my Army pay. But Michael wanted me and he refused to give me up. I loved him dearly before that, of course, but I've always been grateful to him for cocking a snook at that brother of mine. I felt so shamed by my family's treatment and he gave me back my pride. Your father is a good man by his lights, but don't forget I've known him a great deal longer than you have and there's not much you can tell me about him that I don't know!'

'Daddy has never tried to influence me in any way,' Caroline stated firmly. She felt rather more uncertain underneath. She had known that her father had not liked her spending her holidays in Cyprus with his sister when she had been younger, and she had wondered a little at his reluctance when she had told him that Aunt Hilda was ill and had need of her. In fact she wouldn't have come if it hadn't been for her mother's insistence that she had a debt to repay to her aunt and that it was her duty to visit her.

Aunt Hilda raised a languid eyebrow. 'Never?'

'Not about things like marriage——'

'Oh, Caroline!'

'Well, he hasn't! I know he likes Jeffrey and he introduced him to me, but I know heaps of other men that he doesn't know at all——'

'Men like Philip?'

Caroline hesitated. There weren't two men in the world like Philip! 'He doesn't much like Philip,' she agreed reluctantly. 'But that's got nothing to do with it. He hardly knows Philip!'

Aunt Hilda shut her eyes, looking suddenly old. 'He didn't have to. Do you remember when he came to collect you the last time you came to Cyprus? You were sitting in the square with Philip the day before you left and Philip kissed you. Your father saw you both and he said then that you would never return to Cyprus while he could prevent it. You never did.'

Caroline turned away, picking up a pile of shirts that were laid over the chair by her aunt's bed, anything to hide the agitation that had seized her. 'He couldn't have known!' she whispered. 'I ran away. He must have seen me run away!'

Aunt Hilda chuckled. 'I ran away the first time Michael kissed me too. I didn't want him to know that my defences against him were in a very sorry state of repair!' She looked enquiringly at Caroline, making an impatient gesture with her hand. 'Sometimes I think you had more sense at sixteen!' she added crossly.

Caroline didn't answer. She held up the shirts with hands that shook. 'What are these doing here?' she asked. 'Are they Philip's?'

Aunt Hilda nodded. 'They need mending, but I've been too tired recently to do them for him. Put them back, dear. If I see them there for long enough, I'll do them just to get them out of my sight!'

Caroline thrust them back on to the chair. 'You shouldn't have to mend Philip's shirts! He shouldn't expect you to! Surely there's someone else who could do them for him?'

Aunt Hilda smiled faintly. 'I'm not going to fight you if you want to do them for him,' she remarked with considerable asperity. 'He won't thank you if you botch them, but I suppose you have to begin somewhere.'

Caroline stood quite still. 'Begin what?'

Aunt Hilda had the grace to look embarrassed. 'Well, presumably you intend to marry *someone* one day, even if you decide to turn down this Jeffrey of yours, and presumably this future husband will expect you to have at least *some* of the wifely arts!'

'Thank you very much! If my husband's shirts want mending I'll buy him some new ones!'

Aunt Hilda laughed. 'Then you won't mend Philip's shirts?'

'Oh, all right! But I'm doing them for you—not for Philip! Nor shall I botch them, as you charmingly put it. I may not be much of a cook, but I can sew!' She picked up the shirts again and marched with them towards the door, looking back at her aunt over her shoulder. 'Only don't tell Philip, will you?'

'Why ever not? He'll probably want to thank you.'

'No, he won't!'

'How can you know that?'

'It's just that I don't want him to know,' Caroline said stubbornly. 'He'll think it's because of him, and it isn't!' She waited for her aunt to say something, but Aunt Hilda seemed not to have heard her. She had her head back against the pillow and she could have been asleep. Caroline's heart smote her when she saw how tired the older woman was looking. She took another step towards the door when she heard her aunt move behind her.

'Are you sure?' Aunt Hilda said quietly.

Caroline clutched the shirts to her and hurried out of the room, her eyes blinded with tears that she couldn't understand herself. Of course she was sure! She was quite, quite sure! But she couldn't change the lump in her throat, or the way she ran all the way to her own room, ramming the shirts into the nearest drawer, knowing that as soon as she got back from Larnaca and had shaken off Jeffrey for a precious half hour or so she would take them out and moon over them for a while, before repairing them with the neat little stitches she did so well. And she would be glad to do them, jealous of the privilege of doing something for Philip that normally she would not be called upon to do.

She sat down on the edge of her bed, her heart hammering against her ribs, remembering other things she had done for him, willingly, longing for his word of praise if she had managed to dive off an awkward rock, or had run almost as fast as he could himself. Had she loved him then? Did she love him now? And if she did, what would he ask of her now? It was that that set her heart beating and her blood singing through her veins. For the moment she had forgotten all about Ileana.

CHAPTER FIVE

JEFFREY looked at Caroline's new car with approval. He whistled under his breath as she backed it out of the garage and down the concrete ramp to where he was standing.

'You're an extravagant puss,' he said as he got in beside her. 'Whatever induced you to buy a beauty like this when you'll only be here a few days?'

'I may stay longer,' Caroline said. She gave him a quick glance from under her eyelashes. 'Aunt Hilda——' Her voice faded away into silence. There was no way of explaining why she thought she might stay.

'But what about us?' Jeffrey protested.

Caroline turned the car and set it down the hill. The view over the abbey towards the sea was breathtakingly beautiful. 'Do you want to drive?' she asked. 'I mean, I don't mind if you'd prefer it?'

Jeffrey was far from pleased. 'This country is getting at you,' he told her, frowning his disapproval. 'You know you drive better than I do! I'm not Philip Klearchos that I have to take everything into my own hands just because you're a woman. He's a pain in the neck, isn't he?'

'Sometimes,' Caroline admitted.

'Only sometimes?' Jeffrey laughed shortly. 'I shouldn't have thought that all that aggressive masculinity was much in your line.'

'Oh?' Caroline hoped she sounded cool and amused. Inside she was neither. 'There are moments when every girl likes to be swept off her feet,' she went on in the same tones. 'Philip is very good at that sort of thing.'

Jeffrey stared at her. 'What do you mean?' he demanded. 'How do you know?' he added pointedly.

Caroline shrugged her shoulders. She didn't want to

share her knowledge of Philip's attraction for her with anyone, least of all with Jeffrey. 'I've known him a long, long time,' she compromised.

'And he took advantage of that friendship?' Jeffrey concluded, his mouth curling with bitter disapproval.

'Why should you say that?' Caroline reproached him.

'It's obvious! The only thing I can't understand is why I never heard about it before. I thought you were a child when you came out here for holidays?'

'I was.'

'A pretty precocious child!'

Caroline sighed. 'Don't be ridiculous!' she said. 'It wasn't like that at all. I liked Philip—when he didn't drive me mad, bossing me about and making me do a whole lot of things that frightened me half to death, but he was like a brother to me. He still is.'

Jeffrey gave her a cold look. 'Now I know you're lying, Caroline,' he said. 'I know you well enough to know that you don't look on Philip Klearchos as a brother! You may not know it, but you're more than half in love with the man——'

'I am not!'

'Or you hate him,' Jeffrey went on quietly. 'I'm not sure which.'

Caroline uttered a gasp of dismay. She thought it just as well that there was very little traffic on the road just then. 'I don't know either,' she confessed. 'But I think I hate him!'

Jeffrey was silent for a long moment. 'You know I was going to ask you to marry me, don't you?'

The tears gathered at the back of Caroline's throat. She stopped the car, putting up a hand to wipe her cheek before he could see that she was crying. 'It just happened!' she tried to explain.

'And it can't un-happen?'

'*I don't know!*'

She wished urgently that Jeffrey would *do* something and not just sit there, looking at her with hurt, reproachful eyes. Why didn't he kiss her? Or tell her what he thought of her? *Anything* rather than expect her to explain herself, or make the decision for him as to whether he was going to press his suit or not. Philip would have—— Her cheeks burned and her stomach lurched at the mere thought of what Philip would do in similar circumstances. Why couldn't Jeffrey be more like *that*?

'Oh well,' he said at last, 'it doesn't do any good for you to go upsetting yourself. I won't mention it again.'

Caroline could hardly believe her ears. 'Why not?' she asked sharply.

'I think it would only embarrass us both. I thought of you rather differently in England. I didn't realise you had hankerings for something which is quite foreign to me as a man, and an Englishman at that! I am surprised, I must admit, that you find Philip to your taste. He'll take you for granted, make you miserable by denying you any kind of freedom, and very likely you'll find yourself sharing him with any number of other women as well! He isn't the type to see anything wrong in that, it's probably expected in a man, but if you so much as look at another man that'll be a very different story. Have you thought about that?'

Caroline fiddled with her fingers. 'Philip doesn't want to marry me,' she said abruptly. 'He's going to marry Ileana.'

Jeffrey's mouth tightened into a straight line. 'Doesn't that make any difference to you?'

Caroline shook her head. 'I don't think I'm in love with Philip at all,' she said. 'But if you think I'm going to be unhappy, aren't you going to do anything to rescue me from him?'

Jeffrey was startled into looking at her. His eyes were bleak and his distaste for the conversation was clearly visible in the faint twitch at the corner of his mouth. 'I don't think you want to be rescued, Caroline. If you're looking for someone who will demand your complete submission, you've come to the wrong man.'

'There is a happy medium!' she retorted. 'I've told you I'm not going to marry Philip!'

Jeffrey winced. 'I want my wife to be a woman I can admire,' he said slowly, 'a woman who will be an asset to me socially and who will help me with my work. I don't think, after what I've seen of you here in Cyprus, that you are that woman. You would ask too much emotionally and physically—and that sort of thing. I want a nice, calm life, my dear. I'm beginning to think you want to live in the middle of an electric storm. You want the heights and the depths and the excitements, while I want the shallows and a temperate climate——'

'But I don't!' Caroline denied. 'I've always been afraid of getting out of my depth!'

The sardonic look he gave her did little to comfort her. 'You're not being honest with yourself about this,' he told her, quite kindly, but in the same pompous tones that he had used all along. 'You wouldn't be content with what I have to offer you.'

'Wouldn't I?' She turned and looked at him, surprised by her own lack of embarrassment. He was very pink in the face and she felt a little sorry for him. She cast her mind back to the last evening that he had taken her out in London. She had given him her hand to hold in the taxi home and she had thought him unnecessarily awkward about it, it had almost been as though he hadn't wanted the contact, just as he had hardly ever kissed her and, when he had, it had never been more than a chaste salute on her brow or cheek. Only once had he kissed her lips and the caress had left her cold and frustrated, but she had never understood why.

'Have you ever been?' he asked her.

'I don't know,' she admitted. She looked away from him, allowing the silence to grow between them until it, too, irritated her. 'Philip is very Greek,' she went on quickly. 'He has very different ideas about women from yours. He wouldn't be interested in whether I was content or not——'

Jeffrey attempted a small smile. 'You do him an injustice,' he cut her off. 'I think he would be interested, if it ever occurred to him that he could fail to content any woman his eye lighted upon for a moment.'

Caroline felt herself blush. 'That wasn't what I meant,' she said in a low voice. 'What I meant was that no Greek would ever consider a woman to be his equal —in—in any way. I don't think I should like that very much.'

To her surprise Jeffrey laughed. 'I wonder!' he drawled. 'I wouldn't have believed it in London, but now I just wonder if you wouldn't!'

Caroline opened her eyes wide. 'What a thing to say!' she reproached him. 'Even if it were true, which it isn't!'

'No?' said Jeffrey. 'Has Philip ever kissed you, Caroline?'

The colour burned in her cheeks. 'N-not seriously,' she managed.

His eyebrows rose at that. 'You're playing with fire, my dear. But it's none of my business what you do. Only don't get your fingers burned, Caro. Philip could very easily hurt you badly.'

The warning had come too late, Caroline reflected. She was already hurt, and she deserved to be so for dwelling not only on the way he had kissed her in the kitchen, but also for allowing what he had said to her then to come between her and Jeffrey. For she had allowed it to. It had come into her mind again and again every time she had looked at him. Even today it had made her dissatisfied with his company, though no one could have said he was playing the looking-glass and telling her how pretty she was at this moment.

'Philip doesn't want me,' she said.

Jeffrey folded his lips together with smug satisfaction. 'That's as well for you, if you ask me. You'd better come back to England with me and I'll try to forget all that I've learned about you here——'

70

'Well, I won't!' Caroline snapped back. 'I've nothing to be ashamed about! I don't want you to forget *anything*! Nothing, do you hear? I don't want to have anything more to do with you!'

Jeffrey went pinker than ever. 'Am I expected to get out and walk?'

That struck Caroline as funny and she began to laugh. 'Oh, don't be so silly! I'm going to take you to Larnaca.' She bit her lip and another peal of laughter escaped her. 'Don't be so stuffy, Jeffrey! You may as well enjoy your holiday here. You've never really been in love with me, have you? Losing me won't cause you much sadness.'

'More than you know,' Jeffrey murmured dryly. 'Your father will be even more upset, but then I imagine that you know that?'

She turned a shaken face towards him. 'My *father*? What has this to do with him?'

'Don't you know?'

She shook her head, a deep anger growing within her. 'Did he say anything to you about marrying me?' she demanded.

'It would have been—convenient to him from a business point of view, but I daresay he'll get over it.'

Caroline tried not to let this new knowledge hurt her. In a way, she supposed she had always known that her father had had his reasons for encouraging the match. 'He has no business now,' she said quietly. 'He's retired.'

'From drilling for oil. He's quite a young man still, Caroline. He's put a lot of money into my company and has taken an interest in all that we want to do in the next few years. It was understood between us that if he became my father-in-law I'd offer him a seat on the board and see to it that he got other directorships as well. I thought you knew that?'

'No, I didn't know.' She blinked. 'It doesn't matter.'

'Perhaps I shouldn't have said anything——' Jeffrey began, worried by her white, shocked face.

'No, I'm glad I know,' she answered him. She smiled faintly. 'It doesn't change anything, does it?'

'I suppose not,' he admitted. 'But he wouldn't like it if you were to marry Philip.'

Caroline sat up very straight. 'I don't think that's any of his business, or yours either,' she declared. 'I'm of age, you know, and I shall marry whom I like!'

Jeffrey merely grunted. Caroline slipped the car into gear and took off at a great speed, giving him the uncomfortable feeling that his shoulder-blades had stuck to the back of his seat. 'I don't like driving fast!' he complained.

'Too bad!' said Caroline. But she slowed to a more moderate pace and began to point out the various features of the scenery they were passing. He sighed with relief that she was being so sensible about things, for if there was one thing he particularly disliked, it was having his emotions made visible to other eyes than his own. He found it hard to forgive them their discovery that there was very little feeling beneath his rather splendid exterior. The ruling passion of his life was making money, not people. He had no use for money, and none at all for the people who wanted to spend his money for him, but he enjoyed the mere fact of money and watching it grow. It was not something that Caroline would ever have understood, and with a feeling of regret that pleased him rather than gave him pain, he decided he was well out of the whole business of having to marry her. In fact he might even do something for her father nevertheless and moreover. They had a great deal in common and they understood one another very well. He would be a useful man to have on the board once he had got over his disappointment over Caroline. He sat back in his seat with a sigh and looked about him cautiously. This was quite a pleasant island and he thought he might enjoy his holiday after all.

Caroline's thoughts ran along quite different lines. She had almost forgotten the man sitting beside her, so intent was she on the desperate idea that had just occurred to her. She tried to remember exactly what Philip had said to her in the kitchen when they had been discussing Jeffrey, but everything he had said that day had been overshadowed by the moment when he had kissed her. But he had said something—she knew he had! Only what exactly had it been? She remembered he had suggested that Jeffrey was interested in her expectations and she had retorted that one didn't buy someone like Jeffrey—it seemed she had been wrong there! One couldn't buy him for money, perhaps, but there were other ways that her father had known about. It was a piece of knowledge that made her feel cheap and she put it away from her as quickly as she could.

What else had Philip said? She remembered him looking unduly serious, almost as if he had been weighing up in his mind whether to say anything at all to her. He had stood quite still and had said, 'Why don't you try to buy me?' She remembered exactly now. Only he had been joking! He *must* have been joking! But supposing he had really meant it? It wouldn't do any harm to suppose such a thing for a moment. She had turned the suggestion away then, she remembered, by reminding him that he was more interested in Ileana. And he had said—— She took a deep breath, wondering at the gust of crazy excitement that swept through her. He had said that she gave in far too easily, that he was tempted by the Klearchos inheritance and that he might take her along with it—if she asked him nicely. But supposing that she did and he turned her down? It was typical of Philip, she thought angrily, that he would arrange matters so that it was she who had to ask, she who had to strip away her pride before him, before he would even say yea or nay.

But to be married to Philip! Wouldn't that be worth any and every humiliation he might heap on her head? Once she was married to him, he would have the Greek respect for home and hearth and she would have a certain security that no other man she knew would give her. And she would be Philip's wife! From that thought she retreated quickly, afraid of where it would take her. She pulled herself back to the present moment and the road ahead of her with determination.

'It's a pity you won't be here for the Whit weekend,' she said aloud to Jeffrey. 'Larnaca is the best place to watch the celebration of Cataclysmos on the island. It's really the old pagan ceremony of welcoming Aphrodite's emergence from the spray at Paphos, but it was given biblical associations by linking it with Noah's escape from the flood, and then it became linked with Pentecost too——'

'Isn't that stretching things rather?' Jeffrey interrupted.

'Not really,' she answered. 'The Cypriots are a very religious people. They like to cling to all the old customs. I think all people do underneath. Religions come and go, but the holy places are always the same in every country, going right back into the mists of time.'

'I don't think I have much time for such things,' Jeffrey said, yawning. 'Perhaps it's as well that I won't be here for this ceremony of yours.'

Caroline sniffed. 'I enjoy it,' she said positively. 'The priest hurls a cross into the depths of the sea and all the best swimmers compete with each other to retrieve it. I remember Philip tried for it one year——'

Jeffrey yawned again. 'Hot, isn't it?' he remarked. 'How much longer before we get there?'

'Not very long,' Caroline said. She stopped talking then, uncomfortably aware that she was boring him. Funny, because in London she had listened politely to him going on for hours at a time about things that had bored her to distraction. It was funny because she hadn't even realised it at the time. She had taken it as a part of being with Jeffrey and had managed to persuade herself that it was the sort of thing that every

74

girl had to put up with.

'I don't suppose you'd be interested in Lazarus either,' she began again.

'Lazarus? The fellow who was raised from the dead?'

Pleased to have his interest, Caroline nodded with enthusiasm. 'He was the first bishop here for thirty years, during his second life, of course. He was buried here at one time, but his body was taken to Constantinople where it was stolen and taken to Marseilles.'

'Really?' said Jeffrey.

'Yes,' Caroline went on. 'It's interesting because of the salt flats around Larnaca. It was fertile orchards at one time, but the owner refused to allow Lazarus to eat any of the fruit, and so he turned it into the salt flats that are there now. One can see the most marvellous birds there sometimes.'

'I'm not,' Jeffrey said with pained restraint, 'interested in bird-watching.'

'No,' Caroline agreed. He certainly wasn't, not of either kind. 'Perhaps we shouldn't have come,' she added. 'I don't think Mahomet's foster-mother will interest you either. Larnaca *was* an important place, but it isn't now. I'm afraid you'll think it rather seedy and dirty. I should have taken you to Famagusta—you could have seen Othello's tower there. Your friends would be much more interested in hearing about that!'

Jeffrey shot her a quick look and smiled briefly. 'Don't be bitter, Caro,' he advised. 'It isn't my fault that things aren't working out for you.'

'I'm sorry,' she said at once. 'Only I did want you to enjoy today. I've always loved visiting these places and I thought you would too.'

'Did you?' he said quite gently. 'I'm sorry too, my dear, but it wouldn't do to pretend, would it?'

'No,' she admitted. She turned off the main road at the outskirts of Larnaca to go straight to the Tekke and began to tell him about the mosque because she couldn't think of anything else to say. 'Umm Haram means reverend mother. She was called Hala Sultan in Turkish. The local people say this is the third most important shrine in all Islam. I don't think it was ever that, but the Turkish ships always used to salute the shrine every time they went past and, at one time, thousands of pilgrims used to come here. Mahomet's foster-mother, or aunt, was really called Rumeysa, meaning "bright-eyed lady". She sounds rather attractive, don't you think? Anyway, in those days all sorts of people went off on holy wars, and she took part in the first of twenty-four Arab invasions of Cyprus in A.D. 647, and she was given a martyr's burial where she fell. The tomb is a trilithon and was borne on the wings of angels all the way from Mount Sinai. There's a huge floating stone above the tomb which used to be held there by faith alone, but people began to be afraid to go near it, so the authorities put in supports to comfort them——'

'You relieve my mind,' Jeffrey murmured.

'Yes, well, it's a nice story,' Caroline defended the legend she had just repeated, 'And it is an important shrine. One of King Hussein's grandmothers, or maybe it's a great-grandmother, is buried in the mosque too. She used to live in Nicosia.'

Jeffrey patted her hand that was resting on the gear-lever, smiling affectionately at her. 'Why does this place mean so much to you?' he asked her curiously.

She shrugged, half minded to pretend that it meant nothing more than any other place to her. Then she said, so quietly that he had to strain his ears to hear her, 'It's the most peaceful place in the whole island. It has a citrus garden, with palm-trees and singing birds, and there's hardly ever anyone there. It isn't much inside, but it has a friendly atmosphere. Oh, I can't explain! You'll have to see for yourself.'

'I doubt it will mean any of that for me,' Jeffrey said and, for the moment, he sounded almost regretful. But even he was silent when he caught sight of the delicate minaret amongst the trees. 'Is that it?' he asked.

Caroline nodded. 'Isn't it strange that the citrus trees come right down to the edge of the salt flat there? Don't you think it's beautiful?'

'Yes, my dear, I do.'

But when they drove in between the trees right up to the door of the Tekke and bought their tickets to go inside, Caroline knew that the enchantment had already disappeared for him. Not even the scent of the citrus trees and the flowers in the beds could hide the air of neglect that hung over the interior of the building. Caroline stood in the middle of the doorway, sloughing off her shoes with the ease of long habit, and she had to wait for Jeffrey while he seated himself on the step and slowly untied his shoe-laces and put his shoes neatly side by side out of the way where no one could trip over them.

When he stood up, Caroline waited expectantly for the full impact of the dim atmosphere to hit him, but he was disappointingly unmoved. She watched him stroll across the carpet to stare for a long moment, and with an inward shudder, at the niche in the wall called the *mihrab* that pointed out the direction of Mecca.

'What are the clocks for?' he asked the young Turk who had come inside with them.

'They are not working just now,' the youth answered.

'But when they are,' Caroline hurried forward to explain, 'one of them shows the time in Mecca and the other the local time.'

The Turk grinned at her. He waited for Jeffrey to move away, then he winked at Caroline behind his back, shrugging his shoulders slightly in silent enquiry. Caroline pursed up her lips and tried to pretend that she hadn't noticed. 'Do you live in Larnaca?' she asked the young man rather breathlessly.

He nodded. 'I walk here every day. Do you wish to see the tomb now?'

Caroline looked at Jeffrey, but he shook his head. 'You go and look, my dear. I think I've seen enough.'

Caroline hesitated, knowing that he wouldn't like waiting for her, however easy he might seem on the surface, but she couldn't resist a quick look into that dark place where no light ever came. The Turkish youth lit an orange candle and held it aloft for her to see the tomb the better. Shadows jumped out of the wall at her, making her flesh tingle, as he pointed out some green cloth, the purpose of which she had never discovered, lying on the top of the tomb. Caroline stared into the dark corners, imagining all the people who had stood in the same spot where she was standing over the centuries to stare into this holy place. But no message came to her like a bolt from the blue as she had more than half been hoping. Perhaps, if Philip had been standing beside her, she would have known, but he was nowhere near and she could feel Jeffrey's impatience reaching out to her and spoiling the moment for her. She walked back into the prayer hall without a backward look and went straight to her shoes, pushing her feet into them as fast as she could.

'Would you like to climb the minaret?' the Turk asked softly, standing very close beside her. 'I don't mind waiting if you and the gentleman wish to see the view from there.'

Caroline looked enquiringly at Jeffrey. 'Do you want to?'

To her surprise he expressed some eagerness to climb up the narrow stairs inside the minaret. He beckoned to the guide to go with him, calling over his shoulder, 'Are you coming, Caro?'

'No,' she said. 'I want to look at the garden.'

She went out into the dappled sunlight, allowing the peaceful atmosphere to wash over her, bringing balm to her spirit. If Philip had been there that minute she would have had the courage for anything! She looked up at the minaret, shading her eyes, and saw that Jeffrey had not yet appeared on the little balcony that ran round the top, from which the muezzin calls the hours of prayer, and that she had time to walk down the path to the very edge of the salt lake, now quite dry and grey-white with the stranded salt. And, as she watched, a heron took wing and flew out to the centre of the lake, turned in the light wind and skimmed back across the very spot where she was standing. Was that the good omen she had been seeking? She held her breath and told herself that it was. She had always felt superstitious about herons and particularly lucky when she saw one. This one would bring her Philip. It had to! She stood in silence, her shoulders bowed under the burden that she was carrying, for she knew in that moment that there was no one else for her. There never had been. If Philip said no, she would go lonely and alone all her life. She had belonged to him since that brief moment, when she had been only sixteen years old, and he had kissed her and she had begun her long flight from him that had brought her back to the same place she had been then—at his feet!

Jeffrey was full of the view from the top of the min- aret. It was the only part of their visit that he had enjoyed at all. Caroline took him on to Kiti to see the church there, but she knew before they started that the mosaic, beautiful as it was, would barely catch his at- tention, and she herself wanted to hurry home to sort out exactly what she was going to say to Philip.

She drove home at a very fast pace, barely speaking to Jeffrey the whole way to Nicosia and only then be- cause the road was up again and she wanted him to pay attention to the signposts so that they wouldn't get lost somewhere in the suburbs.

When they climbed the hill up the narrow road to Bellapais, she slowed to a more sober pace, trying to think of some way of keeping him out of the house for a while.

'Are you going to send any postcards home?' she asked him, speaking very quickly. 'You can buy them beside the café of the Tree of Idleness. You can get stamps there too.'

'Okay,' he said.

She put him down beside the café, letting in the clutch so fast that she was already moving before he could slam the door shut. A few seconds later she had set the car up the ramp into the garage and was swallowing down the nerves that threatened to overcome her as she let herself into her aunt's house.

'Aunt Hilda? Are you there?' she called out.

Silence was her only answer. She called out again to make quite sure that she was alone in the house, wondering where her aunt had gone. She had looked so tired that morning and it was difficult to believe that she would have gone out anywhere by herself and at this hour of day. There was a faint scuffling noise in the sitting-room and Caroline ran towards the door, her heart in her mouth as she thought what she might find. But when she flung open the door, of her aunt there was no sign. Instead there stood Philip, Ileana standing against him in the close embrace of his arms.

'I'm sorry!' Caroline said abruptly.

Philip's eyebrows rose enquiringly. 'So you might be!' he rebuked her. 'How long have you been home?'

'Long enough!' she burst out, ashamed of the despair that consumed her. 'But don't mind me! I'm going again!'

'Good,' said Philip. 'Shut the door as you go out, will you?' He waited to make sure she was going, a smile twisting his lips as he watched her. 'By the way,' he added, 'don't leave the house, will you? I want to speak to you.'

Caroline slammed the door shut behind her, unable to utter the fierce retort that rose to her lips because of the scalding tears at the back of her throat. But inwardly she shouted the words to herself, "Then want can be your master!"

CHAPTER SIX

SHE ran all the way to the Tree of Idleness, throwing herself into the first chair she came to, unaware of the slight stir she had caused amongst the visiting tourists, as she had come among them. She looked about her for Jeffrey, trying to catch her breath and pretend that she had not been running at all, but she couldn't see him anywhere. Then he came out of the shop and sauntered towards her, unhurried even when she waved urgently to him.

'Hullo,' he said. 'I thought you wanted to be rid of me——'

'I did,' she interrupted flatly.

'But you find you haven't anything better to do after all?' he suggested.

'Yes, I have,' she denied. 'Only Ileana is up at the house and I didn't want to meet her just now.'

'I see,' said Jeffrey. 'Do you want a cup of tea or something?'

Aware that she was not behaving very well as far as Jeffrey was concerned, Caroline flushed. 'You don't mind, do you, Jeffrey? Not really?'

'No, not really,' he agreed, smiling. 'Make use of me all you like, my dear.'

Caroline sighed. 'But that isn't fair either, is it?'

'At least you can accept a cup of tea from me,' he returned. 'After that I shall take myself off and have a look at that ruin of an abbey. I'm sure that that's an occupation that you will approve of!'

'Oh yes!' she said immediately. 'I think you'll find it quite interesting, and the view from the top is terrific.'

'But you're not going to offer to show it to me?'

She shook her head. 'I have to cook the dinner,' she explained in a tight voice. 'It takes me longer than most because I'm no cook. Aunt Hilda says I must learn, and I want to, but in the interim all our meals are rather hit-and-miss affairs.'

Jeffrey looked amused. 'I hadn't noticed,' he said.

'That's because Philip cooked the meal last night,' she told him. 'But there won't be anyone to do it to-night but me, though, and it *has* to be a success. *Everything* depends on it!'

'Why don't you get a girl in from the village?'

She avoided his glance, wondering just how to answer him. 'Philip doesn't think it's necessary,' she said.

'Instead he expects you to make a skivvy of yourself?' Jeffrey shook his head at her. 'Your father would have a fit if he knew that you'd come out here to be cook and bottle-washer to Philip as well as your aunt!'

'It has nothing to do with my father!' Caroline retorted with a glint of anger.

'I wonder if he'd see it that way?'

Caroline's eyes widened in dismay. 'You won't tell him, Jeffrey? I'll never speak to you again if you do!'

'He may come here and see for himself some time, have you thought of that?'

Caroline shook her head positively. 'He wouldn't come here. He hasn't seen Aunt Hilda for years, not since she married Uncle Michael, except once, when he came and collected me—the last time I was here.'

'But he allowed you to come?'

'It was—convenient,' she said evasively. 'But he wouldn't come himself. He didn't want me to come this time.'

Jeffrey scratched the side of his nose thoughtfully. 'Have you thought that he might cut off your allowance if you decide to stay out here with your aunt?'

'*No!*' Caroline gasped.

'I should, my dear. You've never had to fend for yourself financially, have you? There isn't much you could do in the way of work, is there?'

'I could learn!'

'You won't get a work permit to learn!' Jeffrey smiled at her, looking pink and smug and triumphant.

'I thought I'd just give you a word of warning before you committed yourself to something you'll regret. Nothing personal, you understand?'

Caroline sat huddled in misery, scarcely aware of the waiter bringing her tea, or of Jeffrey paying for it and rising to his feet with a well-satisfied air, just touching her on the shoulder as he wandered off across the square towards the ruins of the abbey. If she were to have no allowance, she would have nothing to offer Philip in the immediate future. Would he settle for her expectations of the Klearchos lands? She thought not. Why should he when Ileana had so much more to offer? And he must like the other girl anyway to kiss her as he had been doing when she had interrupted them. Perhaps he more than liked her. Perhaps he loved her as a woman should be loved whom he was going to make his wife. Caroline could not understand her own mixed emotions on the subject. She was almost sure that Philip did not love Ileana, but he had been kissing her just the same, and it was that that hurt. It nagged her like toothache that he should kiss anyone else, and she couldn't understand why she should mind so much. Her whole being cried out against his doing such a thing and the pain he had caused her.

She finished her tea, but she felt too weary to move from her seat. If she didn't go soon, Jeffrey would be back and he would wonder why she hadn't gone back to the house long since. She didn't even look up when a shadow crossed her face and Philip sat down in the chair that Jeffrey had recently vacated.

'I told you to wait in the house,' he said.

She sat up very straight, raising her brows in an expression that was unconsciously borrowed from himself. 'I do as I like,' she answered him.

'So I have observed,' he drawled. 'But you've never done as you've liked as far as I'm concerned, *yinéka mou*, and you're not going to start now.'

'You're impossible!' she informed him, scarlet in the face. 'And I'm not your woman, nor ever like to be!

83

And I don't want to listen to you now!'

Philip looked scornfully at her. 'You always were a jealous little cat——'

'I'm not!'

He leaned forward, shooting out a hand and catching her own in his to make sure that he had her full attention. 'Be very careful, Caroline! Being your father's daughter doesn't excuse everything. People will put up with a lot from you when you can sweeten the pill with all that money, but it has never been like that between us, and it won't be like that now. Understand?'

She nodded, trying to free her hand from his grasp. 'I've never made much of money. It's always been there, that's all.' She bit her lip, not sure how to go on. 'It probably won't be for much longer. If I stay on in Cyprus—with Aunt Hilda,' she added hurriedly, blushing painfully, 'I probably won't get my allowance for very much longer, as Jeffrey has just been pointing out to me!'

'Uncalled for on his part,' Philip commented. 'Are you going to stay on in Cyprus?'

This was her moment, she knew, but she hadn't the courage to seize it. Instead, she bent her head and muttered something that was quite incomprehensible to herself, let alone him, and wished that she could sink into the ground, as quickly as possible, out of his sight.

'Why won't you admit that you're jealous of Ileana?' Philip cut through her agitated murmurs.

'*Me?*' she echoed.

'Is it so impossible?'

'It's ridiculous! Why should I be jealous of Ileana? I've known for days that you're probably going to marry her——'

'Yet you haven't accepted that as definite, have you?'

'No.' She licked her lips, seeing another opportunity slipping slowly past her into oblivion. 'Philip, do you know where Aunt Hilda is? I couldn't find her when I—when I——'

'When you walked in on Ileana and me and jumped to the obvious conclusion that you had interrupted a passionate embrace between us?'

Caroline lifted her head. It was just like Philip to rub salt in the wound, she thought. He wouldn't allow her to ignore it and pretend it had never been, which was what she wanted to do——

'She looked so tired and old this morning,' she said, blinking rapidly.

Philip released her hand and sat back, looking at her through half-closed eyes. 'You're still worried about her? I thought you would have guessed by now?'

'Guessed what?'

'Aunt Hilda thought it time you paid her a visit, but she didn't want to be the cause of a rift in your family. I guess she thought her brother would understand your rallying round more readily if he thought she was at death's door!'

'And she isn't?'

'She has some heart trouble, but it isn't too bad. She gets tired and depressed at times. More than anything else she wanted to see you. She's fond of you, Caroline, and she wants you to be happy. An easy, moneyed contentment of the kind your father will buy for you isn't good enough for her neice!' He pointed an accusing finger at her. 'Is it?' he demanded.

She would have liked to beg the question, but something in his eyes prevented her. 'I prefer to be something more than a business acquisition, either bought or sold. But if I stay on here, I don't know how I shall live, or anything.' She cast him an appealing look, but he made no move to help her. 'I've never been poor!'

'You have the Klearchos inheritance,' he reminded her in a hard voice. 'It will be enough to get you a husband——'

She took a quick breath. 'Would it be enough for you?' she asked, not looking at him.

'That would depend,' he answered dryly. 'I

shouldn't like my wife to be independent of me in any way. She'll eat my bread and bear my children, accepting what I choose to give her. There would be no servants to wait on her hand and foot, and no money to spare for the luxuries that you think of as your right. But there are other men who'd be prepared to do your bidding for a great deal less than your aunt's villa and the Klearchos lands.'

'I don't want a man who would do my bidding,' she said so quietly that she thought for a while he hadn't heard her.

'But then you don't know what you do want,' he said. 'Come on home, my love, and you can talk it over with Aunt Hilda. She went out to tea with a friend of hers, but she should be back any time now.'

Caroline walked up the slope to the house beside him, wondering a little at her own meekness. Half of her wanted to bolt away from him for ever, but the other half knew that she had to stay, to prove to him if possible that in the last few days she had come to know what she wanted and that she had need of his gentleness, even if she couldn't have his love.

She waited until they were out of sight of the square and, indeed, of the whole village. 'Philip, are you going to marry Ileana?'

He turned to her with a smile, but his eyes were cool and wary. 'Are you going to admit you're jealous of her?'

'Why should I be?' she retorted.

He put a hand under her chin and forced her to look at him. 'Because you want to know what it's like to be kissed as a grown woman, with no holds barred. You had a glimpse of what it might be like when I kissed you yesterday and you can't wait for more. Only you're too proud to ask, even if you're not too proud to hate Ileana because you think she's more of a woman that you'll ever be. Now, do you want to find out how you feel about me, or not?'

She jerked away from him. 'How dare you!' she

86

breathed. 'I hate you! *I hate you!* Do you hear?'

'I should think the whole of Bellapais has heard you,' he answered quietly. The expression in his eyes was inscrutable, but she saw only the arrogance of his stance and the challenge in his smile. 'Afraid, Caroline?'

'Why should I be afraid?'

'Because I'm no Jeffrey to dance to your whim. If you don't want to go my way, don't start at all. Well?'

She glared at him, tossing her head in a futile gesture of independence. 'I'm not begging you for anything,' she began. Her eyes wavered and she bent her head. 'Philip, be a little kind to me!'

He held out his hands to her. 'On your head be it, *kori mou*! Come here, Caroline!'

She went into his arms with a sob of gladness that betrayed her eagerness for his embrace, but he did not kiss her immediately. He held her close for a long moment, a hand on the nape of her neck, stroking her back with his other hand in a gesture of comfort that at first soothed her, but then, with a suddenness that shattered her, had quite the opposite effect, arousing a storm of emotion within her that would longer be denied. She slipped her arms around his neck and strained closer to him, offering him her lips with an impetuosity that she would later look back on with surprise at her own daring.

'Oh, Philip,' she answered, 'I didn't know——'

'I don't think it's hate, do you?' he murmured. But he allowed her no time to answer, taking possession of her lips again with a mastery that destroyed all rational thought for quite some time. She was aware only of her delight in him, in the warmth of his body against hers, and of the most delicious weakness in herself that complemented the strength in him. When he released her, she stumbled, half laughed, and leaned against his arm.

'Philip, will you——?' She hesitated, as uncertain as she had been before.

87

'Will I what, *yinéka mou*?'

She flushed with pleasure that he should call her his woman once again, Ileana completely forgotten.

'I don't want to go back to England,' she said shyly. 'I don't have to, do I?'

'Are you asking me or telling me?'

She blinked. 'Asking.'

Philip drew his forefinger along the line of her jaw. The glint in his eyes made her very aware of her ruffled appearance and she made an abortive attempt to smooth down her skirt and to push her hair back into some kind of order, but he seemed to take a delight in making it more difficult for her by riffling his fingers through her hair as fast as she did.

'Philip, everyone will *know*——'

He laughed. 'Do you mind?'

She shook her head, tongue-tied by the look in his eyes. 'Philip, please——' She took a deep breath. '*Philip?*'

He reached out for her and drew her back into his arms, covering her face with kisses. 'Don't tempt me, Caroline, unless you want me as much as I want you. A man can only stand so much!'

'But, Philip, I don't want to be just any woman to you——'

'What do you want?' he repeated.

Caroline shrugged her shoulders helplessly, stepping away from him, shivering a little as she stood there, her eyes frightened and not knowing what to say. How was she to explain that it was all happening too fast for her? That she needed time to think? That she had to steel herself for the time when she could no longer avoid asking him if the Klearchos lands wouldn't be enough for him? If he wouldn't, please, take her to be his wife instead of Ileana?

Ileana! She had forgotten all about her. She swallowed convulsively, trying to regain a belated control of her emotions. 'I need time,' she said at last. 'I—I don't know what to do!'

He put a hand on the small of her back and pulled her close against him. 'Do you want me to tell you what to do?'

How wonderful that would be! But she had no right to put the whole burden on to him. 'I'm not going to marry Jeffrey,' she told him abruptly.

'I could have told you that days ago!' he retorted.

She coloured. 'Yes,' she said. 'But what about Ileana?'

'What about her?' he drawled.

'You—you must like her—to want to kiss her—and —and so on?'

His mouth set in a firm line that frightened her. 'Ileana is none of your business, Caroline.'

She gave him a harassed look. 'No, but——'

'Caro, my love, shut up! Come closer and let me kiss you again.'

But she couldn't afford to lose her head entirely. 'N-not now,' she protested. 'Philip, it isn't *enough*!'

'No? What more do you want?'

She couldn't answer him. 'It isn't enough,' she repeated. 'I d-don't want you to kiss me any more just now.'

His jaw tightened. 'Are you telling me what to do again? I haven't finished by a long way yet, my girl. You let yourself in for this and now you'll stay and see it through——'

'*I won't!*' she declared.

His grip tightened savagely about her. 'Don't ever tell me what you will and won't do again,' he advised her through clenched teeth. 'It is not for any woman to crack the whip over my head, and most certainly not for you! You chose to begin this and now you'll follow the path I select for you. You'll find it pleasant enough if you don't fight me every inch of the way, because I'll not give in to you, Caroline. I am Greek enough to expect to be master in my own house and I have no intention of abdicating any of that authority to you!'

Her heart hammered within her. 'You're—hurting

me!' she pleaded, but his grasp relaxed not at all. He looked very stern and sober and she had no doubt at all that he meant every word he said. 'I'll—I'll do as you tell me,' she said at last on a low note. 'I don't see why you need make such a thing of it!'

'Don't you?' he said dryly. 'You'd have me on a string like a shot if you thought you could get away with it, my dear——'

She raised her head with a return of spirit, looking him straight in the eye. 'I wasn't brought up like a Greek woman to be subservient to any man!' she said proudly.

His lips twisted into a smile. 'You're telling me! But it has its own rewards to give your whole life into another's keeping, as a Greek woman does. She is the heart of the home and sure of her position. What would you be as Jeffrey's wife?'

'He'd love me—in his way,' she insisted. She was silent for a long moment. She knew better than he did what marriage to Jeffrey would be like. There would be money enough for anything she wanted, but she would always come second to his first passion of the money-making business. She would have a room of her own and he would knock on her door when he wanted to come in—and she would have hated every minute of it!

'Philip, if I give you the Klearchos lands and—and all the money I have in the bank, will you marry me? My father—I won't go on getting my allowance, I don't suppose, but you can have anything I have now.'

She felt him stiffen against her and wished the words unsaid again. It was not the right time after all. He was going to marry Ileana! *He didn't want her!*

'The Klearchos lands aren't yours to give,' he said.

She took a swift look at his face, hurt by the cold look in his eyes. Her lips trembled and she felt very close to tears. 'I'm sorry,' she said. 'I didn't mean to embarrass you——' she gulped. 'It'd be a Greek marriage! I wouldn't expect—— Oh, Philip, what else can

I do? I thought you'd understand.'

'Perhaps I do,' he said gently. 'But do you understand——'

She nodded violently. 'I know you don't love me,' she burst out, 'but you don't dislike me, do you? And I would try to be everything you wanted——'

'If I married you, I'd see to it that you were everything I wanted.'

She caught the underlying passion in his words and blushed, hurrying into speech again. 'What did you mean, the Klearchos lands aren't mine to give you?'

He looked grim. 'You don't hold the title to them, that was all.'

'But they will be mine and I want you to have them. They should have gone to you in the first place.' Whatever she said was wrong if he didn't want her, she thought in despair, but having gone this far, there was nothing else to do but to go on and tell him the whole truth. 'It isn't only that,' she said gruffly. 'You know what you said about playing about in the shallows when there's the whole ocean out there waiting? I don't want to stay in the shallows all my life. If I go back to England, the tide will go out and—and I'll be stranded, and—and I haven't the courage to strike out on my own. You've always been there when I've got out of my depth. I—I don't know what to do without you!'

'It's taken you a long time to find that out,' he reminded her.

'I was afraid,' she confessed.

'Afraid of me?'

Caroline shook her head. 'A little, perhaps, but we were children then and people change. I thought it might be different now.'

'And it isn't?'

She averted her face from his gaze. 'If I married Jeffrey, my father would get a seat on the board of his company. He wants it very badly.'

Philip tipped up her face, kissing her lightly on the

lips and smiling a little when she trembled at his touch. 'What would you get out of it?' he asked her.

She attempted a forlorn smile and spoke with a jauntiness she was far from feeling. 'A life of ease and my own way in everything. I'd have a cook, and someone to run the house, and a nanny to look after the children——'

'As my wife,' Philip informed her, leaving no room for any doubt in her mind, 'you'd accept your living at my hands——'

'And eat your bread, and—and bear your children,' she quoted. She tried to avoid his look and, when she found she couldn't, she laughed breathlessly in the back of her throat. 'At least I shouldn't be bored and start looking for something else!'

'No,' he agreed. 'I don't think you'd be bored. And as for looking for something else to amuse you, or some-one else, I don't think you'd try it twice, you'd better make up your mind to that!'

The colour surged up into her cheeks. 'What about you?' she asked in an embarrassed voice.

'My friends are my business,' he retorted calmly. He looked at her thoughtfully, his eyes glinting with some emotion she couldn't guess at. 'I wonder if you know what a Cypriot marriage is like?'

'Aunt Hilda married Uncle Michael——'

'But not according to Cypriot custom,' he cut her off. 'I should expect all our customs to be properly observed.'

Caroline bit her lip. She wished he wouldn't look at her quite like that, his face as hard as granite. 'I—I shouldn't mind that,' she muttered.

His eyebrows rose. 'No quarter asked or given?' he challenged her. 'I wonder why?'

'I've told you!'

He smiled then. 'Have you? My dear Caroline, I've never known you to abase yourself for any reason before and I don't believe you're afraid of being left on the shelf if you don't marry Jeffrey now.'

'I told you! I want more——'

'More than everything money will buy?' His expression mocked her and she wished passionately that there was some way she could turn the tables on him and see him put out of countenance for a change.

'It isn't like that!' she cried out.

'No?' he taunted her.

'No. I wish I'd never said anything at all! I wouldn't have done if I'd thought you'd laugh at me. Well, laugh all you like! I shan't bother you again!'

His hands on her shoulders refused to allow her to break away from him. 'I'm not laughing,' he denied. 'I want a little honesty from you, that's all. Why do you want to marry me, Caroline?'

'Because——' She gasped and put a hand up to her mouth. 'It isn't fair! Why do I have to tell you when you don't say anything at all? I think you're horrid!'

'Because?' he prompted her.

The colour rushed into her cheeks and then abated, leaving her face white and strained. 'I won't tell you!'

He put a hand against her cheek, brushing the tears away from her lower lashes with a gentle finger. 'Sweetheart, why do you have to pretend? I know you lack experience and are scared of your own feelings, but I haven't changed into some ogre behind your back, while you weren't looking. I'm still the same person as I was before. You were a very sweet person when you were sixteen, and very young. I was afraid you'd go away and someone else would stake their claim to you, so I kissed you to give you something to remember me by, but you never came back, and when you did, you had a pretty shell and were trying to pretend you had no feelings at all——'

'And you had Ileana!' she broke in.

'Careful, Caroline! I've already told you that Ileana is no concern of yours! You'll have to learn to keep that jealousy of yours under some kind of control, or I'll think there's more to it than your natural desire to be the only pebble on the beach!'

She jerked her head back, wrenching herself free of his restraining hands, and aimed a kick at his shins, wanting to hurt him again, and again. But he stepped aside, catching her with a long arm round her waist, swinging her right off her feet and holding her so tightly that struggle as she might she could not win free.

He watched her efforts to regain her balance with a mocking smile, amused by her furious face. 'Tell me when you've had enough,' he said blandly.

'You haven't changed at all!' she shouted back.

'But you have. You've discovered all sorts of needs inside yourself that you won't tell me about. Why not?'

She stopped struggling, surprising him into almost dropping her. 'Darling Philip,' she said in dulcet tones, 'drop dead!'

He chuckled and let her go. Caroline landed painfully on her bottom, but not even that could alter her determination not to lose her temper with him again. She had never won any battle with him that way! She sat up and hugged her knees to her, watching him covertly under frowning brows.

'I've decided I don't want to marry you after all,' she said with a painfully achieved dignity.

'Have you indeed?' He bent down and took a firm grasp of her hair. 'What a pity, when I've just decided to accept your very kind offer! I'll talk about your dowry with Aunt Hilda and you'll accept whatever she decides for you and like it! You may not tell me now why you think I'm the right husband for you, but by God, you'll tell me when I've got my ring on your finger and you in my bed!'

She put her hands over her ears. 'I won't listen to you! You can't speak to me like that!' she stormed at him.

Philip took a firmer grasp of her hair and jerked her upwards. 'I'll speak to you how I like, my girl. And I'll kiss you when I like too—and that's right now! Get up

94

and come here. Or shall I pull your hair again?'

She was crying when she turned into his arms, but she wanted his kisses as much or more than she wanted to hurt and humiliate him. His lips took possession of hers and she felt him tremble against her.

'Oh, Philip!' she said brokenly. 'Kiss me again!'

He smoothed her hair away from her face, kissing first her eyes and then her lips again. 'It's my way or not at all, Caroline. I shan't give way.'

Her heart jerked within her and she hid her face in his shoulder, kissing his neck. 'I know,' she whispered. 'Where you lead, I'll follow.' She sighed heavily. 'But you hurt me, Philip! And you know I can't stand anyone to pull my hair!'

He held her closer against him. 'You talk too much,' he told her. 'Be quiet, while I kiss you some more!'

And, for the moment, she was only too happy to oblige him.

CHAPTER SEVEN

'MY dear, where have you been? You look as though you've been pulled through a bush backwards! Surely Jeffrey isn't responsible——'

'Jeffrey?' Caroline sounded so startled by the suggestion that her aunt laughed.

'The young man you brought out here to throw dust in Philip's eyes,' Aunt Hilda said dryly.

But Caroline found it far from funny. 'Where have you been?' she demanded in retaliation, her eyes sparkling with anxious accusation. 'I'm beginning to wonder if there's anything the matter with you at all!'

'Not very much,' her aunt admitted. 'I'm feeling better every day now that you're here. I must say, dear, that you're looking all the better for it too.'

Caroline smiled faintly and gave her aunt the victory. 'It's Philip,' she confessed. 'But he'd better tell you himself. I feel as though I've fallen down a well and found myself in heaven.' She stood a trifle uncertainly before her aunt. 'I still can't quite believe it, but he only has to look at me and I melt inside. The only thing is, it can't last for ever, can it? And what shall I do then?'

'Why shouldn't it last?' Aunt Hilda returned.

Caroline blushed. 'Because Philip has always been unbearably bossy and now he thinks he has me where he wants me, he'll be worse than ever!'

'Very likely!'

'Yes, but that's all right for the moment, but violent attractions often die down——' She broke off, striving vainly to find the right words to express her doubts. 'Aunt, he may still want Ileana.'

Aunt Hilda gave her niece a piercing look. 'If I were you, my dear, I wouldn't waste my time fighting Philip, or wondering too much about his motives. He is very like his uncle in that he has always known exactly what he wanted from life and he won't be stampeded into anything he doesn't want. If he wants to marry Ileana, he will, and neither of us will stop him, but the same goes for if he wants to marry you, my love, and you might just as well make up your mind to it!'

Caroline opened her mouth and then shut it again. She couldn't bring herself to tell her aunt that Philip would never ask her to marry him, if only because she had been reduced to asking him. Her eyes filled with tears. He didn't love her. He probably thought of her with no more than the most ordinary affection. He hadn't pretended he felt anything more than that, and she had no one to blame but herself if that was all she ever had from him. Whereas she—she had fallen flat on her face at his feet, fathoms deep in love with him, and she was more frightened than she had ever been in her whole life.

'I think he will marry me,' she said aloud. 'He—he's going to talk to you about it.'

Aunt Hilda raised her eyebrows. 'Not your father?'

Caroline hung her head. 'I don't know.'

Her aunt frowned. 'Well, we'll have to see about that. He is your father, my dear, when all is said and done. But I'm sure I shan't have to remind Philip of that. I expect he'll write to him and ask him to come over for the wedding. Your mother will come for much longer, I expect. She'll want to have a hand in your dress and all the wedding arrangements. I must say, it'll be delightful to have her here for a while.'

Caroline swallowed. She had not had time previously to give a thought to her family, but now that she had, she found herself shaking at the thought of their reactions to the course she had embarked on. 'It's to be a Cypriot wedding,' she said in a shattered voice. 'I—I don't know exactly what that means, but—but Philip seems to expect it.'

'Well, Philip is a Cypriot,' Aunt Hilda said in a strictly neutral voice, 'but I don't think he can expect——'

'He does!' Caroline exclaimed.

'But, my dear, not even the more sophisticated Cypriots go through the whole rigmarole that used to be considered proper in the villages!'

'Did you?'

'Of course not! Michael and I were married by the Army chaplain. He would have liked to have had a Greek Orthodox church wedding, but the main thing was to get married at all.'

Caroline sighed. 'I'd better go and start cooking the dinner,' she muttered. 'I want it to be particularly good——'

'Do you want any help?'

'No. I've got it all planned.' Her eyes glinted with a fierce determination. 'I'm not going to have it said any longer that I'm helpless round the house! You'll see! I can cook as well as anyone else if I put my mind to it!'

'Bravo!' Aunt Hilda crowed. 'I'll look forward to it!'

Caroline was glad to escape to the kitchen and to be on her own for a while. She found the challenge of producing a worthy dinner acted as a sop to her pride and, by the time she had all the saucepans boiling away on the top of the ancient cooker, she felt her self-respect to be quite restored. She made a moussaka for the main dish and was pleased with the result when she put it in the oven to brown the top and to keep it hot until it was needed. As a first course she made a cold cucumber soup, and for pudding she hulled and washed some strawberries and served them with sugar and cream.

'All your own work?' Philip asked her as they sat down at the table.

She felt suddenly shy of him and nodded quickly, unable to think of anything to say to him. He was the same Philip she had always known, and yet he was not the same, and it was this difference that disconcerted her. She found herself watching his well-kept, tanned hands and imagining them caressing her, and she was more than a little shocked by her own secret thoughts of him, with the result that she turned to Jeffrey with something very like relief and hung on his every word as he recounted all that had happened to him during his brief visit to the abbey.

'Didn't you get the most wonderful sense of peace, looking out towards the sea?' she asked him.

He looked at her. 'I don't think I notice these things for myself, Caroline,' he answered. 'I have to have them pointed out by someone like you. It was better this afternoon at the mosque when I could feed my interest on the fires of your enthusiasm.'

'But you didn't like it much!' she protested.

'I had other things on my mind,' he murmured with a sardonic smile.

'Oh? What things?'

'What things?' he scoffed. 'Why, you, of course!'

She took a quick glance at Philip from under her lashes, rather hoping that he hadn't heard anything that Jeffrey had said, but that hope died the moment she saw the slight frown between his eyes as he looked at the other man.

'J-Jeffrey,' Caroline hurled herself into speech, trying her best to put Philip right out of her mind for a few minutes. 'Jeffrey, what do you want to do tomorrow?'

'I am taking the day off tomorrow,' Philip interposed. 'Jeffrey and I will entertain each other——'

'Oh, but,' Caroline broke in anxiously, 'I want——'

'You have other things to do,' Philip reminded her. 'You must write to your parents.'

'That will hardly take me all day!' she retorted. 'I want to go with you.'

He smiled at her, shaking his head. 'And leave Aunt Hilda on her own again all day? Besides, someone has to do the household shopping and so on. If you like, I'll take you out sailing with me in the evening.'

She dropped her eyes to her plate, struggling against her desire to argue the point with him—all night if necessary! What sort of day would Jeffrey have? He would hate having to make himself pleasant to Philip all day.

'We could go swimming as well,' Philip prompted her. She looked up sharply and her breath caught when she saw the way his eyes crinkled at the corners with amusement and the brilliance of the light in them.

'I—I haven't been swimming for ages,' she stammered. 'I don't want to go too far out.'

His smile mocked her. 'I shall be there!'

She blinked, feeling the colour flood into her face. 'All right,' she said. 'I'd like to.' She made a conscious effort to behave normally, but the electrical excitement that he engendered in her was flowing through her veins, bringing a strange, fearful delight in its train that she found very hard to manage.

'I thought you said you couldn't cook?' Jeffrey's voice roused her. 'I'm always telling you that you underrate yourself.'

'I—I'm learning,' she managed.

He smiled kindly, with only the faintest overtones of patronage. 'I've never thought you were in any need of having to learn any party tricks. I'd prefer a simple English meal myself, but I can recognise the real thing when it's done to perfection like the dish you've just given us. It was very good, my dear. I'll have to tell your father's housekeeper that she must look to her laurels if she wants to keep ahead of you when you return!'

Caroline looked pleased. 'I don't think she'll believe you.' She turned impulsively to Philip. 'Did *you* enjoy the moussaka? Was it right?'

'Sheer delight, my darling!'

She swelled visibly in triumph, though only she knew it was the endearment rather than the compliment that had made her evening. Her eyes sparkled and she gave him an impudent smile. 'You see,' she said, 'Aunt Hilda is right! Anyone can cook if they can read a cookery book. There's nothing to it!'

'No,' Aunt Hilda agreed, 'but it's a little bit more than a party trick to be able to cook.'

'Aunt!' Caroline warned. She tried vainly to change the conversation, but Aunt Hilda had every intention of finishing what she had to say. She glared at her niece and then turned her warmest smile on Jeffrey.

'Every woman should be able to cook and make a man comfortable,' she said firmly. 'If she can't, she's not worth her salt. I can't understand why Caroline has never taken the trouble to learn before. In fact, I can't really understand what she did with her time at all in London.'

'She made a very decorative addition to her father's parties,' Jeffrey said stiffly. 'I think she more than earned her keep keeping all his guests happy——'

'My mother did most of that!' Caroline put in quickly.

But Jeffrey would not agree. 'Your presence never did your father's business interests any harm. What more can one ask of a woman than that?'

Philip gave Caroline a quizzical look, but he said nothing. It was left to her to say uncomfortably: 'I never thought of myself as a business asset, exactly.'

'But of course you are!' Jeffrey insisted. 'Your father trained you very well, but I thought you knew that?'

Caroline shook her head, her spirit baulking at the very idea. 'I don't believe you! He's always looked on me as a person in my own right—and M-Mother too.' Her voice broke a little as she thought of her mother. It was years since she had been anything more than her father's shadow, agreeing to everything he suggested, the perfect, accomplished hostess, who never drew attention to herself and somehow managed to get all the right people talking to one another without any fuss. Had she ever wanted anything more than that?

'A very pretty person!' Jeffrey said, smiling.

Caroline looked at him curiously. The smile was a mere sop to her vanity, she knew, and it didn't reach his eyes. 'Would you marry someone who wouldn't do your business any good?' she asked abruptly.

'I don't know what you mean,' he answered. 'I shouldn't want to marry anyone who worked against my interests, I suppose. Or anyone who was obviously unsuitable, but then that kind of person wouldn't attract me in the first place.'

'How lucky that you're not going to marry Caroline!' Aunt Hilda said brightly.

There was a moment's silence. 'I consider Caroline very suitable!' Jeffrey insisted then.

'You should see her lose her temper if someone pulls her hair!' Philip drawled.

Jeffrey's face turned pink. 'Why should anyone wish to pull her hair?' he demanded.

Philip laughed out loud, throwing back his head and allowing the sound to reverberate round the room. 'Because she always tells the truth when she's enraged. She's a much nicer person without that city gloss!'

'I can't agree,' Jeffrey said primly. 'The truth is the most overrated virtue. I'd much rather be comfortable. Wouldn't you, Caroline?'

Philip looked at her sardonically. 'Well, Caroline?'

'*I don't know!*' she burst out. 'I don't like hurting anyone, and the truth can sometimes do that.'

'I knew you'd agree with me!' Jeffrey sat back smugly, eyeing her with approval.

Caroline pushed her hair back from her eyes with a nervous hand. 'But I didn't agree with you. Not entirely. I mean, it's true that I don't like hurting people, but one can't be comfortable living a lie for long, can one? N-not with someone close to one.'

'Why not?' Jeffrey asked, plainly astonished.

'Because they wouldn't love the real you—they wouldn't respect you!' She shivered, thinking that she would give anything if Philip loved and respected *her*, instead of treating her with a familiar, sometimes even affectionate contempt. 'They wouldn't know what was you at all!'

'One only ever presents a façade to other people,' Jeffrey maintained. 'If my image was right to my wife, why should she care if I was like that through and through?'

Philip took a leisurely sip of wine, his eyes veiled. 'Would you be content with the image of herself your wife wished to present to you? What happens when the image slips?'

Jeffrey grinned. 'Change the model!' he said without hesitation. 'People do it all the time.'

'Not,' said Philip, 'in Cyprus.' He rose to his feet, signifying that the meal had come to an end. 'If you are going to wash up now, Caroline, I will help you this once. I have something to say to you.'

Caroline was tempted to refuse his offer. What had she done now? she wondered. She waited until her aunt had gone to her room and then she began to stack the dishes, carefully not looking in Philip's direction, but she knew the instant he took a step towards her and her hands trembled, making the plates rattle as she held them.

'Would you mind opening the door?' she said in stilted tones.

He took the plates from her, putting them back on the table. 'It's only to consider what we should say to your parents,' he said. 'Having second thoughts, Caroline?'

She cast him a nervous look, picking up the plates again. 'No,' she said in a breathless whisper, almost running into the kitchen. And then, as he followed her more slowly: 'If you don't want to marry me, I shall quite understand.' She dumped the crockery in the sink and sniffed, turning into his arms. 'Sex isn't enough either, is it?'

'It's real,' he said.

'Is it?'

'What lies between you and me is real enough to me. Isn't it to you?'

She blinked at him. 'I don't know,' she compromised.

He shrugged. 'I don't think this is the moment for me to convince you. Pity! I could do with some reassurance myself after watching you sit in Jeffrey's pocket all evening!'

Caroline opened her eyes wide. 'I did not!' she denied.

He ran his hand down her cheek, giving her a sharp tap as he did so. 'Playing social games with him may be amusing, but they are one of the things you have given up to be with me. Remember that!'

'I don't know what you mean!' she said stiffly.

Philip held her hands in his, looking at her through half-closed eyes. 'If you're wise,' he drawled, 'you won't make me explain it to you. Have you told him you're not going to marry him?'

She nodded, afraid of him as she so often was.

'Then stay away from him. He's a long way from being convinced that he won't capture you in the end. And he has your father as an ally, don't forget——'.

'Nobody is going to *capture* me! What an inelegant thing to say!'

He laughed, kissing her firmly on the lips. 'Inelegant or not, my love, you're going to find yourself so firmly hog-tied and shackled to me that you'll never get free for the rest of your life!' He smiled directly into her eyes. 'You don't suppose I'm going to let the Klearchos inheritance get away from me now, do you?'

'Is that all it is?' she cried out, hurt.

'You were always meant to marry me!' he declared. 'You won't escape your fate now and, in your heart, you don't want to! Deny it, if you can!'

Caroline bent her head, longing with all her being for a single word of tenderness from him. 'I won't deny it,' she said. 'You don't have to worry about anything

Jeffrey may do. I've made my choice.'

Philip's face softened. 'You think you have,' he agreed. 'But habit is a funny thing, and you've been away for a long time.'

She didn't understand what he meant. 'There's never been anyone else,' she told him.

He put up a hand and gave a very gentle tug to her hair. 'Keep it that way,' he advised her softly, 'and we'll both be happy!'

She could only hope he was right.

In the end she did the washing-up by herself. Philip stood, silently watching her, until she begged him to go away and leave her to it.

'But we still haven't decided what to tell your parents,' he said.

'I'll write to them both, tomorrow, and tell them I'm going to marry you. Do I have to say anything more than that?'

Philip hesitated. 'I think I should write to your father myself. He isn't going to like it.'

Caroline felt suddenly tired and cross. 'Oh, do as you like!' she snapped at him. 'Only I don't see that a letter from you is going to make him like it any more. Not that it *matters*! I am of age and I make my own decisions, as he'll probably tell you himself.'

'I doubt it!' Philip said dryly.

Caroline turned and faced him. 'Do you want to read my letter to my parents when I've written it?' she asked him.

To her surprise he looked embarrassed. 'Of course not!' he muttered.

Her eyes twinkled, her crossness forgotten. 'You may as well begin as you mean to go on!' she teased him.

The tension between them was suddenly relaxed. 'I shall probably begin by beating you, not reading your letters!' he retorted. 'You should laugh more often, Caroline. I like it!'

She sighed. 'There hasn't been much to laugh about,' she said. 'Though I'm glad Aunt Hilda isn't as ill as I thought. I can't understand why she thought she had to pretend to be dying to get me to come. I didn't really want to stay away so long, but time goes by before one's realised. I feel guilty about it now.'

'Then don't,' Philip said. 'Cyprus has never been a popular subject in your family! Good night, my dear, sleep well!'

'Good night,' she answered him. He could be very nice, she thought, and for the first time that day she began to feel comfortable about her future with him, even if all the love was on her side. She had more than enough for the two of them and that would have to suffice them.

Caroline thought to take her aunt's advice on what she should write to her father, but that lady proved to be surprisingly difficult to pin down on the subject.

'My dear, this is something between the two of you. I daresay Jeffrey would be the best one to advise you—if he will! He probably knows better than any of us how your father will react to the news. Why don't you ask him?'

But Philip's remarks of the evening before made it impossible for her to do that. Indeed, she spent any part of the day that Jeffrey happened to be in the house avoiding having a tête-à-tête with him and it was with some relief that she fell into bed that night, tired out after her sail with Philip, triumphant with the knowledge that her letter was written and that she had not been alone with Jeffrey once that day.

She was not so lucky the following day. Jeffrey watched Philip get into his car and drive off to work with undisguised satisfaction.

'There's something about that fellow,' he said to Caroline. 'I quite enjoyed his society yesterday, and yet there's something about him that I can't stand. He has a very curious attitude to you, my sweet. Anyone would think you were his property——'

'In a way I am,' Caroline said.

Jeffrey looked cross. 'And you accuse me of using people!'

'Did I?' Caroline grinned at him. 'I don't remember!'

'You don't seem to remember much about the times we've spent together. I'm beginning to think I ought to remind you of all that you'll be missing if you insist on falling for that Greek chap!'

'He's Cypriot,' Caroline corrected.

'Same thing! He has very odd ideas about women.'

Caroline looked down her nose at him. 'Oh?'

'Had the nerve to quote Shakespeare to me, just as if it were he who was the Englishman, when he was talking about you too! *"Such duty as the subject owes the prince, Even such a woman oweth to her husband"*! Did you ever hear the like?'

Caroline laughed. 'Don't all men believe that?' she asked.

'In their dreams! But he really meant it. Marry him, my dear, and you won't be able to call your soul your own!' He looked so pink and concerned that Caroline was overcome by an unkind desire to laugh again, this time at him. 'I don't believe you mean to marry him! Not seriously! Carrie, come back to England with me and forget all about him and your aunt. I'll make it up to you, I swear I will. Why, he's not even properly engaged to you, and already he treats you like a servant!'

'Rubbish!'

'Well, he expects you to mend his shirts.'

'I wanted to do them! I *offered* to do them! Oh, shut up, Jeffrey! Would you have me a *"graceless traitor to my loving lord"*? I can't explain it to you, but I'm doing what I want to do. He isn't making me stay here and marry him, you know. I asked him if I could.'

'*Caroline!*'

'I'm sorry, Jeffrey, but that's the way it is.'

Jeffrey was silent for a long time, then he said, 'I can't like it! Your father won't like it either. What's got into you, Caroline, that you have to fall for an obvious caveman like that? I thought you were too civilised and had more self-esteem than to want that sort of thing. If I'd thought——'

Caroline sighed. 'You'd have done more than kissed my hand? Don't be silly, Jeffrey.'

'It isn't too late!' Jeffrey said grimly. 'I'm not giving you up without a struggle. Too many people know——'

'Poor Jeffrey!'

Her mockery hit him on a raw nerve. 'I may not quote Shakespeare at you, but I have other, more potent weapons!'

'What will you do? Present me with another facet of your character calculated to dazzle me into going back to England?'

'I'm not saying what I'll do,' he retorted. 'Why should I warn you and put you on your guard? But I'll back myself to win you in the end. You've lost your head a little to this Greek fellow, but you'll lose your heart to me!'

Caroline felt suddenly bored with the whole conversation. 'What makes you think so?' she asked distantly.

'Because you're not very certain of yourself, my pet. I'm glad I've seen you out here in a way. I've always thought of you as cool and poised and knowing exactly where you're going—all of which qualities I like and admire. I'd overlooked the fact that you haven't had as much experience as I'd thought. There's nothing peculiar in that you should take a toss over Philip Klearchos. He's made you feel like a woman. But almost any man can do that if they try hard enough. *I* can do it, if you'll let me, darling?'

Caroline attempted a smile, wishing that he would go away and leave her alone. How wise she had been not to ask him what she should say to her father, she reflected. He would have twisted everything to suit himself. She felt a cold wind of fear lest he should do anything to come between herself and Philip.

'I—I'm happy as I am,' she said uncomfortably.

'Your father won't think so!'

She half turned towards him. 'Jeffrey, when you go back to England, will you talk to him for me and explain to him that this is what I really want? He'll believe you when he won't believe anyone else!'

'I'll talk to him,' he agreed. 'What will you do for me in exchange?'

Caroline looked at him uncertainly. 'What do you mean?'

He smiled. He didn't look unhappy or disapproving any longer and she drew a deep breath of relief. He had accepted that she was going to marry Philip whatever he had been saying. All that had probably been to punish her a little for bringing him out to Cyprus on a fool's errand, and she thought he was entitled to his revenge.

'Jeffrey?' she said.

He went on smiling. 'I brought you out a present with me,' he explained. 'I had hoped to pin it on your dress in happier circumstances, but I'd like you to have it anyway. You won't refuse me that, will you, Caroline?'

She shook her head. 'It's very kind of you. I'm sorry, Jeffrey. I'm sorry I asked you to come out here for nothing and I'm even more sorry if I've hurt you.'

His face was very pink and he was sweating slightly in the hot sun. 'I'll go and get your present,' he said. 'Don't go away.'

While he was gone, Caroline argued with herself as to whether she wouldn't be wiser to bring her aunt out on to the verandah to have someone there when he gave her her present, but it seemed ridiculous to go to such lengths when she had been alone with him so often before. She pulled a few weeds out of the pot-plants and reminded herself to water them as soon as the sun was off them. She had always loved the rich, luxuriant growth of the Cyprus geraniums, and she particularly loved the bright pink one that grew up the side of the verandah wall, covered with flowers, and giving off its pungent, unique smell, to vie with the other, sweeter smells of the flowers that shared its bed. It made her think of Philip and the way she could tell when he was in the same room without even looking up. He, too, had a bitter-sweet, earthy quality, and made his fellows seem insignificant by his side.

When Jeffrey came back she had almost forgotten all about him. She started when he touched her arm and drew back quickly against the wall, hoping that he would not take long to give her whatever it was he had for her.

He took out a jeweller's box and opened it carefully, laying the brooch inside on the palm of his hand. It was a diamanté brooch, shaped into the letter C, pretty, but not particularly valuable.

'Do you like it?' he asked her.

She nodded, making to take it from him, but he closed his fingers over it, putting out his other hand to draw her closer to him. She thought he deliberately fumbled as he pinned it on to the front of her dress, but she couldn't be sure.

'Thank you very much, Jeffrey,' she said, stepping away from him. 'It was a very kind thought.'

'Don't I get more of a reward than that?' he smiled at her.

'I don't think so,' she said firmly.

'Ah, but that's where you're wrong, my dear!' He pulled her into the circle of his arms, clasping her lightly round the waist. 'I think it's worth a kiss at least!' He watched her struggling to get free, a fixed smile on his face, until he tired of her lack of co-operation and pulled her closer still. 'Don't you want to kiss me?' he asked. And he bent his head and kissed her on the lips, hurting her mouth, and giving her no chance to resist him. 'Here endeth the first lesson!' he said as he released her. 'But don't think it will be the last!'

CHAPTER EIGHT

It was hot on Sunday. Caroline slipped into church through the side door, pulling on a cardigan to cover her arms as she did so. The women greeted her with smiles and squashed themselves closer still to make room for her. It was blissfully cool in the dim interior and the cantors both had beautiful voices as they passed the singing back and forth between them while the priest carried out the intricate mysteries of the Mass, out of her sight, behind the screen doors. A small girl went to sit on her grandmother's knee, offering her own chair to Caroline, and she sat down thankfully, allowing the music to wash over her, her mind a blank.

'*Kyrie eleison; Christe eleison; Kyrie eleison.* Lord have mercy; Christ have mercy; Lord have mercy.' The familiar words echoed round the church and the priest came to the doorway in the screen, looking unexpectedly dignified in his none too clean vestments, his hair neatly pinned in a knot at the back of his neck. There was a rustle all round her as the congregation lit their candles, making little pools of light that flickered and warmed them in their beauty.

It was then that she saw Philip, leaning against a misericord on the men's side of the church. She found that she only had to turn her head slightly and she could watch him to her heart's content. She wished she could sit beside him and share the light and the warmth of his candle, but she knew that such behaviour would never be countenanced in a place like Bellapais. His Byzantine head looked completely at home in the church. Of course the "Abbaye de la Paix" had been founded in Lusignan times, becoming a home first for the Augustinians and later for the Norbertines. It had been a Latin church in those days, one of the great Gothic monuments of the Levant. If one ignored the iconostasis that was a Greek Orthodox addition to the interior of the church, it was still a Frankish Gothic church, but it seemed to Caroline that the Byzantine rites had imposed their own feel on to the building whatever its origins had been.

The candles went out and she couldn't see Philip as clearly as before. His black, curling hair had been brushed down flat but was already kicking up here and there, as restless and as full of life as its owner. It was strange to see his face in repose, to take note of the high cheekbones and the way his skin was stretched tightly over his jaw, accentuating the firm line of his mouth and the moulding of his nose. But it was his eyes that dominated the whole face. Heavy-lidded to the point of weariness, they had only to look at her for her bones to turn to water and arouse such fierce longings within her that she was, even now, made breathless by the thought of it.

When she next looked at him, he was staring back at her and she wondered what had caught his eye. She looked down quickly and saw the brooch that Jeffrey had given her gleaming in the light of the small girl's candle that she had refused to put out with the others. She had forgotten all about it when she had put on her dress that morning. She had meant to take it off and put it away in the back of her drawer while she considered what she would do with it. But it was too late to do that now. She waited for Philip to turn his attention back to the service and unpinned the brooch, tearing her dress in her hurry to be free of it. Perhaps, if she left it on the chair where she was sitting, no one would know it was hers and it would disappear for ever!

There was a flurry of activity as the congregation rose to greet the priest as he came out to give the last blessing and the people began to move towards the open doors and the sunshine beyond. Caroline pushed the brooch well into the shadows and hurried out with the others. A table had been set by the great door on which was piled mounds of diced bread, olives, and glasses of raw red wine. She helped herself to some bread and olives, refusing the wine because the glasses were few and seemed to be all in use by the thirsty men, and sauntered across the square towards the Tree of Idleness café.

When Philip took her arm and stole a couple of olives out of her hand, eating them with relish, she turned and smiled at him.

'You're looking very innocent—and idle—this morning!' he observed.

She laughed. 'I've come to the right place, then, haven't I? Aunt Hilda is cooking the lunch, so I have the whole morning to do nothing in. I'm going to sit here under the tree and indulge myself!'

'Bellapais is said to have that effect on one,' he said dryly.

'I won't make a habit of it,' she assured him. 'But it is a lovely morning!' She peeped up at him. 'You wouldn't like to do nothing with me for a while, would you? Please?'

He grinned. 'I'm not as practised as you are in the art——'

'That's unkind!' she complained. 'It takes a lot out of one, having one's hair done and going to parties! You should try it.'

'Not me! I think I should dislike it as much as you do. A Tree of Idleness is all right for an hour or so, but one wants something better to do with one's whole life.' He seated her at one of the small tables set out in the sun and sat down opposite her. 'This is very pleasant. I was pleased to see you in church.'

'I like to go,' she murmured.

He looked at her in silence for a long moment. She couldn't read his thoughts and after a while she gave up trying, so it came as a shock to her when he suddenly swooped forward, pointing to the tear in her dress. 'Did I say innocent?' he said, his voice cold. 'Why did you take it off?'

Thrown off balance, she tried to prevaricate. 'Take it off?' she repeated.

He sat back again, his eyes veiled from her. 'Oh, Caroline!' he sighed. 'You'll feel much more comfortable when you've told me about it. I wouldn't have commented on it at all if you hadn't taken it off—and don't pretend you didn't, for your dress is torn!'

She swallowed. 'Jeffrey gave it to me. He brought it out from England for me. It—It isn't valuable, or anything—just pretty, so I didn't feel I could refuse it. I saw you looking at it in church, so I took it off.'

'I see,' he said. 'Where is it now? I'd like to see it.'

Caroline looked more uncomfortable than ever. 'I left it in the church,' she confessed. 'I thought I could say I'd lost it—if Jeffrey asked me. But he won't! He'll just think I'm not wearing it.'

Philip gave her a quizzical look. 'And you didn't want me to know about it at all?' he accused her.

'No,' she admitted.

'I'll go and get it,' he said. 'If you don't want it, I shall return it to Jeffrey myself telling him so. Will that do?'

She nodded quickly, wondering if she should also tell him that Jeffrey had kissed her and that she was afraid that he might do so again. She decided not to. She didn't want Philip to think that she couldn't control Jeffrey no matter what he did. It would be weak-kneed to seek his protection against someone she had herself brought to Cyprus. Jeffrey would soon go back to England and she would have nothing further to worry about. She hoped it would be very soon.

Philip came back and sat down again opposite her. He had nothing in his hands, and she thought for a moment that he had been unable to find the brooch, but then he took it out of his pocket and placed it on the table between them.

'I suppose you thought you would go back and retrieve it after I was safely out of the way?' he questioned her. His voice was flat and cool and there was a note of warning in it that Caroline knew she would do well not to ignore. She shook her head silently.

'I didn't want it,' she said.

'Then why wear it?'

She licked her lips, wishing that the brooch would disappear, but it went on winking at her in the sunlight. 'I'd forgotten all about it when I put on this dress. I'd meant to put it away as soon as he gave it to me, but—but something else happened and I forgot.'

'Something else?'

She might have known that he wouldn't let that go by. 'Philip, will you return it to him for me? It would be better if he went back to England, but I can hardly ask him to go.' She looked up with the ghost of a smile. 'Do you think Aunt Hilda could drop him a hint?'

Philip's eyes met hers and held them. 'What else happened?' he repeated.

'He thought he was due something in the way of thanks——' Caroline began. 'Oh, I wish I'd never set eyes on the beastly thing!'

'You told me it wasn't valuable——'

'It isn't!'

Philip gave the brooch a push, sending it spinning over to her side of the table. 'Have a good look at it and then tell me it isn't valuable!'

Caroline picked it up with reluctant fingers. It was better finished than she had thought, with a safety catch on the pin complete with a chain. She turned it over and put it back on the table. 'Diamanté brooches aren't valuable!' she insisted.

'That, my dear, is made of tiny, matched diamonds——'

Caroline stared at it. 'Are you sure?' she asked, feeling hollow inside at the thought. 'I don't believe it! Jeffrey wouldn't——' She broke off, miserably aware that it was exactly the sort of thing that Jeffrey would do. 'But *why*? Why should he want me to have it?'

'I think you can answer that best yourself!' He paused significantly. 'Has he ever given you presents before?'

'Not to me!' she was glad to be able to say. 'He gave my mother a silver tea-set once. She likes old silver and he saw this one in a sale. He told her it was Georgian, but she has always maintained that it was really Victorian, but nice!'

'And your father?'

Caroline shook her head. 'I wouldn't know,' she said.

Philip frowned. 'Didn't it ever strike you as odd that he should lash out on your family like that? Or is that the way it always goes in the business world?'

Caroline wished she didn't have to answer that. 'He's been a friend for a very long time—of us all! After a while it came to be understood that we'd go on from there and that in the end I'd marry him. I did try to say I didn't want to, but it wasn't ever *talked* about, it was just accepted that that was what was going to happen.'

She was more relieved than she could say, to see his expression relax. 'Habit, Caroline! I did try and warn you!'

'Yes, but I told him I was going to marry you and it didn't make any difference. Do you suppose any of them will ever believe that I'm not going back to their life in England?'

'If you're sufficiently determined to convince them.'

She picked up the brooch again and put it into his hand. 'I wasn't going back for it,' she said abruptly. 'I promise you I wasn't!'

Philip smiled at her, and her heart turned over. 'You won't get pretty little trinkets from me!' he warned her.

She found herself smiling back at him. 'I don't want any!' she declared. 'Will you tell him not to give me any more?'

'I think I'll get the idea across to him,' Philip said dryly. 'Your share will be to make sure that you're not alone with him again while he's here——'

116

Her indignation flared at his tone. 'I don't like being ordered about! Jeffrey didn't understand——'

'But I am giving you an order, Caroline!'

'You've always given me orders! But I won't obey you! I'll do as I please!' She stopped, anxious not to provoke him after all. 'Why can't you *ask* me to do something, instead of telling me all the time?'

'Ask you, tell you,' he mocked, 'it all comes to the same thing! A husband commands and a wife obeys in a Cypriot marriage. And you will obey me now!'

'What will you do if I don't?' she demanded, reddening under his stern gaze.

'I'll think of something,' he said cryptically.

'If I do stay away from Jeffrey it'll be because I prefer it that way,' she informed him, 'not because of anything you may do to me!' His mocking look made her crosser than ever. 'I don't want to hear any more about it!'

'You won't—as long as you do as I say!' he retorted calmly. He stood up and smiled down at her. 'Come on, and I'll walk you the long way back to the house, or don't you want to do that either?'

She raised startled eyes to his. 'Can't I have a cup of coffee first?'

'Not if you want me to kiss you as much as I want to make love to you! Are you coming?'

She nodded blindly, following him without a word. She knew that afterwards she would feel humiliated that he had only to beckon to her and she would run into his arms with an eagerness there was no possibility of hiding from him, but for the moment her need for the reassurance of his arms about her and his lips on hers was joy enough to make her blood sing in her veins and for her heart to leap within her in a cascade of delight that took away her breath. 'Oh, Philip, I can't do without you!' she said when she could.

He kissed her again, leisurely, his hand behind her head so that she had no chance of hiding from his insistent lips. 'Is that why you're marrying me?' he

117

asked her.

But she took fright, remembering in time that he had said nothing about loving her, only that he wasn't going to let the Klearchos inheritance escape him.

'I've told you why!'

'Oh no, you haven't! Not properly!' he contradicted her. 'But you will, *yinéka mou*, you will!'

Caroline moved her chair a few inches to make the most of the sun. She was enjoying sitting on the verandah with her aunt through the long, hot afternoon, both of them busy with their needlework. It made her feel as though she had never been away from Cyprus. All over the island women would be doing exactly the same thing, exchanging the gossip of the day and discussing the latest in weddings, births, and funerals, just as she knew Aunt Hilda was warming up to talk to her. It made her feel a part of the long, continuous process of life, where children were loved and old age became an accepted and valued part of living. It was very much what she wanted for herself, no matter what the difficulties.

'I should have thought you would be anxious to take Jeffrey sightseeing,' Aunt Hilda said after a while. 'Or was it Philip's idea that he should take him off your hands?'

Caroline looked up and smiled. 'Need you ask?'

Her aunt chuckled. 'Philip's heart has always been kind to you. He might well have left you to cope with Jeffrey on your own and decided to be jealous into the bargain! Instead, he seems to be intent on avoiding stepping on your sensibilities in any way. He could hardly bring himself to discuss your *prika* at all! I thought he might be waiting for my brother to reply to his letter, but I gather that he is *not* to be asked to contribute?'

Caroline flushed. 'It isn't necessary——'

Aunt Hilda's eyes flashed scornfully. 'My dear, you obviously have no idea of the size of the portion Philip could normally expect his wife-to-be to bring him! A few hundred pounds is neither here nor there!'

'There's a bit more than that——' Caroline began.

'Does Philip know how much?'

Caroline made a few wild stitches, pricked her finger, and watched the small bead of blood form with a hollow feeling of dismay. 'I don't know,' she admitted. 'I wrote to my bank and told them to pay everything I had into his account here. I don't know myself how much it is.'

Her aunt looked with distaste at the blood that was in acute danger of being spread on the collar of one of Philip's shirts. 'Suck it!' she commanded, pausing in her own work to make sure that her niece did as she was told and that her finger had stopped bleeding. 'I suppose you're relying on him accepting that this house and the Klearchos lands will be his eventually through you? It isn't at all the usual way of doing these things!'

Caroline's eyes glinted with humour at her aunt's indignant voice. 'Philip told me I was to accept whatever you arranged for me,' she said with unwonted meekness.

Aunt Hilda gaped at her. 'And is that all you have to say about it?' she demanded.

Caroline grinned. 'What else do you want me to say? You can throw in the car, if you like. Philip chose it, so he must think something of it. I've never been penniless before, without a pound to call my own! I think I rather like the sensation. It makes me feel all helpless and feminine!'

'That'll be the day!' her aunt said dryly. 'But while you're in the mood perhaps we'd better discuss the other details of your wedding. The first thing is the invitations. We'll have to start on a round of visits——'

'But do you feel well enough for that?' Caroline asked immediately, her voice full of concern.

Her aunt had the grace to look embarrassed. 'I'll

manage. I'm rather looking forward to it, truth to tell. They have a very pretty custom here of taking a gourd filled with wine and some biscuits, called *koullouri*, and going round from house to house to ask everyone to come to the ceremony. Philip says it will be quite in order for you to come with me on these visits—and your mother too, if she comes in time.'

'It sounds fun! Where do we get the *koullouri* from?'

Aunt Hilda looked well pleased with herself. 'We make it of bread dough and sesame seeds. You can make it if you want to.'

Caroline sucked on her finger which had long ago stopped bleeding. 'All right,' she said, 'I will, but you'll have to tell me what to do.'

'We'll make it together,' Aunt Hilda suggested after all. 'Then you can blame me if it goes wrong. *I've* never made it before either!'

It had turned out very well, Caroline thought the following afternoon. She liked it well enough to pick at it while it was still hot, until her aunt slapped her fingers and asked if she wanted them to have to begin all over again with another batch.

'Not really,' said Caroline. 'But it is terribly good! Let's save some for Philip and Jeffrey.'

But Aunt Hilda wouldn't hear of it. 'Every family in the village will expect an invitation to your wedding, and each one of them will expect at least a small piece of *koullouri* and a sip of wine. We won't have any to spare for anyone else—and certainly not for you, my girl!' she added on an exasperated note. 'If you're hungry, go and find something else to eat!'

'Yes, Aunt. When do we begin these visits?'

Her aunt wiped a floury hand across her brow. 'This evening, I suppose. Are you sure you want to come with me? I thought I would start with Ileana's family —it's important that they shouldn't feel slighted.' She gave Caroline an uncertain look. 'It could be a difficult situation there. Oh, darling, don't look like that! I didn't mean that Philip had ever seriously considered making Ileana his wife, in fact I'm sure of it, because Ileana isn't the kind to hold out for marriage—if you know what I mean!—and that's important to every Cypriot male. But she was a little in love with Philip and she has awkward manners at the best of times. Oh dear, I'm putting this very badly——'

'No, you're not,' Caroline broke in, her face white and strained. 'I'd forgotten about Ileana. It wasn't all on her side. I wish she didn't have to be hurt! I think Philip encouraged her——'

'My dear, that doesn't mean he ever thought of marrying her! Oh, I know I pretended to you when you first arrived that he might—I thought it time that someone gave you a fright so that you would see what you were losing with all that talk of Jeffrey! But, between ourselves, her parents are desperate to get Ileana married because no one in Bellapais supposes that she is still innocent, and news like that travels faster than fire! They're looking for a husband for her in Greece—they have relatives over there. She has a fine *prika*, she's the only daughter in the family, but rumours of that kind are not the sort of thing that a man like Philip would overlook. You're lucky that Philip is as sure of you as he is!

Caroline blushed a fiery red. 'I don't know how he thinks he can tell,' she murmured. She felt her aunt's anxious eyes on her and went on hastily: 'He's right, of course! But how could he know that?'

Aunt Hilda shrugged. 'The two of you have always been closely in tune with each other. Perhaps he can tell! He seemed very sure after he had seen you that first day at the Tree of Idleness.'

'He's always sure he's right!' Caroline said with remembered resentment. 'He called me a maiden, a callow, green girl with no experience of life! He's the most arrogant creature I've ever met!'

Aunt Hilda pursed up her lips thoughtfully. 'Arrogant? Perhaps. But he's never taken you for granted,

Caroline, or tried to manipulate you into something you don't want to be. Be grateful to him for that. He respects you as a person——'

'He's overbearing and bossy!'

'He treats you like a woman. What more do you want?'

Caroline sighed. 'And the man commands and the woman obeys. I know. He's told me all about it!'

Her aunt began to laugh. 'Do you know what your father once said to me when I wanted to marry Michael? He said Michael would never allow me to be more than a shadow round the house, exuding an anxiety to please! I never felt like that at all!'

Caroline's eyes opened wide. She had a sudden, heart-rending picture of her own mother, but she said nothing. What was there to say after all? Her aunt had said it all.

Kyria Zavallis was seated on a rocking-chair in front of her door. She looked as though it had been a long time since she had last smiled. Her face was creased into lines of bitterness and was grey under her deep tan. Dressed totally in black, there was nothing to relieve the first impression of deep mourning. Caroline, standing awkwardly on the doorstep, did her best not to stare at her, wondering if her husband could have died in the last few days and that she, somehow, had not heard about it. She cast a quick look of enquiry at her aunt, but Aunt Hilda merely shook her head and got down to the business in hand.

'As you can see, *kyria*, we have come to invite you to the wedding. We have come to you first of all——'

'You want Ileana to be one of the bridesmaids?' Kyria Zavallis interrupted disagreeably. 'I can make no promises about that!'

Caroline bent over the woman, offering her some wine and the first of the *koullouri*. 'I would consider it a great honour, *kyria*, if your daughter will consent to be my bridesmaid. Ileana has been so kind to my aunt,

122

visiting her, and doing many of the things that I should have done for her. Everybody knows how dear she is to my whole family——' She broke off, unsure as to how she should continue. She coloured a little as she saw Kyria Zavallis's bright eyes fixed on her face, a painful eagerness in their depths.

'Ileana may be marrying soon herself!'

'Then I'm glad to be able to ask her to be my bridesmaid first,' Caroline responded quickly. 'Once she is married, I couldn't have her, could I?'

Kyria Zavallis made a shaky attempt at a smile. 'Does your betrothed agree to Ileana attending you?' she demanded. She swivelled her eyes round to where Aunt Hilda was standing. 'Did you know of this? It will be our salvation if you agree to it! Who will dare to talk about Ileana if Philip's wife declares her innocent?'

'Oh,' said Caroline, somewhat daunted. She was beginning to think she should have consulted her aunt before she had given way to the impulse of trying to brighten the day for the weary-looking Kyria Zavallis.

'Did you *not* think of this?' the Kyria asked her.

Caroline swallowed, remembering how she had felt when she had seen Ileana in Philip's arms. But it wasn't Ileana he was marrying and he would expect her to be generous. If it hurt her to have Ileana there, what would he care for that? He had always demanded more of her than she had thought she had had it in her to give and she didn't want him to be disappointed in her now.

'Ileana is my first choice, *kyria*,' she said gently. 'I have not even thought as to whom else I may ask. I was hoping—Ileana would advise me about the others, because she knows everyone in Bellapais much better than I do. Do you think she will?'

'I will call her!' Kyria Zavallis said on a note of triumph. She opened her mouth and shrieked her daughter's name, her throat swelling as she did so. She not only looked like a crow, she sounded like one,

Caroline thought with amusement. But that amusement evaporated the moment Ileana stepped out on to the verandah. The Cypriot girl took in the whole situation at a glance and made it very clear that she did not like it.

'How dare you come to ask us to your wedding!' she stormed. 'Did you think we would have so little pride that we would accept your *kind* invitation? Well, I shall not stand by and see Philip married to another woman! If you had not come back to Cyprus, he would have married me! It was all arranged. What can you bring to the marriage? You, whom we have always heard was so rich, so well provided for by your rich father? *Nothing!* You have only yourself——'

'Ileana!' Aunt Hilda protested faintly.

'Ah, you thought I did not know!' Ileana turned on her. 'I have always known! *Your* husband thought so little of you that he left everything to Philip! Why do you pretend that you have any say in the Klearchos lands, or that the villa belongs to you and not to Philip? We all know the truth! You have nothing, just as you had nothing to bring to your husband, just as your niece, Caroline Fielding, will bring nothing but her virtue to her marriage-bed with Philip! At least Philip knows that I am a woman who can love him as he should be loved! I'm not ashamed of it either! Why should I be?'

Feeling slightly sick, Caroline hoped that she was not going to do anything as stupid as faint. She looked round for something to sit on, but Ileana's mother was rocking herself backwards and forwards on the only available chair. In the long silence, Caroline was shocked to see that the Kyria was crying. The tears slid down her walnut-shell skin and on to the knot of her head-scarf and she made no movement at all to wipe them away or to hide them from Caroline or her aunt.

'That a child of mine should be so stupid!' she moaned. 'What did I ever do to deserve such a daughter? To boast of such a thing! Now I have no hope, for who will marry such a one?'

Caroline pushed the wine and the roll of *koullouri* nearer to the Cypriot woman's hand. 'The invitation still stands, *kyria*,' she managed to say. 'The invitation to you and your husband, and to Ileana to be my bridesmaid.'

To her dismay the woman turned her head and kissed the hand in which she held the gourd of wine. With a convulsive movement she forced herself to swallow a sip of wine and answered in formal Greek: 'I will be there, dear. God bless the union and may your path be strewn with roses.'

Caroline thanked her, her own voice shaking a little, before deliberately turning to Ileana and offering the wine and the *koullouri* to her. Ileana glared back at her, her head held high.

'I suppose you will tell everyone what I've said to-day!' she said violently, pushing the wine away from her in an unmistakable gesture of hatred.

'No,' Caroline answered. 'Why should I?'

'Why indeed? You will tell Philip at least!'

'Not even him,' Caroline assured her. 'Least of all him!'

Ileana took a sip of wine with a sulky air. 'I will be there, *dear*! God bless the union, and may your path be strewn with roses!'

Caroline turned away from her with relief. Such roses would have long, sharp thorns, she thought, and could feel them already pricking at her happiness. Was it true that Philip already possessed the Klearchos inheritance? Then why should he have agreed to marry her?

She and her aunt walked away from the Zavallis house in silence, until they were well out of sight of the eyes of the two ladies of the house. Then Aunt Hilda gave Caroline's arm a gentle squeeze.

'I was proud of you today,' she said. 'I was as proud of you as if you had been my own daughter—and I shall tell Philip so!'

But Caroline only bit her lip and shook her head. '*No!* No, Aunt. Philip must never know. I couldn't bear it if he knew——'

'That you know about Ileana?'

She nodded violently. 'He's ruined her life, hasn't he?' she said.

CHAPTER NINE

'I WILL be there, dear. God bless the couple, and may their path be strewn with roses.'

Caroline thought the words would be burned for ever into her consciousness, so often had she heard them spoken. She began to wonder if there would be room in the church for her and Philip, it would be so crowded with their guests, family, and friends. Occasionally she would be asked if they had exchanged betrothal rings and had them blessed by the priest and she had formulated the answer that they were getting married almost immediately, so there had been no time for the betrothal banquet as well.

'Ah well, it will be a splendid week!' the women had one and all sighed. 'We are looking forward to helping your aunt with all the preparations. She is one of ourselves now, but she has never had to arrange an occasion like this!'

Aunt Hilda was not the only one at a loss, Caroline thought wryly. She had hardly seen Philip to speak to for days. He had been busy tying up the loose ends at work so that he could take a couple of weeks off to be married, he had told her, but that knowledge had done little to soothe the edginess and pre-wedding nerves she felt whenever she thought of her marriage to him. And Jeffrey had been no help at all. He had wandered round the house, criticising everything she did, and making snide comments about the local wedding customs—customs which she had to admit she would have found an embarrassment at the best of times!

It was Jeffrey who had brought the news of her parents' imminent arrival.

'Why didn't they write to me?' she had complained to him.

'I expect they thought you were too busy,' he had returned with a superior smile. 'Let's hope the house is in some kind of order when they do arrive. I can't see your father appreciating the peasant humour that we've had to put up with for the last few days. Not when it comes to his only daughter!'

Caroline had sighed. 'Is it much different from champagne and telegrams?'

'Very!' Jeffrey had said with an expressive shudder. 'I'm expecting Aphrodite to look in on the proceedings any moment now!'

Caroline had summoned up a weary smile. 'I wish she would!' she had declared, wishing that everyone, particularly Jeffrey, would go away and leave her alone to sort out her thoughts and catch up on her sleep. 'I could do with her help!'

'The Goddess of Love won't help you with Philip,' Jeffrey had told her, looking rather pleased that he had succeeded in hurting her. 'You'll have more in common with Hera. Wasn't she the goddess of house and home and the wifely virtues?' He had snorted contemptuously down his nose. 'And what a botch she made of it! Zeus having affairs all over the place and leaving poor old Hera to manage on her own. That'll be your role, my love—permanently at your husband's beck and call, while he pleases himself! If I were you, I'd think again, before it's too late.'

But there was nothing to think about. The Caroline Fielding she had always known herself to be had already changed into someone else. She might still be called Fielding, but she was the woman of Philip Klearchos. The wedding ceremony was no more than the seal of authenticity put on an established fact. She had already given Philip her word and her heart; her hand he could claim at his leisure. Though when she looked round at the seething activity in the villa, she couldn't help thinking that leisure had remarkably little to do with it! She wouldn't have credited that a simple wedding could be such hard work!

Yesterday, the Friday before the wedding, there had been the dance. No hall had been considered big enough to contain all the villagers, so they had all gathered in the square outside the abbey and had danced away the night. Philip had hired a couple of violinists and a few *laoutaris*, who played an instrument like a large-sized mandolin, and the men and women had danced together, eating their share of the macaroni, breads and cakes that most of the women had helped to prepare on the Wednesday before. Philip had told her that even a few years ago the men and women danced separately and never together, but nowadays many romances began at such dances as these.

There had been that awkward moment too, when Jeffrey had asked her to dance. She had refused him, of course, but Philip had not been pleased.

'Is he making a pest of himself?' he had asked her.

'Of course not!' she had denied. And he hadn't been then. It had been later that he had found her on her own, trying to repair the lace on the hem of her dress that someone had inadvertently stepped on.

'May one kiss the bride?' he had asked, and had done so before she had been able to dodge away from him. 'Here beginneth the second lesson,' he had muttered in her ear, and had gathered her more firmly to him. Somehow she had managed to free herself and she had given him a stinging slap into the bargain.

'Here *endeth* the second lesson!' she had snapped at him.

'For the moment,' he had agreed, stroking the scarlet patch on his cheek where she had hit him. 'But that isn't the sort of thing I forgive or forget, Carrie my dear. It will be the third lesson that will really count!'

She thought of that now with a shiver of distaste. How glad she was that tomorrow it would all be over and she would be Philip's wife! Though the whispering doubts still came crowding in whenever she was still for a minute. Was the Klearchos inheritance already his? Why had he agreed to marry her? And, worst of all, was he still a little bit in love with Ileana?

Looking out the window of her bedroom, she saw that the women were beginning to arrive for the day's celebrations. This was the day that the whole village had been looking forward to—or so Aunt Hilda had told her—for this was the day when they "spread the mattress", a ceremony the significance of which Caroline could only guess at and which made her blush at the mere thought. She had already decided that the only way to get through the day was to put her feelings in cold storage and to keep to herself as much as possible. It was like Philip that he should insist that she should be embarrassed in this way, but how many times did she have to prove to him that she would be as Cypriot as he liked? *Anything* he liked, if he would only love her a little and let her love him a lot!

She went into the kitchen to help her aunt prepare the inevitable feast that the women would expect before they began work, and then it was that Jeffrey told her that her parents were arriving at Nicosia Airport in two and a half hours' time and that they would expect her to meet them.

'I thought they were coming later!' she wailed. 'What on earth will they make of—all this? Oh, Jeffrey, I can't leave here now! Would you take the car and go and fetch them? You can talk to them on the way back and convince them that I know what I'm doing. Will you do that?'

'Charmed,' Jeffrey smiled. He looked round at the piles of food. 'I'll have a lot to tell them!'

'Yes, well, I don't want them to be upset,' Caroline said uncomfortably. 'And I don't want to get upset myself, come to that.'

His eyes rested thoughtfully on her face. 'Is there any danger of that?'

'No, not really. Only they do make rather a thing of all this and it seems to have been going on for days! I'm tired as much as anything!'

'Adonis doesn't seem to be much in evidence,' Jeffrey commented blandly.

' "Spreading the mattress" is a woman's thing!' Caroline retorted. Adonis indeed! Philip was no Adonis to her way of thinking! He was—he was Philip! 'You won't be missed at all while you're at the airport!' she added, thinking it would do no harm to tell Jeffrey so. He had annoyed her at the dance more than she had thought at the time. She had always thought him so reliable, so very much on her side in everything—and he wasn't! He was on the other side and she had never known it.

'And do you really think that watching this pack of females perform their rites is more important than meeting your parents yourself?' she asked, accepting the car keys from her when she had finally found them in amongst the muddle that had collected at the bottom of her handbag.

'Yes, I think it is,' she said.

Amongst other things, she hoped to get them out of the house before her parents arrived. Surely it couldn't take very long, she consoled herself. But she knew in her heart that the women would be at it all afternoon no matter what she did to hurry them on their way. They had come fully intending to enjoy themselves, and enjoy themselves they would!

Actually, once they got started, Caroline found it all quite interesting. There was no space large enough in the house to hold them all, so they took everything out into the road outside and began to make up the mattress out there. All the bedding was spread out in the sunshine and the women settled down to await the coming of the priest to give his blessing to the proceedings. Inevitably he was late, and Caroline was commanded by her aunt to bring out yet more refreshments to the waiting women.

The priest came smiling and hurried through his part of the business, blessing everything in sight. 'It is good to see these things still being done,' he said with approval to Aunt Hilda. 'It is a fine thing to include the whole community in a thing as important as a wedding. Look at the pleasure it is giving to us all!' He looked round with an air of satisfaction as one of the married women picked up the bedding and began to dance round with it. The others had started to sing now, low, sad folk-songs that they had all known since childhood and which they sang now with the sobbing pleasure of all such chants. The bedding was placed on a mat and the wool sorted into pieces of about the same length as a mattress. Each piece was moved in four directions, making the sign of the cross, before it was finally put into position. Then, when that was finished, aromatic substances were scattered over the top and the women began to sew the bedding into its covering. While their needles flew, a handkerchief was spread on to the centre of the mattress and the wedding presents were produced and put on it. Even those who had only come to watch put a silver coin on to the handkerchief, and, right at the end, the handkerchief was knotted round the coins and they were sewn into the last corner of the mattress.

'Will they go home now?' Caroline asked her aunt. She was becoming increasingly jumpy as the time slipped past and there was less and less hope that they would be finished before the arrival of her parents. 'Daddy won't like this,' she added in an undertone.

Aunt Hilda went white at the thought. 'We *can't* hurry them,' she insisted. 'Perhaps Philip will know what to do?'

But of Philip there was no sign at all.

Three of the stronger married women had come forward to 'dance' the mattress once again now that it had been made up. They took it in turns to raise the heavy mattress above their heads and leap up and down, making suitable comments all the while.

It was at this moment that Mr. and Mrs. Fielding drew up in Caroline's car, looking as though they had arrived in a mad-house and were pretending not to have noticed. Jeffrey got out of the driving seat, grinning all over his face. He helped Mrs. Fielding out of the car, bending over her to say something that brought a slight flush to her face. But Caroline's eyes were not on her. She had seen the furious face of her father and her spirits sank accordingly.

The women stopped dancing for a moment, made shy by the unexpected arrival of these foreigners in their midst. '*Kalispera, kyria, kyrie,*' they murmured, and then gaining in courage, they gave Caroline a little push towards her parents. '*Ine Kypria!* She is a Cypriot!' they laughed.

'What on earth are they talking about?' Mr. Fielding demanded.

'They're getting ready for the wedding tomorrow,' Caroline explained faintly. 'Won't you come inside——'

'How long is it going on?' her father asked angrily.

'I don't know,' she admitted.

Out of the corner of her eye she saw one of the women grab one of the boy toddlers who had come with his mother and roll him in the mattress to the excited murmur of the other women. The child tolerated the indignity twice, but the third time he opened his mouth and yelled as loudly as he could manage, completely drowning Caroline's stammered greetings to her mother.

'Is this what you really want?' Mrs. Fielding asked, looking more anxious by the minute.

Caroline inclined her head. 'I want to be Philip's wife.'

'Oh, darling! Will I like him?'

Caroline smiled and her whole face lit up as she did so. 'Very much!' she exclaimed.

'Well, I shan't!' her father grumbled. 'I've never liked any member of his family yet! I should have known better than to let you come out here to see Hilda. I always knew *she* was unbalanced, but for my own daughter——'

Caroline stopped him with a look, gratified to find that she could. 'You won't make me change my mind,' she said. 'Nothing can do that.'

Her father cast a disgusted glance around him. 'We'll see!' he said grimly. 'You needn't think I'm going to pay for any of this!'

Had meals always been like that, Caroline wondered through dinner, with her father monopolising the conversation, and her mother smilingly agreeing with everything he said? Caroline exchanged glances with Philip, but she couldn't see what he was thinking. He was being definite, but very polite, in everything he said. He expected nothing from his father-in-law. The *prika*, or dowry, had all been arranged and he was quite satisfied with the portion his wife was bringing to him.

'I should think so!' Mr. Fielding exclaimed. 'In England we don't have to bribe a young man to marry a girl as pretty as Caroline! Jeffrey would have had her like a shot *and* taken her empty-handed!'

Caroline screwed up her courage to sticking point and faced her father. 'Philip is taking me empty-handed too,' she said loudly. 'He inherited all the Klearchos lands from his parents and from his uncle. He already has Aunt Hilda living on his charity and yet he has asked nothing from me.'

There was an astonished silence.

'How did you know that?' Philip asked.

Caroline lifted her head defiantly. 'I was told.'

Philip smiled slowly, his eyes warm with—what? She wished it was with admiration and affection and, yes, with love, but of course it couldn't be that, but he did look as though he was *liking* her at that moment.

'I hear from the bank that my balance there has gone up considerably,' he drawled.

She flushed, but refused to lower her head. 'Naturally I had my bank in London send out every penny I had,' she said.

'Your allowance?' her father asked sharply. 'You

can't expect me to continue to keep you after you're married!'

It was Philip who answered him. 'Tomorrow Caroline becomes my responsibility for the rest of her life. My wife lives on what I can give her and I wouldn't have it any other way. Thank you all the same, sir.'

'Thank me for what?' Mr. Fielding blustered.

Philip was silent. He raised his eyebrows and he gave a short laugh. 'For giving me a lovely woman to be my wife,' he murmured.

To everyone's surprise, Caroline's mother turned a sparkling smile on her future son-in-law. 'I've never seen her looking prettier!' she declared. 'If you make her happy, I shall never complain again about her preferring to be out here rather than with us.' She lifted her glass and toasted her daughter, her eyes filled with tears. 'Lucky Caroline!' she said.

Jeffrey put his knife and fork down with a clatter and turned pink. 'I thought you were on my side, Mrs. Fielding. I feel quite cheated. It was I that she sent for to keep her entertained while she was out here *to look after her aunt*, who we are all pleased to see is in blooming health. But since I've been here, she'll hardly speak to me at all. I think she should take pity on me after dinner and show me the garden in the moonlight. You have no objection, have you, Philip?'

'I have every objection,' Philip returned quietly. 'Caroline is tired and should spend this her last night as a girl with her mother. Don't you agree with me, Mrs. Fielding?'

But Mrs. Fielding's spark of independence had already been quenched. She cast a quick, sidelong look at her husband. 'I really don't know——' she began, and stopped, taking a nervous sip of wine. 'Caroline has more in common with her father.'

'Nevertheless,' Philip maintained with a ruthlessness that plainly shocked most of the company, 'it is traditional that a bride should prefer female company at such a time. If Mr. Fielding wishes to be entertained in any way, Jeffrey has been here long enough to be able to take him somewhere——'

'What about you, old man?' Jeffrey put in.

'I, too, must prepare for tomorrow,' Philip answered. Nobody questioned him as to what these preparations might be, Caroline noticed with admiration. Even her father seemed glad to turn the conversation to more impersonal matters, and her mother looked as though someone had presented her with an unexpected bouquet of flowers and actually started a long involved story of her own volition, her eyes sparkling with pleasure when Philip laughed in all the right places. But then Philip could be very kind, Caroline thought. Would he be kind to her?

She went out to the kitchen to bring in the coffee and when she came back Philip had disappeared. Caroline sat down beside her mother, yawning despite herself. 'It's been an exhausting week,' she explained with an embarrassed laugh. 'The Cypriots have more stamina for enjoying themselves than I seem to have!'

'But you have enjoyed it?' her mother asked under cover of the other's talk of the price of olive oil and the remarkable size of the Cypriot lemons to be seen in the shops.

'Yes, I have,' Caroline admitted. 'It's all part of Philip, and I want to be a part of him too. I feel alive when I'm with him. I don't think Daddy will ever understand, but you like him, don't you, Mother?'

Her mother actually blushed like a young girl. 'Yes, darling, I do.'

Aunt Hilda was looking tired too. She made a gesture towards the coffee tray and then asked Caroline to pour out the coffee for her. 'It will be another long day tomorrow.' She smiled fleetingly at her brother. 'It's a good thing your daughter has turned into such a fine cook! We seem to have been feeding the whole village for days. Tomorrow is the climax of that too, with a sit-down banquet for all the guests.'

'Funny idea, getting married on a Sunday,' Mr.

Fielding grunted. He turned rather ostentatiously towards Jeffrey. 'What have you been doing with yourself, my boy? Can't have been much fun for you with all these preparations going on!'

Jeffrey looked suitably modest. 'I've been hanging around hoping to see a bit of Caroline,' he confessed. 'I'd hoped to talk her out of this folly by now, but I've hardly been allowed to see anything of her.'

'I thought she asked you out here?' Mr. Fielding protested, his eyes flashing with indignation. 'It's always been the same! Every time she came to Cyprus, she'd forget her manners and everything else we'd ever taught her! Well, Caroline? You were more than half engaged to Jeffrey when you were in London. Don't you think you owe him more than a cold shoulder now?'

Mrs. Fielding made to say something, changed her mind, and looked worried instead. Caroline looked hopefully at her aunt, but Aunt Hilda had her eyes closed and she should obviously have retired to her bed.

'I was wrong to ask Jeffrey to come here,' she admitted. 'I wasn't sure then of my own mind, but now I am. I'm sorry, Jeffrey, but that's how it is!'

Jeffrey looked down at her smiling. Despite his days in the sun he still looked pink rather than brown. Pink and innocent, she thought. 'I think you owe it to me to hear what I want to say to you before I renounce you for ever,' he said solemnly. 'It wouldn't hurt you, Carrie darling, to allow me to say goodbye to you.' He read the indecision in her face and his smile grew deeper. 'Good heavens, my dear, what do you suppose Philip is doing but saying goodbye to his girl-friend? He doesn't seem to share your scruples about having friendships with the opposite sex!'

'But there's nothing to say!' Caroline protested.

'You haven't heard what I have to say yet. I won't hurt you, Caroline. Never that! Don't you know yet that I love you?'

'Yes, go with him, Caroline my dear,' her father

137

chimed in. 'You have your big day tomorrow, but what has Jeffrey to look forward to? He knows how to toe the line. It will do you good to have a breath of fresh air before going to bed. You and Hilda look like a couple of ghosts—I'm not at all surprised, seeing the racket that was going on when we arrived! Still, no excuse for forgetting how civilised people conduct themselves, do you think?' He looked straight at her, opening his eyes wide in a way he had when he wanted something very badly. For a wild moment Caroline wondered if he and Jeffrey had cooked up the whole conversation between them, but she dismissed the idea as ridiculous and felt her own stand weakened in consequence.

'I'm tired,' she said. 'And Aunt Hilda is half asleep now. I think we should all go to bed——'

'A quarter of an hour?' Jeffrey begged. 'That's hardly asking for the moon, Caroline!'

She stood up stiffly, resenting the ease with which they could overset her determination. She didn't want to listen to Jeffrey. She was very much afraid that he would lead her into saying something that she would regret. It wasn't his fault that he had paled into insignificance as far as she was concerned the moment she had seen Philip again.

'Ten minutes,' she said briskly, 'and then I for one am going to bed!'

He put a stole about her shoulders and opened the door for her. She had never seen the stole before, but she supposed it must be one of her mother's and she was so impatient to get the interview over that she didn't bother to argue about using it. It was cool in the garden and she was glad of its borrowed warmth. It was not the first time that she had felt suddenly cold in Jeffrey's company.

She turned and faced him. 'Well, what do you want to say to me?' she urged him.

'We can be overheard so near the house. Let's walk a little way down the road. No one will see us in the dark, and the abbey looks particularly romantic in the moonlight.' He took her hand and drew it through his arm, leading her out of the garden on to the steep road down to the square.

'What do you want, Jeffrey? We have nothing left to say to each other. You must be able to see that!'

'I have a great deal to say,' he contradicted her. 'I'll begin by telling you how beautiful you look tonight. Philip is a lucky fellow.'

'I'm lucky too,' she said sincerely. 'In fact, I can hardly believe that Philip really wants to marry me and that tomorrow I'll be his wife. I seem to have spent all my life getting ready for that moment. Does that sound impossibly sentimental?'

'It doesn't make pleasant listening, but then you haven't heard what I'm going to say yet. That will change your mind for you!'

'Nothing could!'

'Not even the fact that Ileana is with him now? I thought you'd have too much pride, Caroline, to share your husband with another woman—especially on your honeymoon! He won't give her up now, or he would have done so the minute you came back to Cyprus.'

Caroline stiffened. 'Philip has Greek ideas about these things——'

'You can't even deny it! I thought not!'

'I trust Philip,' she forced out.

'Not quite the same thing, is it, my sweet? From where I'm standing it looks a mighty unfair arrangement that you have with him, my dear. You, like Caesar's wife, have to be above suspicion, while he does as he pleases!'

Caroline broke away from him, cold with anger. 'I won't listen to you! Why can't you keep your nasty suggestions to yourself and leave me alone? I'm going back to the house! I don't want to be alone with you again, Jeffrey, not ever! I'm sorry I gave you false hopes that there might be something between us, but

I've always tried to behave honestly and I told you as soon as I could. Please don't try to get in touch with me again!'

'Oh, Caroline!' His laughter struck like splinters against her ears. 'You don't really think you can get away with that? Have you forgotten about the third lesson I promised you? This seems to be just the time and the place, don't you think? Come here, sweetie, and have a little fun with me, just like your swain is doing with Ileana!' He made a grab for her and pulled her close against him. In vain she struggled to get free, but he was ready for her this time. 'Oh no, you don't, not this time!' he warned her. 'This time you'll kiss me and like it. Nobody slaps me twice!'

She twisted her face away from him and, when he tried to put up a hand to hold her more firmly against him, she bit his finger as hard as she could and kicked him in the shins for good measure. The stole she was wearing came away in his hands, but she was able to tear free and she ran as fast as she was able, down the hill, away from him, towards the abbey. Her high heels made any speed difficult and after a few steps she cast them off and ran on in her bare feet, scarcely feeling the rough ground beneath her feet.

When she paused in the shadows to catch her breath, she thought she heard Jeffrey crashing after her, and she took fright all over again. There seemed to be nowhere where she could hide from him, nowhere where he would not find her, and she might not be so lucky a second time as to get free of him. Without pausing in her stride, Caroline launched herself up the nearest tree, pushing herself upwards from branch to branch until she could feel the top of the tree swaying beneath her weight and knew that she could not go up any higher.

'Caroline! Don't be such a fool! Where are you?'

She didn't answer him. She froze to her uncomfortable perch and waited for him to go away, but he was coming nearer all the time. At intervals she could hear him calling out to her in a hoarse whisper and she hugged the trunk of the tree with hands that shone white in the moonlight and shut her eyes against the great gulf of blackness below her. She would never be able to get down by herself! She was afraid to move in any direction! All she could do was hang on tight and pray that he would go away and leave her to her panic. If she were alone, she might be able to unfreeze her muscles and move slowly downwards, but when she tried it, she nearly fell out of the tree and found she was sobbing with fright under her breath and that her dress was completely ruined.

It was a long time later that she heard Aunt Hilda's voice calling to her. 'Caroline, it's me! Jeffrey is with your father, so you can come back now! Where are you, Caroline?'

'I'm here,' she whispered, and then a little louder, 'I'm here, Aunt Hilda. I can't get down!'

'Nonsense!' her aunt declared robustly. 'You got up there, didn't you?'

'It moves!' Caroline explained in despair. 'I'll *never* get down!'

Aunt Hilda peered up the tree at her. 'I'll get Philip,' she said decisively.

'*No!* You can't! He told me not to be alone with Jeffrey. He'll be furious and I couldn't bear it!'

'Better than being stuck up there all night!' her aunt opined. 'Wait there! I shan't be long.'

As if she had any choice, Caroline thought bitterly. She tried to move her leg into a more comfortable position and the tree swayed dangerously beneath her. She shut her eyes again and the panic within her subsided a little. She began to wonder how long she had been up the tree. If someone didn't come soon, she didn't think she could hold on much longer.

When she opened her eyes, Philip was standing in the moonlight below her. 'It isn't very high,' he told her. 'What's all the panic about?'

'I can't move!' She attempted a laugh. 'It's high

enough for me to break my neck if I jump!'

'And that would be no more than you deserve!' he returned brutally.

'*I know!*' she sobbed.

'You don't have to jump,' he said in soothing tones. 'All you have to do is let go and I'll catch you. You trust me to see that you don't hurt yourself, don't you?'

'*I can't!*'

'Yes, you can! Let go now, Caroline, or I'll leave you up there all night. I'll count and when I say three, let go. One, two, *three!*'

She let go blindly and fell awkwardly from the tree straight into his arms. They felt hard and strong about her and she hid her face in his shoulder, trying to still the shudders that racked her body. 'I'm sorry, Philip! I should never have gone with him! If you hadn't come——' She gulped and began to cry in earnest. 'I couldn't have let go if you hadn't been here, *and I didn't think you'd come!*'

He hugged her tightly against him. 'Never mind, love, you're forgiven. I'll always be there. Don't you know that even yet?'

'Is that a promise?' She looked up at him, wiping her damp face on the back of her hand. 'I can't do without you!'

'I promise,' he said. 'Now, do you think you can walk home on your own feet?'

She nodded, but she still clung to his hand. 'I've lost my shoes.' She put her bare feet tentatively down on the ground. 'I should never have agreed to go with him even for ten minutes. I didn't mean to put myself in such a silly position!'

Philip gave her a crooked smile. 'Habit, my dear,' he said. 'Old habits stick like burrs until you have others to put in their place. They counted on that!'

Caroline sighed. 'I wish I were married to you now!' she exclaimed. 'Philip, I didn't mean to disobey you——'

He laughed and kissed her cheek, his expression very gentle in the moonlight. 'Come on home, my love,' he said. 'Your mother is waiting to put you to bed. Jeffrey won't bother you any more.'

She shivered again. 'My mother likes you,' she said shyly. 'You don't suppose she'll wonder——'

'No one will ask you any questions tonight,' he assured her. 'Come on home, dear!'

CHAPTER TEN

CAROLINE slept late that Sunday morning. She heard
the clanging of the church bell in her dreams, but she
was not yet ready to wake up properly and embark on
the day that was to see her married to Philip. She tried
to think about him clearly, but she found it impossible. She had only to call up a picture of him in her
mind and her heart began to knock against her ribs
and she was as aware of him as if he were standing
beside her. It was unfair that he could do that to her
when she had no similar hold over him. Yet, and it
had been this that had consoled her all through the
night, he had not been with Ileana last night. He
couldn't have been! And he had come when she had
needed him most—and he had been kind in a way she
had not deserved.

Was it habit that had made her agree to talk to Jeffrey last night? Her father had been so insistent and
Jeffrey himself had been so reasonable, it would have
been silly and petulant to have refused. Or that was
what she had thought at the time. Habit? Yes, she
thought Philip was right. Jeffrey had been a habit with
her for a long time now. She had fallen in with her
father's suggestions that he should meet him, go out
with him, and almost fall in love with him. She had
been lucky that she had not married him out of habit!
That she wasn't committing her life into *Jeffrey*'s keeping that day, for there would have been no hope for
her then. Philip had been right about that too. Jeffrey
was nice, but he wasn't the man she wanted. It would
be like living with a looking-glass to be married to
him. Whereas being Philip's wife would make demands on her inmost being and she would be hard put
to it to keep up with him. Habit didn't come into it!

A soft knock on the door preceded her mother's

anxious face. 'Caroline, are you really going to have *ten* bridesmaids?'

Caroline laughed and stretched, enjoying her mother's scandalised expression. 'It's quite usual,' she said. 'Philip has ten young men attending him too.'

'Oh dear, how *strange*! I wish the ceremony were a little more normal, darling. Your father has the idea that it's all completely uncivilised! Jeffrey says you'd prefer to call it pagan and talked a lot about Aphrodite, of whom your father had never heard, but I thought Philip was a *Christian*?'

'He is,' Caroline said with a giggle. 'Unlike Jeffrey, he even goes to church on Sundays! As for Aphrodite, Cyprus is sometimes considered to be her special realm. Why don't you try to introduce Daddy to her while you're here? It would do him good.'

'*Caroline!*'

Her daughter gave her an unrepentant smile. 'Well, he doesn't often think about anything else but work and its rewards, does he?'

Her mother was silent for a moment. 'I'm glad you're marrying someone like Philip,' she said. 'I never thought Jeffrey was right for you, but I didn't do anything about it. Sometimes one's loyalties are stretched in two directions at once and I've always taken the line of least resistance.'

'Philip would say your first loyalty is to Daddy,' Caroline said awkwardly. She tried to reintroduce a note of levity by adding: 'He's left me in no doubt as to whom I owe all my loyalty for the rest of my life! But he was nice last night. I thought he'd be far angrier than he was. I was a fool to agree to talk to Jeffrey.'

Mrs. Fielding looked at her with a flicker of curiosity. 'Do you want to tell me what happened?' she asked.

Caroline flushed. 'He tried to kiss me—not for the first time! He's quite strong, you know, when he's roused, and I took fright and climbed up a tree to get away from him. It was all rather horrid. I found I couldn't climb down the tree again, but then Philip came and everything was all right.'

'Yes, it would be,' Mrs. Fielding agreed.

'You *do* like him!' Caroline exclaimed.

'I liked Michael too,' her mother said unexpectedly. 'I used to envy Hilda when we were younger, though of course I could never have taken to the life here as she did! I used to tell myself that she was a strong candidate for Women's Lib, or whatever its equivalent was in those days, to get to work on, but I never really believed it. Michael may have been the head of the house, but he made her happier than any of my other girl-friends were. Philip is very like him.'

Caroline swung her legs off the bed, looking ruefully down at her still sore feet. 'Philip isn't exactly biddable,' she said.

'No?' Mrs. Fielding looked amused. 'You used to hate it when he called you to order when you were both children. You used to write me long, mostly illegible, letters complaining about how he ill-used you. You won't be able to do that when you're married to him!'

Caroline averted her face. 'No. But it will be different now. I've given him the right, if you see what I mean. Ours is going to be a Cypriot marriage. Those were his terms and I accepted them. You see, I asked him to marry me, not the other way round. I thought he'd agree because I could bring him the Klearchos lands that Uncle Michael owned. I thought Uncle Michael and Aunt Hilda had arranged things that way, but I think Philip has owned them all along—ever since Uncle Michael died, so now I don't know why he's marrying me. And I can't ask him.'

'Why not?'

'Because he won't lie to me and I'd rather not know the truth if it's because he's in love with Ileana and won't marry her because—well, because he's already had what he wanted from her. He has very Greek ideas

146

about these things!' she ended, daring her mother to find his attitude less than admirable.

'Isn't he in love with you?'

Caroline shrugged her shoulders. 'I don't think so.'

'I see,' Mrs. Fielding said gently. 'Isn't there a Cypriot saying that if the stone hits the egg, poor egg; and if the egg hits the stone, poor egg? I'm sure I heard Michael say it once.'

'You're a great comfort!' Caroline smiled.

'I've always been the egg,' her mother said dryly. 'There's nothing egg-like about you, darling. I was wondering what happened when stone hit stone?'

'The sparks fly!' Caroline suggested, laughing. 'I'm not feeling sorry for myself, Mother, so there's no need to look like that. Even if he doesn't love me, I'll be his wife. I'd rather that than nothing at all. Philip's wife will always count with him. He *is* very Greek, you see!'

'You know,' her mother said, 'you've grown up quite a bit in the last week or so. I missed so much of your growing up when you were small that I swore I'd be there when you turned into a woman, but Aunt Hilda had that pleasure too. I suppose I should be thankful to be here to see you married!'

Caroline looked concerned. She had seldom heard her mother complain about anything in her life before. 'It isn't Aunt Hilda's fault,' she began.

'No,' her mother sighed. 'But I hope Philip allows you to bring up your own children——' She broke off, seeing her daughter convulsed with laughter, and began to laugh herself. 'I suppose it is funny! As if Philip would ever consider anything else! You'll have your hands full being the "woman of his house"!

Tell me, do the Greeks always use the word woman when they mean wife, or is it just common usage that makes them do so?'

'There is a word, but it hasn't the comfortable sound of the other. The man is nearly always referred

to as the master, or the lord, and his wife as his woman
—a much lower being! I minded terribly as a child,
but I don't seem to mind at all now.'

'You must be in love,' her mother teased her.

'I am,' Caroline said, and she didn't care who knew
it, as long as Philip didn't.

Her wedding-dress had been laid out in the hall for
the many visitors of the last few days to look at and
admire. Caroline stopped now and fingered the stiff
material thoughtfully. It had been lovingly embroidered from head to foot by her aunt's many friends and
the train was encrusted with tiny pearls, making hundreds of little stylised flowers that caught the sun and
gleamed when the material was moved. It was a beautiful dress and she was glad that she was going to wear
it for Philip, but otherwise it was remarkably unim-
portant to her. It wasn't the trappings of the wedding
she wanted, but to know herself safely committed
to Philip once and for all time.

She had wasted too much of the morning and now
she had to hurry to help with the preparations for the
banquet that the bride's parents traditionally provided for all the guests. They were due to sit down to
the meal at noon and Caroline felt rather guilty that
she had left almost all the preparations to the others,
especially as her aunt had been looking so tired the
evening before.

'Oh, Caroline, there you are!' Aunt Hilda exclaimed, catching sight of her in the hall. 'My dear
child, you haven't begun to *dress*! Don't touch anything! Go back to your room and I'll try and find those
bridesmaids. They were here a minute ago, asking if
you wanted the dress "danced" before you put it on. I
told them there wasn't room. By the way, Ileana is *not*
in a very happy mood. The young man she's supposed
to be marrying from Greece was supposed to arrive
yesterday and didn't come. I do hope you're not going
to regret asking her to be one of your *coumera*. Does

Philip know?'

'He never asked.'

'Well, I'm beginning to regret it, even if you're not! Kyria Zavallis says the young man may come today, but her hopes have been raised so often that she doesn't rely on it. Keep telling Ileana that he's coming, though, won't you?'

'If you think it will do any good,' Caroline returned. She came up close to her aunt and shook her head at her. 'Aunt Hilda, would it be any use suggesting that you don't try and do everything yourself? I'll need you for afterwards and, frankly, you look as if you could do with a week in bed!'

'But I'm loving every minute of it!' Aunt Hilda claimed triumphantly. 'I wish Michael had been here. It's just as we always dreamed it would be and I'm not going to miss any part of it! I can rest afterwards.'

'We-ell,' Caroline compromised, 'Mother makes a splendid lieutenant——'

'She's suffering from shock hearing about your culinary skills!' Aunt Hilda retorted. 'For heaven's sake, go and get dressed!'

Caroline went obediently back into her bedroom, not quite sure what was expected of her. She sat on the edge of the bed, feeling increasingly nervous, and not at all like herself. She didn't have long to wait before Ileana slipped into the room and stood in silence, looking round the room with heavy eyes.

'It's a nice room, isn't it?' Caroline said, not much liking the silence.

Ileana shrugged indifferently. 'It's old-fashioned. I prefer modern houses, not ones like this one where one is always cleaning and nothing is convenient. The plaited reed ceilings are pretty, but they attract the dirt.'

'They're cool,' Caroline smiled. 'I like the old, traditional things.'

Ileana glared at her. 'One day Cyprus will have to be as modern as other places! Then there will be nothing to choose between the two of us. Philip is a fool! How can he be happy with someone like you as his wife?'

Caroline looked away. 'Isn't that his decision?' she returned quietly.

'I shall make a modern marriage!' Ileana informed her. 'It's all arranged. I am to marry a man from mainland Greece. I shall live in Athens. He is a very important man, and I shall be important too as his wife.'

Caroline felt sorry for her, though she supposed she would be happy enough. She hoped that she would find it enough, but couldn't bring herself to believe that she would—not when she might have had Philip!

'I hear your fiancé is coming to Cyprus very soon?' Caroline tried to instil the right amount of enthusiasm into her voice. 'You must be very excited.'

Ileana shrugged again. 'Why should I be? Why must you pretend all the time that you don't know about Philip and me? He may be marrying you, but you will never know him as I have known him. You are welcome to be the mother of his children! You have never given anything freely. Would you love him if he did not offer you marriage and the chance to live in this house, and everything else that you want—all the things that brought you back to Cyprus?'

Caroline gasped. 'I didn't have to marry Philip——'

Ileana looked her disbelief. 'Would you have married the other one? The pink and white one?' Her eyes half closed as she walked towards Caroline. 'Why does Philip believe that nothing has passed between you and the other one? How did you convince him of that when half the village saw him kissing you—in the road too!—last night?'

Caroline didn't answer.

'I was in the road too,' Ileana went on relentlessly. 'I was coming to see Philip. He had *asked* me to come! The other one came with the message——'

'*Jeffrey?*'

'So, when you are married to Philip, how do you

know he will come home to you? If I am here, you will never be sure where he is, will you? Think of that in church today, *Anglitha*, when you make your vows to him!'

Caroline roused herself with difficulty. 'I don't believe a word of it!' she said in a voice that trembled. 'Especially not if Jeffrey had anything to do with it. *I won't believe it!*'

Ileana uttered an hysterical laugh and then began to cry. 'He didn't come yesterday. No one believes he will come now! So why should I give up Philip to you? No one in Cyprus will have anything to do with me now!'

'He will come,' Caroline said with a great deal more confidence than she was feeling. 'He may even come today.'

Ileana went a brick-red colour, biting her lips to restrain her tears. 'It would be wonderful if he came today! He would see me as one of your *coumera*, and then he would never believe anything bad of me. If he comes today, I will never see Philip again!'

Which was cold comfort to Caroline. What she wanted was for Philip not to *want* to see Ileana. If he did want to, it didn't seem to matter much whether Ileana was still in Cyprus, Greece, or Timbuctoo.

'I think I should start dressing,' she said aloud. 'Would you mind helping me, Ileana? There are some rather awkward fastenings on the dress and I'm afraid of tearing the material.'

She scarcely recognised herself when she was dressed. She looked a stranger and not quite real. She stuck out her tongue at herself in the glass and thought she looked good enough to eat, but good enough for very little else. Her eyes were shadowed and without their usual gleam of humour, and her face was pale and serious even when she attempted a smile to brighten up the cool, elegant vision that looked back at her.

'Oh well, here we go!' she said to herself. She crossed her fingers and, shutting her eyes, wished earnestly that it would all go well. Only another few hours and she would be alone with Philip, but she wouldn't think about that because it set her trembling inwardly, and she still didn't know why he was marrying her. How could she have been so silly as to think it didn't matter? It mattered to her more and more every minute!

'Caroline, are you ready?' Her mother appeared behind her in the looking-glass, her face wiped clean of all expression. 'I didn't know you were so lovely,' she said finally. 'Oh, Caroline, it's a beautiful dress!'

'It rather outshines the bride,' Caroline said wryly. 'But I don't suppose it matters. Philip knows what he's getting!'

'None of us know what we're getting!' Mrs. Fielding retorted with robust good sense. 'Pull yourself together, darling, and come and do whatever it is you have to do next. Hilda sent me to get you. And'—she went on hastily, seeing that Caroline was about to feel sorry for herself all over again—'if you can't see for yourself that you're wearing the dress very successfully, and not the dress you, then you ought to go into spectacles and look a perfect frump!'

'Yes, Mother,' Caroline said meekly. She met her mother's eyes squarely and thought how pretty she could look when she was excited—and out of sight of her father. She hoped that this day at least, nothing would happen to quench her mother's pleasure, and kissed her warmly on the cheek to give things a good start. 'Are you hungry? I believe it's traditional for everyone to eat far too much at a wedding!'

'Everyone but the bride,' her mother said in reproving tones. 'You won't have time if you have to circulate amongst that crush outside! Oh darling, this is fun, isn't it?'

Caroline saw Philip from the other side of the room. He looked up and his eyes widened as he saw her. He jerked his head at her to come and stand beside him

and she went, her eyes on his, just as if there was no
one else there. She felt more and more unreal and she
was only partly reassured when his hand squeezed hers
under cover of her veil.

'Mother's having a lovely time!' she said, unnatur-
ally bright.

He smiled. 'And her daughter?'

'Not quite here!'

His eyes lit with a brilliance that warmed her
through and through. 'We'll have to do something
about that as soon as we can!' His voice dropped to a
whisper.

> *'My love in her attire doth show her wit*
> *It doth so well become her:*
> *For every season she hath dressings fit,*
> *For Winter, Spring, and Summer.*
> *No beauty she doth miss*
> *When all her robes are on,*
> *But Beauty's self is she*
> *When all her robes are gone.'*

That brought her back to the present with a venge-
ance! How dared he quote such nonsense to her? How
dared he even know such verse, especially in what to
him was a foreign language? Her face grew heated
with indignation and she longed to make some retort
that would put him firmly in his place, only she
couldn't think of anything except that he had no right
to read her mind with such accuracy—and over her
own wedding-dress too!

'Don't you like it?' she stammered.

'Dear heart, when I tell you that there won't be a
crowd of people all round us. I've never seen you love-
lier!'

'But not quite me,' she said on a sigh.

The brilliant look was back in his eyes and she
thought must be reflected in her own. 'You look like
yourself to me *yinéka mou*: the self you've never seen

153

as yourself, a young, green girl——'

'Philip, you do indeed want to marry me?'

His eyes mocked her, bringing a blush to her cheek. 'I hope to convince you of that too,' he drawled softly. 'Take courage, Caroline, the Klearchos inheritance will be quite safe with me!'

'But you already have it——'

'Not yet,' he said, 'but I have every hope that it will soon be entirely mine!'

Afterwards Caroline was to remember very little about the banquet. She was seated by Philip's side, to her father's immense disapproval, and they shared a pair of roasted doves so that they might have a peaceful married life.

'There won't be time later,' Aunt Hilda told them, fussing over their comfort and looking tireder than ever. 'Everyone is coming back here for wine and snacks, but we can't put on two banquets in one day! I hope everyone understands. It's unusual to have the bride and groom both living in the same house. Caroline, you must try and eat something. Don't you *want* to have a happy married life?'

Caroline struggled through a few mouthfuls of roasted dove, hiding the rest of it beneath her knife and fork. 'Do we have to come back here?' she asked Philip in an undertone.

He raised his eyebrows and smiled. 'We needn't stay long.'

It occurred to her that she didn't know yet where they were going and she turned to ask him, but there was a sudden shift of interest among the guests away from the food and out into the street and she realised, with a sudden lurching sensation inside her, that it was time for them to go to the church.

White of face, she walked on her father's arm, with Philip beside her, and Aunt Hilda on the other side of him, where his father would have stood if he had been alive. Ahead of them went first the priest, then the

154

violinists, and behind came the ten *coumbari,* the bridesmen, and the ten *coumera,* the bridesmaids, and the great crowd of guests and well-wishers, which was practically everyone in the village and the neighbouring villages as well.

Caroline avoided looking at Ileana as they entered the church. She avoided looking at anyone. She had a horrid feeling that she was never going to breathe properly again, that the whole of life was suspended on a tight-rope that might give way at any moment. She had a sudden longing for an English country church and the familiar words of the English marriage service. Then she raised her eyes to the iconostasis, the screen that separates the sanctuary from the congregation in an Orthodox church, and was fiercely glad that she was where she was. The icons of the Old Testament prophets gazed down at her from the top row of the screen, Our Lady of the Sign in the middle, with Christ Emmanuel on her breast. The second row was taken up by the saints and scenes from the life of the Virgin and of the life of Christ. Beneath these, seated in glory, sat the enthroned Christ Pantocrator, judging the world, with his mother and St. John on either side, pleading with him on behalf of all humanity. 'Pray for me,' she said under her breath.

Her father was at a loss. He stood away from her with a gesture of distaste, but Caroline scarcely noticed. She stood by Philip's side, lost in the beauty of the sound as the psalmists threw the chant from one side to the other of the church, their golden voices echoing the splendour of the Orthodox marriage ceremony. Then the priest was speaking alone, repeating the vows for first Philip and then for herself. When her turn came she found herself looking straight into Philip's face.

'—to love and obey——' said the priest, and Philip stepped sharply on her toes, making her gasp with sheer pain.

'Lest you should forget!' he whispered in English

with a taut smile. The priest frowned and went on in Greek. Caroline spread her toes in her shoe and winced again. She should have been expecting it, she thought. This was not the first Cypriot wedding she had been to, and she had seen the groom remind his bride of the duty she owed him before. Only that other bride had not been running over rough ground in her bare feet the night before! Had Philip remembered *that*? Very likely, she thought, her anger kindling against him, but that had not made him more gentle with her! On the contrary, he had probably thought that it would make the lesson all the more effective and, when she thought of the circumstances that had led to her flight down the stony road the previous evening, she could hardly blame him.

She looked down at the golden band he had put on her finger and hoped he hadn't noticed how her hand had shook when she had put her ring on to his finger. The touch of his strong hands beneath hers had roused an unexpected feeling of delight within her, and she had wondered if he had felt it too, but he had given no sign that he had felt anything at all, only pushing the ring more firmly home with the same abrupt movement he had made when placing his ring on her finger.

Then at last, the blessings over and the marriage crowns put away, they left the church again and led the procession back to the house on a wave of happiness, the bridesmaids following behind them. Caroline looked down at her feet and saw the black mark Philip had made on the white satin of her slippers.

'You've ruined my shoes!' she accused him, swishing her skirts to one side so that he could see the damage more clearly.

'So I see,' he said.

'Is that *all* you've got to say?' she demanded, allowing her anger full rein.

'For the moment. Caroline, where has Ileana gone?'

Instantly she felt dead inside. 'Ileana?'

'She's your bridesmaid, remember? Where has she

gone?'

'How should I know?' she said on a high note.

'Caroline, it's important.'

'Only to you!'

Philip grasped both her hands, forcing her round to face him, no matter how many people were looking on. 'What is that supposed to mean?'

With difficulty she swallowed her anger. 'N-nothing,' she stammered.

'It had better not! Where is she?'

'I don't know! Truly, I don't know. She was here when we went into church. That was the last time I saw her, though I didn't exactly look at her then.'

He rasped out a laugh. 'Still jealous of her? If you felt like that, why did you ask her to be one of your *coumera*? It wasn't a particularly suitable choice, if I may say so.'

'*You* can say that! I only did it for you—because of what you've done to her! And I don't care if she has disappeared. In fact, I'm glad! I don't care if I never see her again! So there!'

'Caroline——'

'Why should you care where she is?' Caroline went on, almost in tears.

'I don't! Caroline, shut up before I slap you! Now *think*! Where did you last see her? Did she slip out of the church? Can you catch Aunt Hilda's eye and ask her?' His fingers bit into her wrists. 'And just what is it that I am supposed to have done to the girl?'

Caroline opened her eyes wide. 'Well, if you don't know, I'm certainly not going to tell you!'

His mouth closed in a grim line. 'That's what you think, is it? But find her we must! Her fiancé has arrived at last——'

'Perhaps that's why she's gone,' Caroline suggested smoothly.

'*Her mother* won't survive another rebuff to Ileana,' Philip continued, just as if she hadn't spoken. 'It was bad enough when I refused to have her, having led

157

them all on to believe I would——'

'You mean you might have married her?'

His face lost its grim look and he laughed. 'It was about as likely as your marrying Jeffrey, but her parents didn't know that. As it turned out, I shouldn't have married her anyway.' He gave her a wry smile that set her heart beating frantically against her ribs. 'I prefer my wife to be a young, green girl with eyes for no one else but me.'

'Then it wasn't you——' she murmured.

'I do not seduce innocent girls, which is not to say that I don't take what I'm offered by the not so innocent,' he said dryly. 'You should have come home a long time ago. There are many Ileanas to be had in Cyprus!'

Aunt Hilda was as concerned as Philip was at Ileana's disappearance. 'She will have to be found,' she stated firmly. 'If only the young man had come earlier, but I suppose she thought he wasn't coming.' She swayed slightly, her face grey with fatigue. 'Philip, you'll have to find her,' she said.

Philip nodded. 'I'll take the car. But I can't go yet. We don't want to draw attention to her disappearance. Caroline will go and talk to her fiancé and tell him all about her being one of her bridesmaids and that she was overcome by the atmosphere in the church. I'll slip away as soon as I can.'

'But you won't know where to look!' Caroline protested.

He lifted a mocking eyebrow. 'I have a better idea than most. She'll probably be more than half expecting me!'

Caroline took a deep breath. 'I'm coming with you!' she announced. She hoped she sounded as decided as he would have done, but she could hear for herself the note of entreaty in her voice. 'It's much better that I should. Everyone will be expecting us to go together.'

'Quite right,' said Aunt Hilda. 'I'm sorry, both of you, but I must sit down. Caroline, will you go and fetch your mother? I think I'm going to need her help.'

Mrs. Fielding took one look at her sister-in-law and whisked her off to bed, for once completely in command of the situation that faced her. 'She's thoroughly overtired and needs rest, and that's what she's going to have. Don't worry, I shall look after her for the next few days, whatever anybody may say. If necessary, your father can go back to England without me.' She smiled at her daughter and her brand new son-in-law. 'Why don't you disappear while you can?' she suggested. 'The car is all ready for you.'

Philip grinned back at her. 'Good idea!' he said. And he kissed her, hugging her tight against him. 'A very good idea!'

CHAPTER ELEVEN

MRS. FIELDING freed herself from her son-in-law's clasp with a heightened colour and sparkling eyes. 'I don't know when I've enjoyed myself so much!' she said impulsively. 'Caroline, I think you might slip away and change now. The party, and Aunt Hilda, will both get on very well without you.'

Caroline looked uncertainly at Philip. 'What shall I change into? Should I pack a few things to take with me?'

'Do you mean you have nothing ready?' Philip demanded.

'How could I have?' she excused herself. 'I don't know where we're going even now!' The look in his eyes unsettled her oddly and she found she couldn't bring herself to return his glance. 'I'll go and get ready,' she said in a shaken voice.

'Wear something warm,' he bade her, 'and bring some shoes you can walk in. I'll go and see to the car.'

It took her longer than she had thought possible. The house was in turmoil from the celebrations of the last few days and it was almost impossible to find anything in the resulting chaos. Caroline put a small suitcase on her bed and flung in the first clothes that came to hand with abandon. Outside, the violinist was striking up a jaunty tune and most of the guests had started to dance. It was a merry scene, with all the villagers in their best clothes doing their best to attract the right eye with their fripperies and Sunday elegance. What was it they said locally? 'Buy a shoe from your own country, even though it be mended'? Meaning that a young man should choose his wife from his own village. Philip had done that, or had he? Did she count as an inhabitant of Bellapais because she had spent so much of her childhood there? She liked to think so, because, in a

160

way, that day she had come home, more so even than on the day she had come back to Cyprus.

She was further delayed because she couldn't find her sponge-bag. She went into the kitchen to get a plastic bag that she thought would do as well and found a strange young man seated on one of the wooden chairs, his hat resting on the knees of his dark suit. He stood up as she came in, striking an attitude of attentive deference that seemed quite foreign to the sulky, over-fleshed lines of his face.

'Kyria Caroline? But of course the wedding-gown means that you must be she! I have been hoping to speak with you, *kyria*.'

'Why?' Caroline asked abruptly.

'I have come this day from Greece, to become acquainted with my fiancée, Ileana Zavallis——'

'But what are you doing here?' Caroline asked. 'You ought to be with her family.'

'I was there,' the young man said. 'I was told Ileana was here, that she is one of your bridesmaids, but when I came here to take her home she was not here——'

Caroline gave him a guilty look. 'She is—she is helping me change my dress,' she claimed.

The young man shook his head. 'Forgive me, *kyria*, but she is nowhere in the house. I think you know this, no?'

Caroline blinked at this attack on her veracity, feeling cross that she should have been put in this ridiculous position in the first place. 'I don't know where she is,' she admitted. 'But she was here, and she is one of my *coumera*——'

'You do her too much honour,' the young man remarked.

Caroline favoured him with an icy stare, conscious of the bitter irony that she was about to defend Ileana to the best of her ability when it was the very last thing she had ever thought she would do, let alone of her own free will.

'*Kyrie*, Ileana is a friend of mine——'

'And of your husband's? Oh yes, I have not been here long and already I have heard much that is not to my fiancée's credit! I have been misled by her family, but I mean to get the truth before I leave here. I mean to have the whole story from her own lips!'

'That is your business, not mine!' Caroline snapped back. 'I can only hope that when you find out that you owe Ileana an apology—and a great deal more—she'll be sensible enough to send you straight back to Greece! What kind of a man are you that you can only condemn where you ought to protect? Ileana deserves a great deal detter than you!'

The young man looked first astonished and then he smiled reluctantly. 'Is there no truth in these rumours?' he asked.

Caroline busied herself with looking in one drawer after another for the plastic bag she was seeking. 'Isn't it enough for you that I should ask her to be one of my bridesmaids?' She saw with satisfaction that she had shaken him and pressed home her advantage. 'Why come here and question me about your fiancée, *kyrie*? I find it most improper!'

'Would you rather that I asked your husband?'

'I would rather that you asked Ileana's father, or Ileana herself. But I will fetch my husband if you wish to speak to him?' It was the first time that she had named Philip as her husband and it gave her a glow of satisfaction to be able to do so. 'But I don't think he will have anything to say to you!'

The young man looked thoughtful. 'I apologise, *kyria*, for troubling you on such a distasteful subject. My name is Aristotle Aghreus. I have not seen Ileana since she came once to stay with my mother, who is her godmother. It has been arranged between our two families that I should marry her. It is time I married, you understand, and it is a suitable match for us both. But then, when I arrived here, I am told of your own wedding and that I shall find Ileana here. She is not here, but there are plenty of people ready to tell me why she may have run away sooner than come face to face to me. I want to know the truth of this matter. My name is an honourable one——'

'Oh, really!' Caroline exclaimed. 'What good is your honour to you? Why don't you show a little humanity and understanding instead?'

He looked amused. 'That is the remark of a woman, *kyria*. Who can tell what I shall show Ileana when I find her? I am told she has grown into a remarkably pretty woman.'

'And the size of her *prika* has nothing to do with it, I suppose?'

'It has everything to do with it!' he assured her earnestly. 'Why else do you think I am here? But it is better if we can like one another also.'

Caroline produced a plastic bag from the back of the last drawer she had looked in. 'Ah, here it is! I'm sorry, *kyrie*, but I must finish changing my dress and my packing. My husband is waiting for me.'

'You are leaving the party already?'

Caroline coloured. Would he guess that they were going to look for Ileana? And if he did, would Philip blame her for giving the game away? She hoped not on both counts. 'We have some way to go,' she explained, determined that he shouldn't ask their destination if she could help it. 'I don't know where exactly. It's to be a surprise for me.'

He stepped aside from the door, the sulkiness gone from his face. 'Have you someone to help with your dress?' he enquired. 'I see all your bridesmaids, except Ileana, are outside dancing and enjoying themselves.'

'I can manage,' Caroline informed him stiffly. 'If I can't, my mother will help me. Why don't you join the dancers?'

He smiled without amusement. 'Because I wish to see Ileana as soon as possible.' He laid his hat carefully down on the table. 'Kyria Zavallis suggested that I should enlist your help in finding her and I mean to do so.'

163

'*Kyrie*, I am setting out on my *honeymoon*——'

'I shall wait for you in the hall,' he cut her off. 'Oh, I forgot,' he added as he turned away, 'I wish you every happiness in your marriage. *Sto kalo!*'

'Thank you,' she said blankly.

It didn't take her long to finish her packing after that. She pulled her wedding-dress up over her head and allowed it to fall in a pool of embroidered silk at her feet. Why should everyone suppose that she knew anything about Ileana? It wasn't in the least likely that the Cypriot girl would choose her as a confidante. They didn't like each other and they never would, not while they both wanted Philip! She threw the last of her things into her suitcase and snapped it shut. Now, she thought, what was she going to wear?

She settled for a pair of plum-coloured corduroy trousers and a long-sleeved shirt to match. With a heavy silver pendant round her neck, bearing the representation of Aphrodite on one side and a rolling wave on the other, she thought she looked feminine but far from the usual image of the just married which was what she most wanted to avoid.

There was quite a crowd round the car when she went outside. Kyrios Aghreus was not in the hall, much to her relief, as she tiptoed out the front door, and no one said a word to her when she quietly came and stood beside Philip, suddenly shy as she silently handed him her suitcase. Her parents were there, and she was astonished to see her father was smiling. Caroline went up to him and gave him a quick kiss.

'How long are you staying?' she asked him, encouraged by his relaxed expression.

'As long as Hilda will put up with us.' He lowered his voice and went on confidentially, 'Hilda is not at all well, my dear, and your mother insists that we stay on and look after her until you get back from your honeymoon. Poor Hilda always worked too hard when Michael was alive, and she's paying for it now! Don't make that mistake, will you? There's no need for *you* to turn yourself into a servant for any man. You have only to ask and I'll go on with your allowance, Carrie.'

'Thank you, Daddy, but I won't ask. Philip can give me everything I want——'

'Very romantic!' her father scoffed. 'I'd think more of him if he didn't expect you to cook and wash for him! Quite unnecessary when your husband is as well off as that young man. However, I suppose you won't listen to me——'

'No, I won't,' Caroline agreed, laughing.

'I thought not!' He patted her shoulder, his eye transfixed by the sight of a number of women struggling out of the house with the heavy wedding-mattress being carried between them. 'Do you have to take *that* with you?' he demanded.

Caroline turned helplessly to Philip. 'D-do we?'

By way of answer, he wrenched open the rear door of the car and helped the women to bundle the mattress on to the back seat. 'Get in!' he said to Caroline. 'It's time to go.'

There was a flurry of embraces all round and then Caroline stepped into the car, feeling quite exhausted and with a strong inclination to burst into tears. She managed to control this last, however, until Philip was seated beside her and then she said in a voice that broke dangerously: 'Ileana's fiancé has arrived. He was sitting in the kitchen, and he more or less accused me of hiding the wretched girl from him!'

'Why should he think that?'

Caroline sniffed. 'He's heard rumours about her already——'

'What did you say to him?' His tone was cold in the extreme.

'I said she was helping me change my dress, but he didn't believe me. He said he was going to wait for me in the hall, but he'd gone when I came outside.'

'What made him come to you?'

'Kyria Zavallis. Philip, can't you tell *him* where to find her? Why do *we* have to chase all over the countryside looking for her?'

He put a hand over hers, rubbing his forefinger against her ring. 'Don't argue about this, Caroline. If you don't want to come, you don't have to. You can wait here for me if you prefer. No one will hold it against you.'

'No, I'd rather be with you!'

'Good! I thought we were going to have a row about it and I don't feel strong enough at the moment to win any arguments with you. It's been quite a day!'

'Have you ever thought,' she asked him as he slipped the car into gear and they started off, edging their way through the villagers who had crowded round to wish them a safe journey, 'have you ever thought that all you have to do is to explain things to me? I'm on your side!'

'Over Ileana?' he mocked her.

'I asked her to be my bridesmaid!'

Philip glanced into the driving mirror. 'There's a car following us. Take a look and see if it's the fiancé, will you?'

Caroline shifted the glass until she too could see the driver in the car behind them. 'Yes, that's him. Philip, I don't think he means to marry her. He was full of the honour of his name and—and that's why you didn't marry her, isn't it?'

'That is something I do not intend to discuss with you!'

Caroline sighed. 'Yes, but, Philip——'

'Drop it, Caroline! I'm going to stop and have a word with this fellow. If he doesn't intend to marry Ileana, he seems to be going to a great deal of trouble to tell her so!'

He brought the car to a rather forceful stop at the side of the road and got out, waving to the car behind them. Watching them over her shoulder, Caroline saw the second car come to a stop beside them. Kyrios Aghreus swept a hand up to the hat he was wearing and removed it, using it as a fan while he waited for

166

Philip to walk round the car to the open window beside him. Caroline couldn't hear what they said to one another, but in the end they shook hands and Philip came back, throwing himself into the driving seat beside her.

'Says his name is Aristotle!'

Caroline giggled despite herself. 'Yes, I know.'

'Very funny!' But he laughed too. 'He's going to follow on behind. Ileana is luckier than she knows.'

Caroline made a face, but she said nothing. She was disturbed that the thought of Ileana had such power to hurt her. It was jealousy, she told herself, and shouldn't be surprising to her, for she had already admitted to herself the other side of that particular coin. She was fathoms deep in love with Philip and she just had to face the fact that he was not in love with her.

The swallows cavorted in the sky, swooping in and out of the glassless windows of the abbey refectory, which had once been used as a miniature rifle-range by British troops. Caroline turned her head to see them better, enjoying her last glimpse of the golden ruin and church on her wedding day.

'Regretting it already?' Philip teased her.

She shook her head. 'Never that!' she murmured.

They took the road to the east, going through practically deserted country that later in the year would be full of blue and orange tents, and the bronzed bodies of the tourists as they stretched themselves out on the practically deserted beaches.

'I think we'll take the forest road,' Philip said after a while. 'The views from up there are fantastic. Cheer up, love! You may not be enjoying this very much, but I swear I'll make it up to you afterwards. It isn't half as bad as you think!'

But it was, every bit as bad. Surely she had been entitled to Philip's whole attention today of all days? Surely that wasn't asking too much? The thought of Ileana cut her to the quick and it was only with difficulty that she raised a smile and enquired if their dust wasn't going to be rather trying for the driver of the car following on behind.

'He'll have to put up with it!' Philip responded heartlessly. 'His time is coming. I want to enjoy my inheritance right now!'

The road led upwards, falling into disrepair here and there with the weight of the lorries going backwards and forwards carrying the materials for the new road that was being built alongside. Below lay the navy blue sea, the waves whipped into a startling white by the evening breeze. Between the coast and themselves were hundreds and hundreds of grey-green olive trees, mixed with carob trees which produce the locust bean that is the staple diet of most of the farm animals too, and neatly tilled land on which are still used the old-fashioned wooden ploughs and the wooden spades and forks that can also be seen rather less surprisingly in the folk museums of Kyrenia and Nicosia.

A man on a donkey, leading his flock of goats and sheep as multi-coloured as Jacob's homeward, held them up on a breathtaking corner of the road. The liquid sound of the animals' bells became more agitated as the beasts rushed hither and thither in their anxiety to stay with him. And then as suddenly as they had come, they had gone, and only their heavy smell was left behind as witness to their passing.

On the other side of a neglected village, where the goats seemed to be as numerous as the inhabitants in the streets, the road went on upwards into the afforested hills that were dominated by the five rocky fingers of the Pentadactylos, so named because it is linked in memory with the legendary Cypriot hero who defended the island from the invading Saracens in the eighth and ninth centuries. Of Greek father and Oriental mother, Dighenis is the symbol of the history of Cyprus, and it was here, as he vaulted over the mountains in pursuit of his enemies, that he left the huge imprint of his hand to be looked up to for ever more.

Caroline caught sight of a bird scratching amongst the fir-cones and pointed it out to Philip. It had a black chest, bright chestnut collar, and a spotted back.

'What is it?' she asked.

'A francolin—a black partridge. That's the male with the fine feathers!' he added with a grin. 'There weren't many of them around when you were last here because they make very good eating, but it's protected nowadays.'

'Do you remember the eagle we saw by the side of the road once?' she reminded him. 'You made me crawl up a cliff on my stomach to get closer to it—and then it flew away!'

'I'm not surprised, with you complaining every inch of the way!'

Caroline's eye kindled. 'I did not! You always blamed me when anything went wrong with one of your hare-brained schemes! Besides, I wouldn't have made a murmur if you hadn't told me to hang on to that bush. I might have been killed because it came straight out of the ground, just as I'd known it would, and if you hadn't been behind me, there would have been *nothing* to stop my rolling right down to the bottom!'

'There were other bushes!' he retorted.

'I was bruised from head to foot!'

'Served you right! You had a kick like a mule even in those days.' He laughed suddenly. 'You were a menace to my peace right from the word go, falling from one scrape into another, and never being in the least grateful when I rescued you from the results of your folly! How I missed you when you went back to England!'

'Did you?' The eagerness in her voice humiliated her. 'I was grateful—sometimes,' she added. 'I was very grateful last night!'

'Philip was silent for a long time and she jumped visibly when he suddenly exclaimed, 'Damn Ileana!'

169

He lapsed into silence again and then went on equally forcefully: 'Damn the lot of them!'

The road became worse and the views got more spectacular. They passed a signpost to Halevka, a small hill retreat, and another pointing down an impossible track to the Armenian monastery of Sourp Magar.

'Are we going to Antiphonitis?' Caroline asked, remembering at last where this road led to. 'But why there?'

'Ileana frequently goes there when she's unhappy. I'm hoping that's where she's gone now.'

'I thought nobody ever went there,' Caroline said in a small voice.

'That, my dear, is its attraction.'

Caroline swallowed hard. 'But how does she get there? She couldn't walk all this way.'

'She gets a bus to Ayios Ambrosios and walks up from there. It comes of giving women too much freedom to go off by themselves! Her parents should have kept a stricter watch on her.'

'*You* can say that!' Caroline gasped, stung.

'Why not? I shan't allow you to go wandering off on your own, not even when you have a couple of children to keep you busy!'

She raised her chin indignantly. 'I shall do as I like!'

He touched her cheek with one finger, giving her a look of such warm affection she thought she must have imagined it. 'No, my dear,' he said, 'you'll do as *I* like!'

The setting sun cast an orange glow over his features, making him unbearably handsome to her. 'You'd better keep your eye on the road,' she bade him. 'I shouldn't like to go over the edge round here!'

She heard his laughter, but she bent her head so that she could not see anything but her own nervous fingers pressing into the corduroy of her trousers. Had he really said 'Damn Ileana'? Could it possibly be because he wanted to be alone with his wife as much as she wanted to be alone with him?

It was almost dark when they reached the turning for Antiphonitis. The road curved steeply downwards, revealing the octagonal dome of the old monastery church that lay hidden in a fold in the mountains. There were no monks there now to share in the surrounding silence and only the mellow sandstone walls remained of the monastery where they had once lived and contemplated the majesty of God. Marigolds reflected the dying colours of the sun as they massed about the walls of the courtyard, sharing the last of the warm rays with the fig-trees that were just bursting into leaf. A small spring ran below them, disappearing into the conifer trees that covered the slopes back to join the road that fell away to end eventually in the village of Ayios Ambrosios that huddled by the sea in a different world of tobacco hanging from sun-bleached eaves, old men in black sashes and wide Turkish trousers sitting on well-shaded doorsteps, and old women, their grey hair completely covered in uniform black head-scarves, tending to the needs of their husbands and sons, stopping occasionally to throw a word of their own into the general pool of ceaseless masculine conversation.

'She isn't here,' Caroline said.

'She has to be!' Philip retorted. He got out of the car and went into the courtyard, ringing the green copper bell that was slung from the bough of a tree close to the church. 'That ought to raise her!'

The second car came creeping down the slope and stopped beside theirs. Aristotle Aghreus looked about him, breathing deeply with the relief of having arrived somewhere. He, too, got out of his car and went into the courtyard. His stocky figure moved awkwardly over the loose pebbles before he was lost to Caroline's sight, somewhere beyond the church.

It was peaceful in the car and she was close to sleep when they came back to her. 'Have you found her?'

she called out to them.

Philip shook his head. 'But she'll be here. It'll take her longer, coming by bus, and it's a good climb up from Ayios Ambrosios. We shall have to wait until she comes.'

Aristotle Aghreus kicked at a pebble at his feet. 'You have met Ileana here before?' he accused Philip.

'I have seen her here.'

'What's the difference?'

Philip shrugged. 'Ileana has never made an assignation to meet me here. There was someone once, someone her family were never to know about, and I saw him here with her. Afterwards many people thought that she came here to see me and I never denied it. I thought the truth would do far more damage.'

'The truth?' Caroline burst out, unable to contain herself a moment longer.

'Ileana used to walk in the hills behind Bellapais, sometimes even as far as the fort of St. Hilarion, despite it being in the hands of the Turkish community. She met one of their soldiers and they fell very much in love. They used to meet here——'

'What happened to him?' Caroline could hardly hear the words herself, so stiff and constricted was her throat as a new hope burgeoned within her.

'There was an incident and he was killed. It happens very seldom. A lot of people died a few years ago and the two communities are still apart. It can happen. . . . Someone fired a gun and two men died one Greek, one Turk. He was the Turk.'

'Oh, poor Ileana!' Caroline whispered.

Aristotle Aghreus looked thoughtfully down at the ground. 'She could never have married him,' he said abruptly. 'She will be happier when she is away from here and with me in Greece. I will arrange matters as quickly as possible. Once she is married to me, she will not look back.' He was as superbly confident of himself as any Greek is when he speaks of his wife. 'It is better that her family never know of this,' he added. 'It is enough for them that she is marrying well.' He smiled, not quite looking at them. 'Her dowry is considerable —enough to make me overlook much! When she comes, I shall talk to her about it this once, then we shall never talk about it again. She will make a good wife, and that is all that matters.'

Poor Ileana, Caroline thought again, and then changed her mind as quickly. She wouldn't expect anything more from marriage. Perhaps she was lucky in a way. It might be a better fate than wanting anything as romantic as to be the light of a man's life and the keeper of his heart!

It was very dark when the sun had slid down below the sea. Caroline found it increasingly difficult to stay awake. There was something soporific about the two men talking in lowered voices. There were long bits of their conversation that she couldn't understand because her Greek, good as it was, was not as idiomatic as theirs, and anyway, she couldn't bring herself to concentrate properly.

'Why don't you lie down in the back seat?' Philip suggested, seeing her head nod uncomfortably against the back of her seat.

'The mattress is there.'

'All the better,' he smiled. 'It will make it more comfortable for you. I'll wake you when she comes, *ylikia*!'

'*If* she comes!' she muttered, yawning.

'She'll come,' he said with such certainty that she found herself smiling back at him. 'Come on, love,' he urged her. 'I'll spread the mattress for you and you can have my coat to cover you.'

His hands were unexpectedly gentle as they helped her into the rear of the car. Caroline lay down, her heart thumping at his nearness, and he put his coat over as much of her as it would cover, flicking her nose with his fingers. 'Sleep now, while you can!' he whispered, and left her, disappearing into the black darkness, to where Aristotle was standing, waiting for him.

For a long time she could hear their voices just out-side the car and she thought that that was how it would often be in the future: Philip outside, talking with his friends, and her inside, waiting for him to come in to her. She allowed her thoughts to stray cautiously to what he had said about Ileana. Was it possible that he had never been in love with the Cyp-riot girl? It was a thought to go to one's head and leave one shaking. But she had seen him kiss her! She had seen that with her own eyes. Could it be that he had done no more than try to comfort the other girl? Could *that* be why he had married her? But she wouldn't let herself probe further in case she was wrong. If she didn't think of it, there could be no heartbreak when he admitted he could not love her as she wanted to be loved—as she loved him!

The mattress was more comfortable than she had expected. It smelt nice too, a strange mixture of raw wool and aromatic herbs. It was a smell she would re-member all her life. She burrowed her face further into its softness and she slept.

She knew it was Philip who had touched her im-mediately. She rolled over sleepily and blinked into the darkness, searching for his shape beside her.

'*Kyrie?*' she murmured uncertainly.

His hand tightened on the nape of her neck and she could feel his breath on her face. 'I've told you before,' he said, 'that Philip will do!' And he kissed her, hard, before she could answer him.

174

CHAPTER TWELVE

'Is she here?'

'She is, my dear delight——'

Caroline wriggled away from him, trying to see his face in the darkness. The moon had risen while she had slept, but even so she could not see more than his outline against the open door. '*What* did you call me?' she whispered.

'I shall call you what I please!'

'Oh *yes*! Yes, of course. Only you startled me, calling me *that*. You never have before——'

'Must we argue about it now?' His voice was full of laughter. 'I'd much rather get rid of Ileana and her swain, but if you insist I don't mind telling you some of the other things I intend calling you. Though perhaps not, if you persist in addressing me as *lord*!'

She blinked, finding it quite delightful to spar with him in this way. 'I thought you meant to be my lord, my husband——' She broke off, suddenly unable to say what she had intended after all.

'And?' he prompted her, a new note in his voice.

'Just that,' she said. 'What more would you want to be?'

'Your lover?' he suggested.

Her breath deserted her as if she had been winded and she scurried round in her mind for some way of changing the subject before she humiliated herself further by telling him that that was all she wanted him to be—all she had ever wanted.

'Was—was Ileana surprised to find us here?' she asked him.

'You'd better come out and see for yourself. She'll feel better when she sees you have come with us to chaperone her while she has things out with her Aristotle!' He gave her rather a hard pat on the cheek and, taking her hand in his, yanked her out of the car after him. Caroline thought to brush the creases out of her trousers, but he retained her hand with a firmness that surprised her, linking his fingers with hers as if it were the most natural thing in the world.

Ileana was indeed glad to see her. She took one look at Caroline and burst into overwrought tears. 'I thought he wasn't coming!' she gasped out. 'I thought he would *never* come!'

'And how was running away going to help?' Caroline demanded.

'I was miserable!'

Caroline cast her an exasperated glance, thinking that if Aristotle still wanted her, seeing her now, Ileana could be more complimented than she knew. 'Well, he's here now, so wipe your eyes and do something about your hair. You look a sight!'

Apparently this was the treatment that Ileana needed, because she achieved a rather wretched smile and tried to tie her hair back from her face more tidily, peeping at the stocky young Greek out of the corners of her eyes, her curiosity about him overcoming her sense of devastation.

'Does he know about Mustafa?' she enquired, re-arranging her skirts with a nervous hand.

'I have heard about him,' Aristotle answered her. 'But you will tell me all about him—everything, you understand! Then I shall consider the question of our marriage and what is best to be done. Is that what you want too?'

Ileana nodded obediently. 'You will still marry me?'

'I will tell you that when I have heard all about you,' Aristotle told her grandly. 'Your parents are offering a very generous *prika* with you and I shan't lightly throw that away. My wife will have a respected position in Greece, though. Are you worthy of that respect?'

Ileana seemed to shrink into herself. 'No,' she whispered. 'But if you marry me, I will try to be. You can't understand how it was for me. There was no one in our village for me. I used to pretend to myself that Philip might ask for me, but he was always determined to marry Caroline as soon as she came back to him. He would have no other. Caroline was his wife as surely as if she had already been married to him! I was lonely. Then I met Mustafa. He was lonely too. He didn't like being a soldier up at St. Hilarion's Fort. Often and often, he could see the coast of Turkey from up there, but he had never been there and all he could do was wonder what it was like. He was the most beautiful of men, yet when he saw me, he wanted only me! One day, he said, we would be married and go away from Cyprus. He would take me to England and we would have a shop there—he had a lot of friends there already—and we would have been happy together.' She seemed to be in danger of breaking into tears again, but Aristotle appeared quite unmoved by her distress.

'And you met this Turk here?' he demanded.

'We came here sometimes—when he could get away from the Fort. No one ever comes here, especially not in winter. I didn't think anyone would ever know about him—until Philip saw us here together.'

'You knew it was wrong to meet like this! Is this why you wanted to keep your assignations secret?' Aristotle flared up.

'In a way,' Ileana admitted. 'I knew my parents wouldn't like it.'

'I should think not! A man they knew nothing about, a Turk, a man of a different religion and with different customs. What happiness could you expect from that?'

'He was—Mustafa. And I loved him.'

'He kissed you?'

Ileana nodded. 'But he only kissed me. He wanted to marry me. It wasn't at all what you're thinking!'

'It is bad enough!' Aristotle told her sternly. 'Enough to start people talking about you!'

'But they think——' Ileana began, and then stop-

177

ped, looking at Caroline with wide, appalled eyes. 'I am sorry now,' she added, 'but I didn't think it would hurt anyone.'

'You behaved very badly,' Aristotle bore down on her. 'You were silly and thought about nothing but yourself, risking your reputation for a few kisses, when you should have been better occupied preparing yourself for marriage. Isn't that so?'

Ileana bent her head. 'Yes, Aristotle,' she agreed meekly.

'I blame your parents,' he went on more kindly, though he still sounded remarkably angry. 'They must have been blind not to have noticed that you were more often out of the house than in it——'

'They thought I was with the Kyria Hilda,' Ileana muttered.

'You told them lies as well?'

'No, but I didn't contradict them when they said that was where I had been,' Ileana excused herself. 'Please, Aristotle, don't say any more!'

'Do you intend to tell lies to me too?'

For an instant Ileana could scarcely believe her ears. 'Then you do mean to marry me? Oh, Aristotle, you are much too good to me! I swear I will do everything you tell me and be a good wife to you. Mustafa——'

Aristotle patted her kindly on the shoulder. 'You will forget all about Mustafa once you are married to me. Young girls have these fancies, but all they need is a husband to love and they never think of them again. Once you have been loved by me, you will have something else to think about!'

Ileana would have cast herself into his arms there and then, but he held her off with a gesture, pointing towards his car. 'I'll take you home to your parents and there you will stay until I take you back to Greece with me.' He stood back, watching to see that she obeyed him. Then he turned to the others with a flashing smile that showed up clearly in the moonlight. 'She is not to know that I would have taken her anyway, however far it had gone between this Turk and herself! It is nice to have a woman who is pretty enough to attract the eyes of other men, but it is better that she doesn't know how beautiful she is, at least until I have her safe in Greece!'

'Well, really!' Caroline exclaimed, and in English the better to give vent to her feelings. 'You Greeks certainly think well of yourselves!'

'What did she say?' Aristotle asked, and laughed when Philip translated. 'No men make such good lovers as the Greeks,' he told Caroline. 'We know how to hate and we know how to love—more than any other people in the world! Why should we deny it?'

'Why indeed!' Caroline said dryly.

Aristotle shrugged his shoulders, holding out his hands in dismay. 'She does not believe me! But I am thinking that by morning she will have changed her mind.' He laughed again, turning his back on Caroline as more important matters came to mind. He held out his hand to Philip, putting his other arm around his shoulders. 'You are owed an apology by Ileana. I hope you will accept it from me? I will take her home now and put her parents' mind at rest. We both thank you for all you have done.'

'It was nothing,' Philip returned. 'I was pleased to help.'

Aristotle nodded and strode away to the car with as much dignity as his pudgy figure would allow him. He settled himself in front of the driving wheel with another wave of his hand, and then the car started into life, misfiring as it slipped and slithered on the loose pebbles on the steep slope that led back to the road.

'What about me?' Caroline said, watching the departing red lights of the car.

'What about you?' Philip's fingers tightened on hers.

'He could have thanked me too!' she complained.

'He probably didn't like to, with me standing here, watching him.'

'But it was *I* who asked Ileana to be my bridesmaid,

and it was *my* wedding that we had to leave to come and find her for him——'

'So it was!' Philip murmured.

'Well then,' said Caroline, 'he could have said *something*!'

'He did—to me. He knew that I'd say all that was necessary to you after he'd gone. Quite right too! And now that I have you to myself, I mean to make the most of it!'

'But we can't stay here!' she protested. 'Philip, where are we going?' She pulled at her hand, but found it more tightly held than ever. 'I'm hungry!'

'Are you? You should have eaten more at lunchtime. Traditionally we should have had the roasted doves in the evening, but Aunt Hilda had enough to do without giving us dinner as well. Can you last out another hour or so?'

'I suppose so.' She longed to ask him about something else, something that Ileana had said, but she couldn't raise her courage high enough to do so. Instead she pulled at her hand again, this time breaking free, and then wished she hadn't because she didn't know what to do with her freedom. 'Are we going to stay here?'

'We can come back in the morning,' he answered her. 'One has to fetch the key from Ayios Ambrosios if one wants to go inside. You may like to see the frescoes. They're rather fine ones, mostly from the fifteenth century, I think.'

'Oh?' Caroline tried to sound interested, but failed dismally. She took a step closer to Philip, wishing that it wasn't so dark and that she could see what he was thinking. 'If we're not going to stay here, where are we going?'

His laughter made her heart somersault within her. 'I have a small summer house back there, in the forest. It's fairly primitive, but I thought you'd prefer it to going back to Bellapais?'

'Do you own it?' She wasn't prepared to give voice

to her preferences at that moment, but it sounded like heaven to her.

'Yes. I bought it a few years back.'

'Then it isn't part of the Klearchos inheritance?'

'No, my sweet love, it is not! Not even in the way that you mean it. But that's another thing we'll talk about when we get there. For the moment you'll have to make do with this, and this!' He kissed her twice, once on the cheek and once full on the lips, almost before she was aware, and she wished she felt less shy of him and had the courage to kiss him back as she longed to do.

Instead, she made a little rush towards the car and pulled open her door before he could do it for her, falling into the seat as fast as she could, her knees feeling as though they would no longer support her. She pretended not to notice when he got in beside her, though the light came on when he opened his door and she was very conscious of his thick, black, curly hair and the smoothness of his olive skin. It was a relief that it was still the same Philip. The same, and yet not the same, she reminded herself. The Philip of the past had never called her his dear delight, nor his sweet love, and his touch hadn't raised a storm of pleasure when they had gone creeping through the undergrowth to get a better view of the eagle. It did now. It had first happened to her when she had been sixteen and he had kissed her, but even that had been no more than a pale shadow of how she felt about him now.

'Darling,' she said, when he slammed the door and the light went out again, engulfing her in the former darkness, 'were you ever in love with Ileana?'

He chuckled. 'Still jealous?'

'No!' She was silent for a long moment. 'I think you might have told me that it was all a mistake. I had a right to know!'

'You had no rights in the matter!'

She sighed. 'Crushed again!' she said. 'What if I was

jealous? I saw you kiss her with my own eyes, and you can't deny it, because you did!'

'Ah,' he said, 'so you do admit to being jealous?'

'Yes,' she said into the darkness. 'I hated you both!'

'Ah, that sounds much more like you! It was rather a petty revenge,' he added, 'but you had Jeffrey and were busy stuffing him down my throat——'

'It was despicable!' she exclaimed, very cross indeed.

'It had the desired effect!' he retorted dryly. 'Don't you agree?'

She cast him a speaking look which was unfortunately lost in the darkness. 'I hated you then and I hate you now!' she informed him in a voice that shook. 'And I don't believe you already have the Klearchos inheritance, or you wouldn't have married me! Though I would have given it to you anyway.' She bit her lip. 'Is it—is it a great deal of land?'

'No land at all,' he told her cheerfully.

'But there must be! There always has been! Where is it now?'

'I sold most of it on my father's death. I'm no farmer, Caroline, and I didn't think you would be either——'

'Then—then what is the Klearchos inheritance?' she stammered.

His laughter rang round her ears. 'A young woman called Caroline Fielding. You were always intended to belong to the Klearchos family—we all agreed about that. My parents, my Uncle Michael, and your Aunt Hilda!'

'But the dowry? I must have brought you something! Aunt Hilda was so pleased with herself!' Her voice caught in the back of her throat. 'I wanted you to have everything.'

The car lurched and he uttered an exclamation as Philip pulled it back on to the road. 'You gave me all you had,' he reminded her.

'I don't care! If I had been a Greek girl you wouldn't have taken me with so little. You must see——'

The car came to a stop outside a pavilion-like building that nestled amongst pine-smelling conifers on the brow of a hill. Philip leaned over and grasped her hand, pressing painfully on the ring he had put on her finger.

'Why, Caroline? Why did you marry me?'

And she heard her own voice saying, 'Because I love you, and love you, and love you! Is that reason enough for you?'

Philip threw open all the windows, but the musty smell that closed houses are apt to gather still lingered in the two small rooms that made up the interior.

'There's a verandah out front,' he told her. 'We may be reduced to sitting out there—sleeping too!'

'It'll make a lovely place to eat!' she enthused, ignoring the second part of his remark. 'Are there any lights?'

'There are some storm-lamps somewhere. I'll take the torch and go and find them.' He put his hand on her shoulder, making her heart jump within her. 'I'm sorry, Caroline, that it isn't all ready for us. I thought we'd be here in daylight and that it would be fun to get everything ready between us. You're not afraid of the dark, are you?'

'I'm not afraid of anything as long as I know you're here too,' she answered. 'But don't be long getting the lamps, will you?'

She could see his black eyes looking at her over the light of the torch and turned her own face away so that he wouldn't see that she was indeed scared of the long shadows that the frail beam cast round the room. 'Shall I wait here?' she asked him.

He smiled at her. 'I shan't be long,' he promised.

Caroline found herself standing by a white-painted wicker-chair and sat down in it, listening to him as he flung open the cupboards, pulling everything out on to the floor as he looked for the lamps. She heard his grunt of approval as he found them and then the scraping noise of a match as he lit the first lamp and brought it back to her.

'Still hungry?' he grinned at her, putting the lamp down on the table with an air of triumph.

'Ravenous!'

'There's a hamper of food in the car. Your mother and Aunt Hilda put it up between them, so it ought to include all our old favourites. I'll bring it in and you can find us something to eat while I get the mattress and try to get that stale smell out of the bedroom.'

Caroline went with him to the car, astonished by the size of the hamper of food that had been put in the boot. It was as big as a laundry-basket; she had no hope of carrying it by herself and had to ask Philip to help her. Once she had it inside, however, she set to with a will, unpacking the contents and finding some cold cuts of meat, pickles, freshly baked bread and some of the soft sheep's-milk cheese that is made in Cyprus during the spring months. To finish the meal, she found some *halva*, a sweet, sticky concoction, made of ground sesame seeds, and which is only obtainable during the fifty days before the Greek Easter, the forty days before Christmas, and, for some reason, during the first fortnight of August.

When it came to it, however, Caroline's appetite deserted her. She picked at some ham and a piece of cold lamb, envying Philip's robust approach to the meal before him. He poured her out some wine, a gleam of humour sparkling in his eyes. 'I never thought to see you without zest for the battle!' he teased her.

'What battle?' she said defensively.

'You didn't suppose I was going to leave it there, did you? Oh no, my darling, I want to know all about this love of yours—and so I shall, before you sleep to-night!'

'I don't want to talk about it!'

'Of course not!' he mocked her. 'But you will all the

same.'

'There's nothing to tell. I told you that I didn't want to go back to my life in England—that I'd rather stay in Cyprus and—and that I couldn't do without you!'

'You did without me very successfully for six years!'

That made her look up with a start. 'Not very successfully,' she said.

'No?'

'It was a bit like today when I put on my wedding-dress. It was me, and yet it wasn't me. I did all the right things in London, went to all the right places, and knew all the right people, but I couldn't be my-self.'

'You could have come back before,' he murmured.

'I was afraid——'

'Afraid of what?'

She licked her lips, blinking into the flame of the lamp. 'I can't tell you that!' she whispered.

'Why not?'

She thought he looked very stern and unyielding and she shivered. 'You wouldn't understand,' she managed. 'I *can't* explain!'

He gave her a little more wine and she saw that he was smiling. Perhaps, she thought, she could tell him if only he wasn't angry, but he wasn't much given to tenderness and her feelings bruised easily—they always had!

'I'd thought of you as a friend,' she began. 'You don't know how *young* I was! I thought I could say anything to you, whatever came into my head, and it wouldn't matter. I thought it was like that for you. I didn't have to be braver, or cleverer than I am, because you knew exactly what I was. I didn't mind when you teased me and made me do things I thought I couldn't. It was like having a *brother*, and wonderful to me, because I barely knew my parents. You were my family—and Aunt Hilda, of course.' She stopped, not knowing how to go on. She looked helplessly across the table at Philip, but could read no sympathy in his expression and she felt worse than ever. 'I was only *sixteen*!' she reminded him.

'Hardly a child,' he retorted. 'Many girls are married then, or betrothed at least.'

'But not *English* girls! Not girls like me!'

'Why not you? You knew I wasn't your brother, and that my interest in you was far from brotherly——'

'But I didn't!' she declared.

'Then why did you suppose that I allowed you to tag along with me wherever I went, losing your temper whenever I tried to teach you anything, and always talking at the wrong moment, just when the fish was about to bite, or the bird settle on her nest, or when I wanted to be silent for a few minutes?'

'I thought you liked me,' she advanced timidly.

'My dear girl, of course I liked you!'

'That's what I thought,' she said, 'but it wasn't what I meant by liking. I didn't know that you saw me as a girl at all——'

He grinned, making her blush. 'Not even when I pulled your hair?'

She shook her head. 'Not until you kissed me.'

'And that made you afraid? But, Caroline, it was hardly a kiss at all! I was only staking my claim——'

'I didn't know what you were about,' she cut him off. 'I only knew how I *felt*! You might as well have turned into a—a frog, or something! I didn't think I'd ever be able to face you again. It isn't funny to discover that you've been carrying around a bomb inside you and that whether it goes off or not doesn't depend on you at all, but on someone else, someone who has always seemed perfectly ordinary and not at all dangerous. I felt as though I'd been blown up sky-high and that I'd never feel the ground under my feet again. I was scared stiff!'

'So you took to your heels and ran?'

'I ran as hard and as far as I could! I didn't want such a thing to happen to me again. Not ever! I wanted to be in control of my own feelings, not have them at the mercy of someone else!'

Philip raised his eyebrows. 'Very understandable,' he drawled, 'especially when one is sixteen!'

'Yes, well, I stayed sixteen for rather a long time!' she snapped, her temper getting the better of her. 'No one else ever had that effect on me. No one ever has. It seemed quite a reasonable attitude to take, to want a calm, adult relationship with someone who would respect my point of view about things, as I would respect his. It would be much more civilised than—than an elemental clash of wills——'

'That you would be destined to lose?'

'In a way,' she said with dignity. 'In a way there isn't any winning or losing, is there? But I didn't know that—not until today, as a matter of fact.'

Philip looked at her in quick interest. 'And before today?'

She swallowed. 'I was content to lose—to you,' she said simply.

'Very generous of you!' he exclaimed without a trace of sarcasm. 'I'm ashamed to say that I would have been very much less than content to lose to you!'

'Yes, I know,' she said in a low voice.

'I swore you wouldn't find any softness in me! I knew you had to go back to England, but I thought the most I'd have to wait was a couple of years and that then you'd be back, ready to marry me and live here with me. Two years was long enough, but *six years* was a humiliation I intended you would pay for day by day. When I saw you sitting in the café of the Tree of Idleness, I didn't know how you could look so much the same and yet not admit that you were mine!'

'I would have come to your parents' funeral if I had known,' she blurted out. 'Oh, Philip, I longed to come so often! You could have come and got me! I thought you would if you really wanted me. It would have been quite in character for you to have ridden roughshod over any ideas I might have had and ordered me into marriage with you. But you didn't!' She tossed her head, pushing her hair back from her face. 'I thought it was just a casual kiss and that I had over-reacted and made far too much of it!'

'Just like the kiss I gave you at the Tree of Idleness?'

She tried to laugh it off. 'If you like,' she agreed.

'I don't. I think you made enough of it to send for Jeffrey, though what good you thought *he* was going to do you——'

'My father likes him.'

'A likely recommendation!' he said dryly.

'I did consider marrying him. Only I knew I couldn't the moment I saw you again. But I thought you were in love with Ileana and I couldn't bear it——'

'So you asked me to marry you?'

Caroline nodded. 'I would have done anything——' She made a tentative search for a handkerchief, found too late that she hadn't got one anywhere on her, and sniffed instead. 'I love you so much! I can't explain any better! It's like finding the source of my being in you—I'd be condemned to a living death without you. I *told* you!'

'You didn't tell me you loved me. You had only to say that——'

'It wouldn't have changed anything. You were so angry—and not at all kind! And you said I had to be a Cypriot wife and obey you in everything. And I *wanted* to! I still do! I want to be with you, and have your children, and be your wife. I don't ask more than that.'

Philip pushed back his chair and stood up, pulling her up into the circle of his arms. 'I'm sorry I wasn't kind, darling, and I'm sorry I was angry, but I think you want a great deal more than that. I meant to punish you for turning your back on me, but I thought you knew I was the same underneath. I hadn't realised that I'd turned into a frog!' He laughed shortly. 'A *frog*! You could have chosen a kinder metaphor yourself——'

'But it was the frog who turned into the prince!' she explained eagerly, afraid that she had hurt his feelings.

He put a hand behind her head, rubbing his thumb along her jaw. 'Only when he's kissed! Is that why you were so willing to kiss me?'

'That—and other things.' She tried to turn her face away from his searching look. 'I thought you were marrying me because you wanted the land, and then because you wouldn't marry Ileana because'—the colour rose in her cheeks—'because you didn't have to, and you had to marry *someone*. But it wasn't any of those things, was it? Darling, tell me why.'

His kiss was very gentle. 'Gladly, my dear delight. I love you, it was never more than that. I loved you to distraction then, and I love you even more now.' He pulled her closer, his lips closing over hers with a fierceness that made her gasp. 'I intend to blow up at least half a dozen bombs tonight, so I'm sorry if you don't like it——'

Caroline laughed against his lips. 'I think I'm going to like it very much—when I've got used to it!'

He joined in her laughter. 'And you won't be afraid any more?' he teased her.

She peeped up at him through her eyelashes, consciously flirting with him and a little bemused by her own daring. 'Not as long as you're there to hold my hand,' she said.

Mills & Boon
Best Seller Romances

The very best of Mills & Boon
brought back for those of you
who missed reading them when they
were first published.
There are three other Best Seller Romances
for you to collect this month.

THAT SUMMER OF SURRENDER
by Rebecca Caine

After her father's death Perdita's happy relationship with Olivia,
her stepmother, had brought no problems. But when Olivia had the
chance of making a new life for herself Perdita found herself dealing
with considerable problems – not the least of which was the arrival
on the scene of the insufferable Blake Hadwyn!

THE HOMEPLACE
by Janet Dailey

Her grandparents' farm in Iowa had always meant so much to Cathie,
and she couldn't help resenting the stranger, Rob Douglas, who
had come along and bought it. But resent him or not, she certainly
couldn't ignore him – and soon she found she wasn't resenting him
any more. What was going to become of her engagement to Clay?

THE JAPANESE SCREEN
by Anne Mather

Susannah met and fell in love with Fernando Cuevas in London.
She little thought when she travelled out to Spain to work for a
wealthy family that the child she had come to teach was Fernando's
child and that she would be meeting Fernando himself far sooner
than she had expected . . .

If you have difficulty in obtaining any of these books through
your local paperback retailer, write to:

Mills & Boon Reader Service
P.O. Box 236, Thornton Road, Croydon, Surrey, CR9 3RU

Mills & Boon
Best Seller Romances

The very best of Mills & Boon Romances
brought back for those of you who missed
them when they were first published.
In March
we bring back the following four
great romantic titles.

DARK HILLS RISING
by Anne Hampson

When Andrew MacNeill married Gail he made it clear that he did
not want a wife but a mother for his children; Gail, having thought
marriage was not for her since she had been badly scarred and
injured in an accident, told herself that all she wanted was to have
some children – any children – to mother. But was either of them
being completely honest?

LOVE IN DISGUISE
by Rachel Lindsay

Because Mark Allen, a high-powered tycoon, preferred his
housekeeper to be an elderly woman Anthea assumed a disguise
to get the job. But no disguise could hide her awareness of her
acid-tongued employer or help to conceal her dislike of the lovely
Claudine, who seemed determined to marry Mark. Yet . . .

HEART IN THE SUNLIGHT
by Lilian Peake

Norway, Noelle found when she went to work there, was a land of
sunlight, glorious scenery and charming people – with the exception,
unfortunately, of her boss, the infuriating Per Arneson!

DEAREST DEMON
by Violet Winspear

Destine felt that her life had ended when her young husband was
killed only hours after their wedding. In an effort to forget she took
a job in southern Spain – and met the man who, in all the world,
was the most likely to remind her of that tragedy she only wanted
to forget . . .

If you have difficulty in obtaining any of these books through
your local paperback retailer, write to:

Mills & Boon Reader Service
P.O. Box 236, Thornton Road, Croydon, Surrey, CR9 3RU

GW00359863

Older

and a whole Lot

Wiser

ALLSORTED.

Published in 2017 by Allsorted.
Watford, Hertfordshire,
WD19 4BG
U.K.

© Susanna Geoghegan Gift Publishing 2017
Compiled by Michael Powell
Concept by Milestone Design
Designed by Bag of Badgers

Illustrations by Dave Williams

ISBN: 978-1-910562-95-6

Printed in China

Older and a whole Lot Wiser

We used to think of brain cells as a finite resource, beans in a jar that are taken out and lost forever, so that we are left with diminishing mental powers as we get older. Fortunately that old-fashioned cognitive model has been thrown out of the window.

In fact, our brains are constantly rewiring, learning new things, solving problems and being super-flexible. This amazing neuroplasticity allows the brain to reorganise itself throughout life, no matter how old we are.

The more you challenge your brain to form new neural connections, the sharper and better it will become. Research has shown that doing puzzles increases the flow of blood to the brain, boosting its oxygen uptake and fighting the effects of ageing.

It loves a good challenge and hates inactivity, so this book is designed to put your brain through its paces. It contains dozens of puzzles, conundrums, lateral thinking and trick questions to tickle your synapses and to blow away the cerebral cobwebs. They may even help to improve your mood and memory, decrease stress and keep those neural pathways firing on all cylinders.

Cruise Ship Ladder Puzzle

The metal ladder of a cruise ship has fifty rungs, spaced 30cm (12in) apart. The bottom rung is 1 metre (three feet) from the water. The tide is rising at 30cm every 15 minutes. How many rungs will be underwater in four hours' time?

Red Coat, Blue Coat

Two old friends sit next to each other on a park bench. One is wearing a red coat and the other a blue coat. 'I'm wearing a red coat,' says one. 'You're wearing a blue coat,' says the other. Only one of them is lying. What colour coat must the liar be wearing?

Clock This

The time is twenty past two. How many degrees is the acute angle formed between the two clock hands (there are 360 degrees in a circle)?

CRAZY OLD CAT LADY 1

A crazy old cat lady has nine cats. Each cat sleeps next to one or more cushions, scattered across a large tiled floor. Each cushion is numbered to indicate how many adjacent tiles contain a cat. Place a C where you deduce each cat is sleeping.

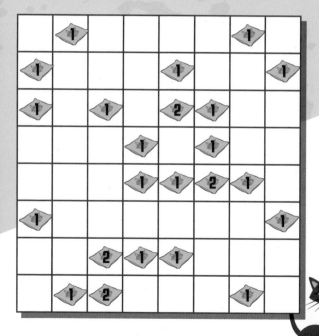

SLITHERLINK 1

Connect adjacent corners horizontally or vertically to form a single closed path, with no extra branches. The path cannot cross itself. A number tells you how many lines surround that square. There is one unique solution.

	1	2	3			1
1			2	2		0
2	2			1		
			1			
		2			2	1
1		1	0			1
2			1	1	1	

MAGIC SQUARE 1

1	13	7	16
15	8	10	4
12	2	17	6
9	14	3	11

Fill in all the blank cells to form a magic square in which each column, row and diagonal adds up to the same number.

1	12	6	
	7		
11			5
	14		

WORD LADDER 1

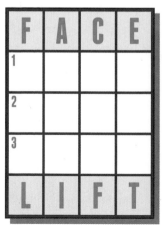

F	A	C	E
1			
2			
3			
L	I	F	T

Change the word from FACE to LIFT. Change one letter each time, so that every step forms a new word.

7

ARITHMAGON 1

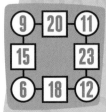

The number in each square is the sum of the numbers in the two adjacent circles. Fill in the missing numbers.

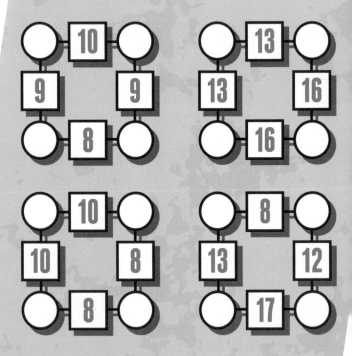

STROOP TEST

Here is one of the most commonly used tools for determining attention problems. It is also a test of Executive Function and Working Memory. Ready to test your mental vitality and flexibility? Quickly – say aloud what colour you see in every word, NOT the word you read. Go from left to right, from top to bottom. Ready. Set. Go!

Don't worry if you found it tricky. Overcoming automatic behaviour (in this case, reading) is challenging (and at least it means you're a fluent reader!). It takes your brain longer to name colours than read colour names.

Grandson or Granddaughter?

A man has two grandchildren. One of them is a girl. What is the probability that the other is a boy?

Hint: the correct answer is NOT fifty per cent.

Mint Humbugs 1

Gladys and Bernard are the fastest mint humbug eaters in the world. Together they hold the world record for eating twelve packets of mint humbugs. Bernard can eat twice as fast as Gladys. If it takes Bernard three minutes to eat four packets, how many minutes is their world record?

Say What You See

What is the next number in this sequence: 1, 11, 21, 1211?

a) 111221
b) 312211
c) 13112221

OUROBOROS 1

Fill every blank square with a letter by answering all the clues. The direction of each word is indicated by an arrow on its initial letter.

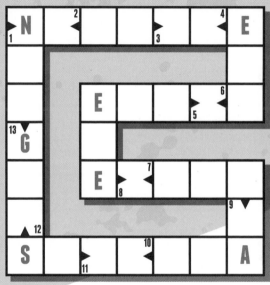

CLUES

1. Nuclear weapon
2. Archaic form of until
3. Dark granular rock used to make abrasive powder
4. Quiet and submissive
5. Combustible funereal heap
6. Greek princess, after whom the Pyrenees is named
7. Sexual indulgence
8. Wide open rural landscape in Southern Africa
9. Small pointed missile
10. Weakens
11. Latin word which means 'stars'
12. Secret language
13. Hold firmly

SUDOKU 1 - EASY

Fill in all the blank squares. Each of the nine 3 x 3 square blocks must contain all the numbers 1–9, but each number can only appear once in the same row or column.

7	4		2	1	9		8	3
		8	6		4	9		
1		6	3		5	4		2
5	1		7	6	3		4	8
	2	3				7	6	
				5				
9	6			3			1	4
	8			9			2	
4	5		1	2	8		9	6

LETTER FILL 1

Words on the same row must be completed using the same missing letter. Complete all eight rows to discover the hidden word.

_AIN	CO_E	RA_E	◯
DIR_	PAC_	_ARS	◯
_ACK	SLA_	KNO_	◯
CAR_	_ARN	BOL_	◯
_ACK	_AIN	_EAR	◯
B_KE	B_LE	CH_P	◯
BEA_	FLA_	BU_K	◯
MA_T	_ATE	_IZE	◯

13

ISLANDS IN THE STREAM 1

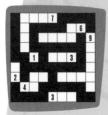

Shade some squares so that each number is inside a white island with that given number of squares. The white islands may only touch diagonally, the black 'stream' must be continuous (i.e. no shaded squares cut off on their own) and shaded areas may not form or exceed 2 x 2 squares.

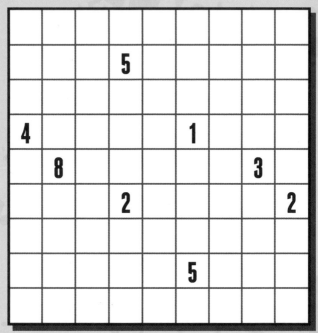

TANGRAM 1

The seven yellow pieces have been arranged, without overlapping, to form the blue shape. Draw straight lines on the blue shape to show how they fit together.

LOGPILE 1

Each number is the sum of the two directly below it. Fill in every blank circle with a positive whole number greater than 1 (no zeros).

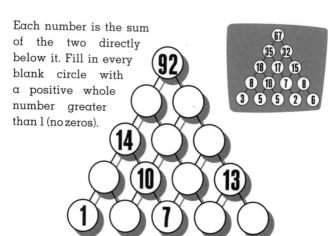

Floating or Sinking?

An inflatable air mattress is floating on the surface of the water in a swimming pool. How can you raise the level of the water the most: by placing a coin on top of the mattress or throwing it into the water?

Cheap Hotel

The Lone Ranger rode into a Texan hotel on Tuesday and asked the owner how much it would cost him to stay there. The owner replied, 'It's normally ten dollars per night, but you're the Lone Ranger, so for you it's only eight dollars per night.' The Lone Ranger checked out on Friday morning, delighted with the excellent service he had received, but he only paid eight dollars. Why?

Coloured Dice Puzzle 1

If the blue die has a value of 13 and the green die has a value of 12, what value should you assign to the red die?

SKIP TO THE LOO

Brian's prostate isn't what it used to be. Can you help him find the bathroom before he taps a kidney?

FUTOSHIKI 1

Fill every blank square so that each row and column contains the numbers 1, 2, 3, 4 and 5 with no repeats. An arrow indicates that the number in the square is greater than the adjacent number to which the arrow points.

ARITHMAGON 2

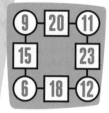

The number in each square is the sum of the numbers in the two adjacent circles. Fill in the missing numbers.

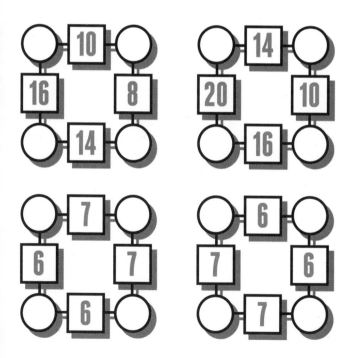

CRAZY OLD CAT LADY 2

A crazy old cat lady has nine cats. Each cat sleeps next to one or more cushions, scattered across a large tiled floor. Each cushion is numbered to indicate how many adjacent tiles contain a cat. Place a C where you deduce each cat is sleeping.

20

MAGIC SQUARE 2

1	13	7	16
15	8	10	4
12	2	17	6
9	14	3	11

14	7		2
	4		9
			16

Fill in all the blank cells to form a magic square in which each column, row and diagonal adds up to the same number.

WORD LADDER 2

C	L	E	A	N
1				
2				
3				
4				
5				
S	H	E	E	T

Change the word from CLEAN to SHEET. Change one letter each time, so that every step forms a new word.

21

Missing Ingredient

This rye bread recipe is lower in gluten than your average white loaf but what's the missing ingredient?

200g   rye flour, plus extra for dusting
200g   strong white or wholemeal flour
7g   sachet fast-action dried yeast

½ tsp   fine salt
1 tbsp   honey
1 tsp   caraway seed (optional)

Ding Dong

If a clock takes 5 seconds to strike 6 times, how long will it take to strike twelve times?

Number Series Puzzle 1

What number comes next in each sequence?
1) 3, 8, 4, 7, 15, 19, 26 . . .
2) 1, 2, 6, 42, 1806 . . .

PATH HUNTER 1

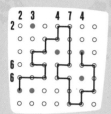

Draw a continuous line from one green dot to the other. You may move vertically or horizontally but NOT diagonally. Your line cannot pass through a red dot. The numbers tell you how many white or green dots your line passes through in that row or column.

OUROBOROS 2

Fill every blank square with a letter by answering all the clues. The direction of each word is indicated by an arrow on its initial letter.

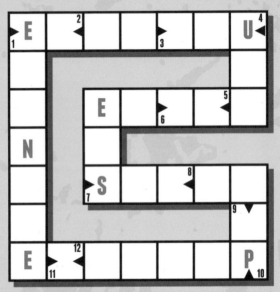

CLUES

1. Muslim military commander
2. Black garnet crystal
3. French word meaning 'study'
4. Plural of uterus
5. Articles offered for sale
6. Reverential respect and wonder
7. Member of a monotheistic religion founded by the guru Nanak
8. Osculation
9. Opposite of downtime
10. Exert force to move something away
11. Send money
12. Light-sensitive tissue at the back of an eye

DOMINOES 1

The numbers 0, 1, 2 and 3 can be arranged in 10 unique pairs. Find them here to solve the puzzle.

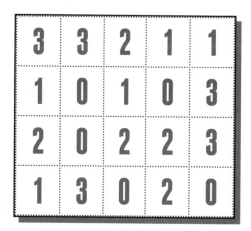

Missing Fish

Two fathers went fishing with their sons. The fathers caught two fish each and the two sons caught three fish in total. They returned home that evening with their catch of five fish. If they didn't eat them or throw them back, what happened to the other two?

LETTER FILL 2

Words on the same row must be completed using the same missing letter. Complete all eight rows to discover the hidden word.

_ACE	_ACK	CA_E	◯
_AEK	_IFE	_AFT	◯
P_KE	DR_P	SH_P	◯
_AIL	ROO_	_APS	◯
AC_D	B_ND	B_LL	◯
O_EN	_AIN	_EST	◯
SL_M	S_CK	B_TE	◯
CO_E	_ODE	HA_E	◯

CIRCUIT BOARD 1

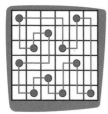

Connect adjacent squares horizontally or vertically to form a single closed path which passes through every square only once. Your path must change direction at every red dot and once between each red dot.

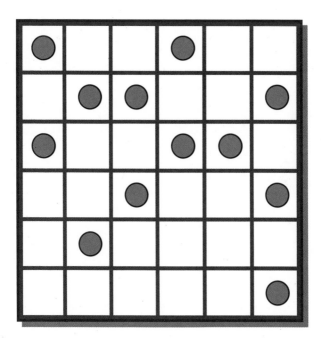

Wedding Planner

Six friends – Robert, Jeannette, Richard, Elizabeth, Sandra and Joe – share a round table at a wedding breakfast.
Joe wants to sit between Robert and Elizabeth;
Richard wants to sit between Sandra and Jeannette;
Sandra does not want to sit between Richard and Elizabeth;
Richard wants to be second to the right of Elizabeth.
Draw a seating plan that keeps everyone happy.

Number Squares 1

By looking at the existing numbers and their locations, can you work out what numbers should be in the blank squares?

3	3
5	4

2	3

5	8	

3	5	3
3	5	3

Two Ropes

You have two ropes, both of which take exactly one hour to burn. However, neither rope burns uniformly. Half of one rope could take ten minutes to burn and then 50 minutes for the rest of the rope. How can you measure 45 minutes of time using just the two ropes and a lighter?

OLD LADY HANDBAGS 1

Solve the puzzle by giving every old lady her own handbag (mark with an x) horizontally or vertically adjacent to her. Handbags must not touch, even diagonally. The numbers indicate how many handbags are in each row or column.

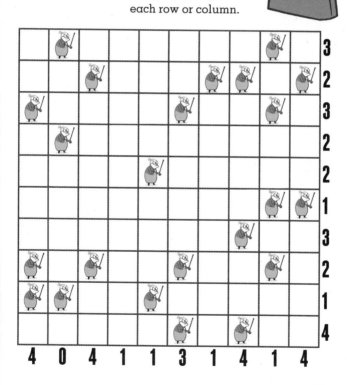

3D Odd One Out 1

Which is the odd one out?

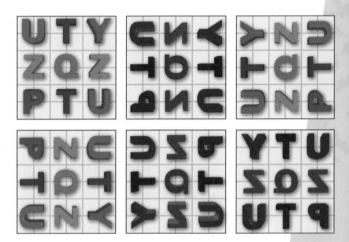

MAGIC SQUARE 3

1	13	7	16
15	8	10	4
12	2	17	6
9	14	3	11

16			
		12	17
			8
9	4		14

Fill in all the blank cells to form a magic square in which each column, row and diagonal adds up to the same number.

Old Age Wordsearch

S	C	H	S	L	G	A	U	F	R	Y	L	I	M	A	F
J	E	I	J	W	O	Z	C	I	F	P	D	E	G	A	G
B	J	N	N	C	L	Y	P	O	S	A	V	O	J	C	D
G	M	P	I	I	F	E	L	G	B	R	E	L	E	D	S
P	L	N	G	O	L	D	G	E	R	E	M	V	L	E	H
N	P	L	U	B	R	C	J	N	Q	H	I	O	S	U	T
S	I	T	I	R	H	T	R	A	O	T	T	S	Y	M	L
D	V	K	Q	W	S	I	R	C	C	I	A	G	X	V	A
C	F	H	Z	U	M	E	V	A	F	L	S	R	U	A	E
A	R	V	E	E	B	L	D	Q	G	R	T	N	F	I	H
Q	K	T	M	P	P	K	J	D	D	E	T	Q	E	Q	B
W	W	O	J	R	O	F	G	M	H	T	W	C	V	P	S
J	R	N	D	M	L	O	D	C	Z	I	C	N	K	C	Z
Y	R	Y	R	U	V	U	C	T	M	R	O	D	W	R	Q
E	F	E	T	R	A	V	E	L	R	E	T	T	H	M	A
Z	J	X	A	K	T	R	I	P	S	G	E	Q	O	F	K

Golf	Family	Arthritis
Old	Clinic	Aged
Travel	Ripe	Glasses
Senior	Nurse	Will
Retire	Pension	Time
Memory	Health	Active
Trips	Therapy	

Word Fill 1

Find a three-letter word that completes each trio of longer words:

1. MANIF _ _ _
OVERS _ _ _
EMB _ _ _ ENS

2. MILI _ _ _ Y
SEC _ _ _ IAN
S _ _ _ VING

3. L _ _ _ RATED
DEF _ _ _ S
GRIM _ _ _ S

4. CH _ _ _ ELIER
R _ _ _ OM
GR _ _ _ ST _ _ _

5. G _ _ _ BY
CHE _ _ _
SH _ _ _ LAND

6. STRI _ _ _ T
CA _ _ _ CE
CRE _ _ _ CE

SLITHERLINK 2

Connect adjacent corners horizontally or vertically to form a single closed path, with no extra branches. The path cannot cross itself. A number tells you how many lines surround that square. There is one unique solution.

			1		1	2
1	2		1	1		1
	0	2		3		1
0		2		2		1
0		2		1	2	
1		1	1		2	2
0	2		2			

The Priest and the Vicar

A priest and a vicar meet at an ecumenical conference. The priest lies on Mondays, Tuesdays and Wednesdays and tells the truth on the other days of the week. The vicar only lies on Thursdays, Fridays and Saturdays. The priest announces: 'Yesterday I was lying.' The vicar replies, 'So was I.' What day is it?

Mint Humbugs 2

Bernard has three great-grandchildren who can devour three packets of mint humbugs in three minutes. How many additional great-grandchildren would be needed to help them finish off 100 packets in 100 minutes? (Bernard doesn't eat any.)

Coloured Dice Puzzle 2

If the blue die has a value of 10 and the red die has a value of 6, what value should you assign to the green die?

TANGRAM 2

The seven yellow pieces have been arranged, without overlapping, to form the blue shape. Draw straight lines on the blue shape to show how they fit together.

MATHS SQUARE 1

Use the numbers 1 to 9 once only to fill in the blank squares to make the equations work vertically and horizontally (perform multiplication and division before addition and subtraction).

3	+		−		4
x	■	−	■	+	
	x	5	−		11
−	■	+	■	−	
	+		+	6	21
5		5		4	

DOMINOES 2

The numbers 0, 1, 2 and 3 can be arranged in 10 unique pairs. Find them here to solve the puzzle.

3	1	1	1	3
1	3	0	0	2
2	2	1	2	0
2	0	0	3	3

LOGPILE 2

Each number is the sum of the two directly below it. Fill in every blank circle with a positive whole number greater than 1 (no zeros).

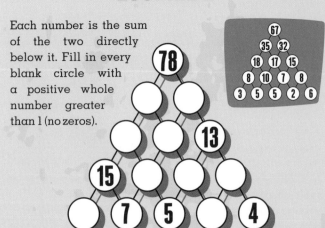

HITORI 1

Black out some of the cells in the grid so that each row and each column contains no duplicated numbers. Blacked out cells must not touch horizontally or vertically and all white cells must form one continuous area

5	6	2	4	1	1
3	5	5	1	2	6
6	1	4	2	3	5
1	3	5	2	2	1
3	4	1	5	3	2
1	3	6	2	5	4

LETTER FILL 3

Words on the same row must be completed using the same missing letter. Complete all eight rows to discover the hidden word.

D_A_FT	M_A_LT	S_A_ND	(A) E
SHI_N_	_N_EST	_N_OUN	(N) N
_D_UMB	_D_AME	_D_EAR	(D) D
M_A_TE	L_A_TE	L_A_ST	(A) U
_R_AIN	_R_ASP	_R_ASH	(R) R
L_I_MP	F_I_RE	M_I_ST	(I) I
_L_OCK	_L_OSY	_L_AME	(L) N
_C_LUE	_C_ROW	_C_ASH	(C) G

38

MEDICATION MISSION

Pat has to collect a prescription. Can you help her reach the chemists before it closes?

Padlocked Chest

Two pensioners, Brian and Derek, live in separate care homes and they don't trust the staff. They each own a padlock and its key. How can Brian send a padlocked chest of valuables securely to Derek so that only Derek can open it, but without sending his own key? (Hint: three separate deliveries are required).

Potting Challenge

Gladys is a keen gardener. She has some sunflower seeds and some plant pots. If she were to plant one seed in each pot, she would have one pot too few. If she were to plant two seeds in each pot, she would have one pot too many. How many seeds and plant pots does she have?

Number Series Puzzle 2

What number comes next in each sequence?

1) 8, 12, 18, 27, 40½ . . .
2) 3½, 5, 6, 8, 10, 13 . . .

SUDOKU 2 – EASY

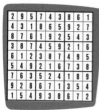

Fill in all the blank squares. Each of the nine 3 x 3 square blocks must contain all the numbers 1–9, but each number can only appear once in the same row or column.

9	1	3	5		4	6	7	
			9	3		2	5	
		5		7	6			
3	2		1					5
	5	8	2		3	7	1	9
7	6		4					3
		2		4	8			
			6	5		3	8	
6	8	7	3		9	5	4	

SHIKAKU 1

Divide the grid into a set of rectangles (including square rectangles if necessary), each containing one number and composed of that many squares.

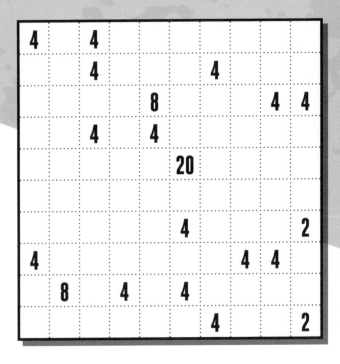

Word Fill 2

Find a three-letter word that completes each trio of longer words:

1. COEX _ _ _ SIVE

AT _ _ _ UATE

PRE _ _ _ DING

2. DISPA _ _ _ ING

ST _ _ _ GLING

ANCHO _ _ _ E

3. TIP _ _ _ D

_ _ _ HOLD

VE _ _ _ D

4. LOG _ _ _ _ S

PY _ _ _ _ AS

UN _ _ _ _ S

5. AF _ _ _ _ M

CON _ _ _ _ M

_ _ _ _ ETRAP

6. _ _ _ _ OGRAPHIC

PETRO _ _ _ IES

B _ _ _ _ GER

MAGIC SQUARE 4

1	13	7	16
15	8	10	4
12	2	17	6
9	14	3	11

13			8
	6	15	
	17	12	

Fill in all the blank cells to form a magic square in which each column, row and diagonal adds up to the same number.

WORD LADDER 3

B	R	E	A	D
1				
2				
3				
4				
5				
6				
T	O	A	S	T

Change the word from BREAD to TOAST. Change one letter each time, so that every step forms a new word.

PATH HUNTER 2

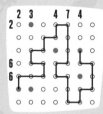

Draw a continuous line from one green dot to the other. You may move vertically or horizontally but NOT diagonally. Your line cannot pass through a red dot. The numbers tell you how many white or green dots your line passes through in that row or column.

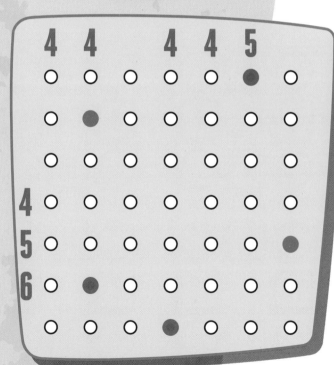

45

ARITHMAGON 3

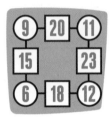

The number in each square is the sum of the numbers in the two adjacent circles. Fill in the missing numbers.

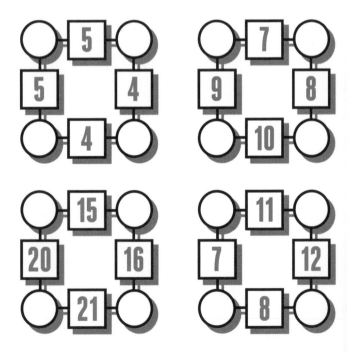

Fifteen Bottles

Starting with 15 empty bottles standing on the wall, you and one other player take turns to remove either one, two or three bottles. Whoever removes the last bottle loses the game. You make the first move by removing two bottles. Then how can you guarantee to win the game?

Number Squares 2

By looking at the existing numbers and their locations, can you work out what numbers should be in the blank squares?

1	0	1
1	1	1
1	0	2

7	3	7
5	8	6
7	4	7

	29	45
33		33
45	29	

Cocktails

Three old friends meet for cocktails at a hotel. Violet is wearing a red hat and always tells the truth, Rose is wearing a blue hat and always lies and Agatha is wearing a green hat and only tells the truth on Mondays. They each order a cocktail. One is red, one is blue and the other is green. Violet says, 'We all have drinks that are a different colour to our hats.' The woman with the green drink replies, 'Yes, Violet you're right.' Which day of the week is it?

TANGRAM 3

The seven yellow pieces have been arranged, without overlapping, to form the blue shape. Draw straight lines on the blue shape to show how they fit together.

MATHS SQUARE 2

Use the numbers 1 to 9 once only to fill in the blank squares to make the equations work vertically and horizontally (perform multiplication and division before addition and subtraction).

	x	8	+		73
/		/		+	
3	x		−		-1
+		x		−	
	x		+	4	34
8		24		4	

CIRCUIT BOARD 2

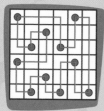

Connect adjacent squares horizontally or vertically to form a single closed path which passes through every square only once. Your path must change direction at every red dot and once between each red dot.

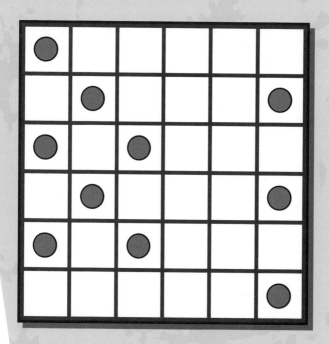

SHIKAKU 2

Divide the grid into a set of rectangles (including square rectangles if necessary), each containing one number and composed of that many squares

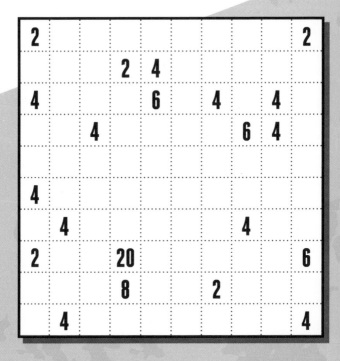

OUROBOROS 3

Fill every blank square with a letter by answering all the clues. The direction of each word is indicated by an arrow on its initial letter.

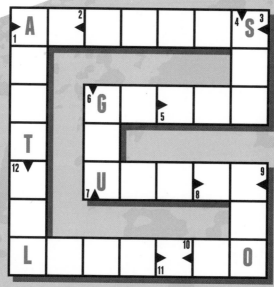

CLUES

1. Person who excels
2. Young trainee in the armed services or police force
3. Criticise severely
4. Latin prefix meaning 'half'
5. Component quantity of measurements used to sequence events
6. Brusque
7. Strong impulse
8. At an end
9. Short, explosive burst of breath
10. Middle of the brain
11. Open area of hills often covered with rough grass and heather
12. Call attention to indirectly

Poisoned Quiches

A greedy old billionaire has three delicious quiches delivered to his penthouse apartment. His loyal personal assistant warns him that two of the quiches have been laced with poison but he's too miserly and greedy to throw all three quiches away. So he gives the first quiche to his cat, the second quiche to his dog and keeps the third. His cat nibbles at its quiche and drops down dead, poisoned. So now the old billionaire knows that one of the remaining two quiches is safe to eat but he doesn't want to share any, so he snatches the quiche from the dog bowl and starts eating it because he now knows that this quiche is less likely to be poisoned than his own. Is his reasoning correct?

LOGPILE 3

Each number is the sum of the two directly below it. Fill in every blank circle with a positive whole number greater than 1 (no zeros).

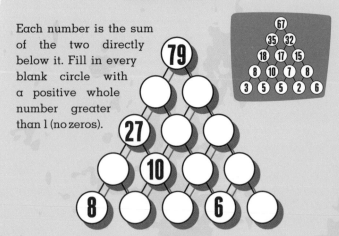

OLD LADY HANDBAGS 2

Solve the puzzle by giving every old lady her own handbag (mark with an x) horizontally or vertically adjacent to her. Handbags must not touch, even diagonally. The numbers indicate how many handbags are in each row or column.

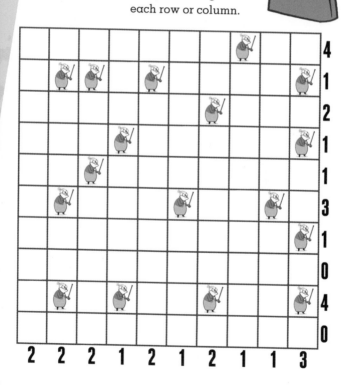

Golf Wordsearch

Q	G	V	R	I	U	L	E	Z	F	R	F	L	O	I	J
B	A	C	K	S	W	I	N	G	A	E	L	I	H	N	G
I	B	D	R	E	L	G	A	E	I	K	A	N	N	N	Y
U	S	P	D	I	L	P	G	O	R	N	G	K	L	R	V
K	O	G	P	K	L	O	A	W	W	U	O	S	I	Z	X
T	E	X	B	A	E	T	H	E	A	B	A	X	T	U	K
A	S	K	Y	T	T	I	Z	E	Y	G	L	O	V	E	D
E	W	O	H	E	W	R	D	D	Y	M	G	I	D	R	S
E	F	M	E	Z	E	W	W	R	B	K	S	A	N	D	E
F	I	H	X	T	T	U	V	D	I	C	F	P	A	H	W
C	F	G	T	B	S	J	C	N	I	B	L	I	S	S	Z
D	W	U	H	E	I	D	D	A	C	V	P	U	N	G	W
F	P	R	D	T	Y	P	E	W	D	A	O	J	B	B	F
L	F	H	E	R	E	H	Y	R	O	Z	L	T	V	J	B
Y	J	C	F	M	R	E	L	O	O	L	B	P	L	G	Q
G	I	A	F	G	U	S	N	H	W	V	S	D	S	S	X

Caddie	Eighteen	Club
Hole	Glove	Putter
Fairway	Divot	Wedge
Wood	Links	Backswing
Birdie	Tee	Eagle
Fade	Playoff	Flag
Sand	Bunker	

FUTOSHIKI 2

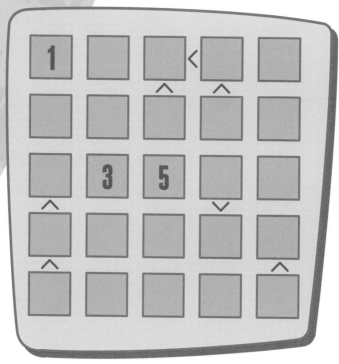

Fill every blank square so that each row and column contains the numbers 1, 2, 3, 4 and 5 with no repeats. An arrow indicates that the number in the square is greater than the adjacent number to which the arrow points.

Word Fill 3

Find a three-letter word that completes each trio of longer words:

1. PRO _ _ _ ION
INTU _ _ _ E
SUN _ _ _ HE

2. PRO _ _ _ EROLE
PRO _ _ _ WISE
BE _ _ _ TING

3. NE _ _ _ _ IATE
E _ _ _ _ IST
MAG _ _ _ _ Y

4. C _ _ _ _ IATE
G _ _ _ _ ITE
P _ _ _ _ DIAL

5. CA _ _ _ _ TE
MOU _ _ _ _ RAP
COR _ _ _ _ ED

6. SO _ _ _ _ SIST
CA _ _ _ _ HATE
S _ _ _ _ PAGE

DOMINOES 3

The numbers 0, 1, 2 and 3 can be arranged in 10 unique pairs. Find them here to solve the puzzle.

1	2	0	3	2
1	0	2	3	1
1	0	1	2	3
0	3	3	2	0

MATHS SQUARE 3

Use the numbers 1 to 9 once only to fill in the blank squares to make the equations work vertically and horizontally (perform multiplication and division before addition and subtraction).

	+		x	1	11
−		x		+	
5	−		/		3
−		+		x	
	+	3	x		25
-3		19		25	

57

The Thirteenth Hole

Two old golfers, Alastair and Hamish, were playing a round on a glorious summer afternoon in the Scottish Highlands. On the thirteenth hole, Alastair hooked his tee shot and his ball ended up in the lake. Hamish laughed and boasted, 'I bet you fifty pounds I can play the exact same shot, with the same club and same type of ball from the exact same place and even hook my swing shot without losing my ball.' His friend reckoned this was impossible so he accepted the bet. 'OK, then,' replied Hamish, 'let's meet here in six months' time, when I'll demonstrate my skills.' How did Hamish win his bet?

Coloured Dice Puzzle 3

If the blue die has a value of 12 and the green die has a value of 18, what value should you assign to the red die?

SUDOKU 3 – MEDIUM

Fill in all the blank squares. Each of the nine 3 x 3 square blocks must contain all the numbers 1–9, but each number can only appear once in the same row or column.

7		3	4	6				8
				1			6	
				7		3		
			7			9	2	6
	4			3	5			1
			8			4	5	3
				5		2		
				2			9	
5		2	9	8				7

PATH HUNTER 3

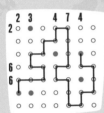

Draw a continuous line from one green dot to the other. You may move vertically or horizontally but NOT diagonally. Your line cannot pass through a red dot. The numbers tell you how many white or green dots your line passes through in that row or column.

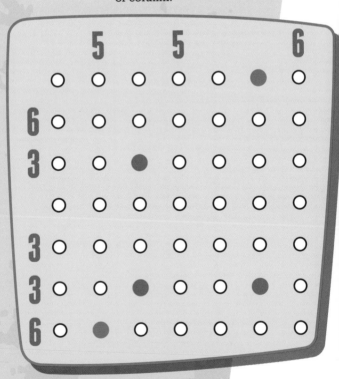

HITORI 2

Black out some of the cells in the grid so that each row and each column contains no duplicated numbers. Blacked out cells must not touch horizontally or vertically and all white cells must form one continuous area

4	5	2	5	1	5
2	1	5	3	5	5
5	5	3	2	4	1
1	2	4	5	3	5
5	3	4	1	6	4
4	6	5	2	2	5

SLITHERLINK 3

Connect adjacent corners horizontally or vertically to form a single closed path, with no extra branches. The path cannot cross itself. A number tells you how many lines surround that square. There is one unique solution.

			1	1	2	3
1		0		1		
2	3		3		1	
			2			
	1		0		1	1
		3		0		0
2	2	1	3			

LOGPILE 4

Each number is the sum of the two directly below it. Fill in every blank circle with a positive whole number greater than 1 (no zeros).

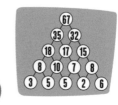

123
55
22
9   20
4   3

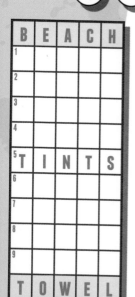

B	E	A	C	H
1				
2				
3				
4				
5 T	I	N	T	S
6				
7				
8				
9				
T	O	W	E	L

WORD LADDER 4

Change the word from BEACH to TOWEL via TINTS. Change one letter each time, so that every step forms a new word.

63

Mint Humbugs 3

Gladys made Bernard an offer he couldn't refuse.

'I bet you one packet of mint humbugs, that if you give me two packets of mint humbugs I promise I will give you three packets of mint humbugs in return.'

Should Bernard accept her bet?

Number Squares 3

By looking at the existing numbers and their locations, can you work out what numbers should be in the blank squares?

3	2	2
2	6	1
4	5	2

10	5	5
5	25	0
15	20	5

	120	-5
70	95	

Millie's Grandma

Millie's grandma is two years older than her mother.

How is this possible?

ISLANDS IN THE STREAM 2

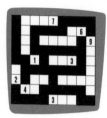

Shade some squares so that each number is inside a white island with that given number of squares. The white islands may only touch diagonally, the black 'stream' must be continuous (i.e. no shaded squares cut off on their own) and shaded areas may not form or exceed 2 x 2 squares.

						5		
	3				1			
						4		
		3						
						3		
		4						
			2				2	
		5						

LETTER FILL 4

Words on the same row must be completed using the same missing letter. Complete all eight rows to discover the hidden word.

IO_A	RI_E	_EAL	◯
L_EU	LA_N	A_DE	◯
SA_E	_ACE	SEE_	◯
B_LT	L_SS	M_LD	◯
_ICK	_ASH	HA_K	◯
CL_P	CL_Y	CR_P	◯
B_AN	OVE_	PAI_	◯
_EAP	S_AP	S_IP	◯

66

SHIKAKU 3

Divide the grid into a set of rectangles (including square rectangles if necessary), each containing one number and composed of that many squares

								2
	10		4					
4		4						
						20	4	
								4
2			2	4				
	5					2	4	
		3	2	4			2	
				8				
4		2					4	

TANGRAM 4

The seven yellow pieces have been arranged, without overlapping, to form the blue shape. Draw straight lines on the blue shape to show how they fit together.

3D Odd One Out 2

Which is the odd one out?

CRAZY OLD CAT LADY 3

A crazy old cat lady has nine cats. Each cat sleeps next to one or more cushions, scattered across a large tiled floor. Each cushion is numbered to indicate how many adjacent tiles contain a cat. Place a C where you deduce each cat is sleeping.

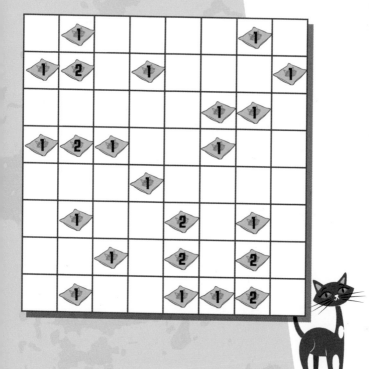

How Many Drops of Whisky?

How many drops of whisky can Arthur put in his empty
6oz hip flask?

Circle of Sweets

Florence has arranged all the sweets she has in a circle.
They are evenly spaced and the 8th sweet is directly
opposite the 20th sweet. How many sweets are there in
the circle?

DOMINOES 4

The numbers 0, 1, 2 and 3 can be
arranged in 10 unique pairs. Find
them here to solve the puzzle.

3	2	2	2	3
0	2	3	2	1
0	1	0	0	1
3	3	1	1	0

CIRCUIT BOARD 3

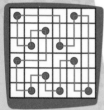

Connect adjacent squares horizontally or vertically to form a single closed path which passes through every square only once. Your path must change direction at every red dot and once between each red dot.

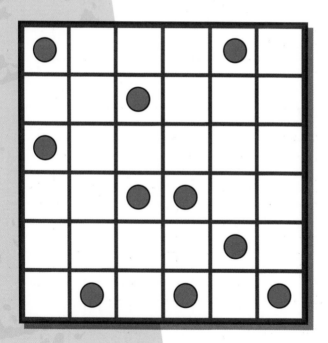

MONEY RUN

John has to meet his financial advisor to discuss an annuity. Can you help him reach her office before the next financial crisis?

MAGIC SQUARE 5

1	18	7	16
15	8	10	4
12	2	17	6
9	14	3	11

Fill in all the blank cells to form a magic square in which each column, row and diagonal adds up to the same number.

		15	
16			17
		20	
		8	14

CUTTING PATTERN

Take a square sheet of paper and fold it corner to corner three times to form this triangle:

Cut a square from the longest side.

When you open out the paper, which pattern will you see?

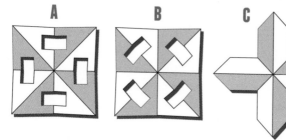

A   B   C

Knitting Wordsearch

C	E	T	X	E	Q	O	Y	B	P	R	S	E	H	S	P
H	G	Z	S	S	D	I	K	A	G	A	S	M	T	X	O
E	U	P	R	A	R	V	T	W	R	I	T	I	C	S	O
A	A	B	O	E	C	L	D	E	W	N	T	T	L	P	L
N	G	C	T	R	T	I	F	L	S	C	V	I	E	L	V
A	M	N	Y	C	Z	R	R	B	H	I	P	P	F	R	O
F	U	C	X	N	P	U	A	F	O	R	W	A	R	D	N
L	O	O	W	I	P	E	U	G	Y	C	W	T	M	Q	A
Q	U	C	Z	Y	L	L	L	B	S	R	P	B	I	N	D
B	I	P	Z	B	C	S	B	Y	F	I	P	Q	V	N	I
K	J	F	A	U	H	F	G	W	F	B	U	Q	J	M	K
S	X	C	Q	N	I	J	O	S	K	B	R	O	C	K	R
S	S	M	H	V	T	R	I	Y	N	I	L	Y	H	T	I
E	Y	Z	G	A	V	D	L	N	G	N	K	J	A	L	B
E	L	D	E	E	N	V	K	A	L	G	U	P	M	X	V
G	I	H	K	R	X	I	Z	R	A	E	W	T	I	N	K

Bind	Purl	Garter
Forward	Gauge	Cast
Pattern	Slip	Increase
Knitwear	Stitch	Purlwise
Yarn	Wool	Loop
Row	Needle	Ribbing
Knitwise	Cable	

FUTOSHIKI 3

Fill every blank square so that each row and column contains the numbers 1, 2, 3, 4 and 5 with no repeats. An arrow indicates that the number in the square is greater than the adjacent number to which the arrow points.

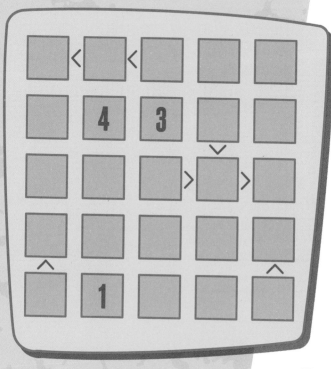

Number Series Puzzle 3

What number comes next in each sequence?

1) 300, 1200, 3600, 7200, 7200 . . .
2) 1, 4, 10, 22, 46 . . .

WORD LADDER 5

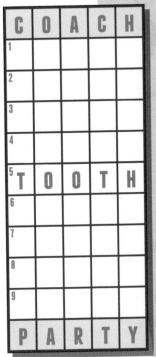

Change the word from COACH to PARTY via TOOTH. Change one letter each time, so that every step forms a new word.

OLD LADY HANDBAGS 3

Solve the puzzle by giving every old lady her own handbag (mark with an x) horizontally or vertically adjacent to her. Handbags must not touch, even diagonally. The numbers indicate how many handbags are in each row or column.

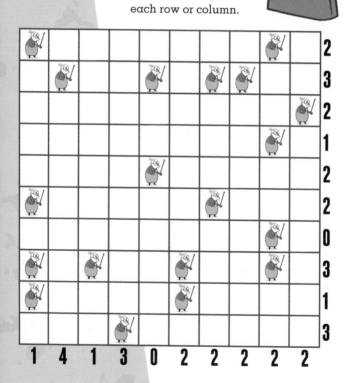

SUDOKU 4 – HARD

Fill in all the blank squares. Each of the nine 3 x 3 square blocks must contain all the numbers 1–9, but each number can only appear once in the same row or column.

	2	4				5	6	
6			2	5	3			8
				4				
1								2
	4						5	
	8						4	
7			5	2	6			4
			7	9	4			
	5						2	

3D Odd One Out 3

Which is the odd one out?

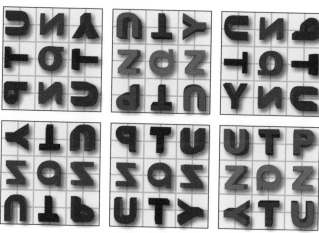

LOGPILE 5

Each number is the sum of the two directly below it. Fill in every blank circle with a positive whole number greater than 1 (no zeros).

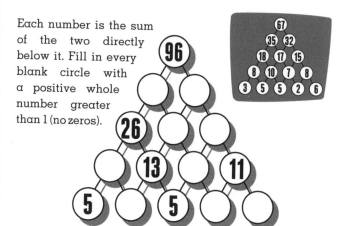

OUROBOROS 4

Fill every blank square with a letter by answering all the clues. The direction of each word is indicated by an arrow on its initial letter.

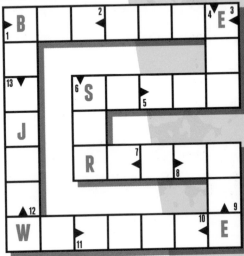

CLUES

1. Medieval term for a gold coin

2. Humped cattle originating in South Asia

3. Active stratovolcano on the east coast of Sicily

4. Ancient Jewish ascetic sect, authors of the Dead Sea Scrolls

5. Municipality on the Romsdal Peninsula in Norway

6. Raw or painful places on the body

7. Greek god of love

8. Single sheet of glass

9. Short sleep

10. Unmanned light tank used by the United States Army

11. Conical church tower

12. Small and elegant

13. Native American people from the area around Lake Superior

ARITHMAGON 4

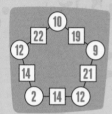

The number in each square is the sum of the numbers in the two adjacent circles. Fill in the missing numbers.

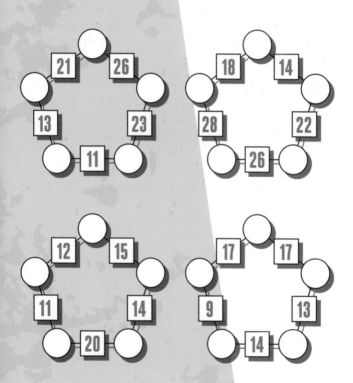

The Inheritance Race

Bertie has a son and a daughter. He sets them a challenge to see who will inherit his money, asking them to have a motorbike race. However, he adds a twist to the challenge: it's the one whose bike is slowest who will inherit.

The siblings set off, but after much swerving, wobbling and delaying, it's soon clear that this race may never be won. Eventually, Bertie's friend Bob asks the son and daughter to stop and he has a word with them, telling them how to resolve the stalemate. Then the son and daughter jump back on their bikes, rev up and race full-pelt for the finish line.

What did Bob tell them to do?

Number Squares 4

By looking at the existing numbers and their locations, can you work out what numbers should be in the blank squares?

2	1	3
7	5	6
9	8	4

8	4	12
28	20	24
36	32	16

152		228
532	380	456
	608	

Word Fill 4

Find a four-letter word that completes each trio of longer words:

1. PO _ _ _ _ ATE
INAT _ _ _ _ IVE
PENI _ _ _ _ IAL

2. B _ _ _ _ LET
DISG _ _ _ _ D
T _ _ _ _ ABLE

3. COM _ _ _ _ R
E _ _ _ _ PTIC
RECOM _ _ _ _

4. SEAP _ _ _ _
P _ _ _ _ TARY
WARP _ _ _ _

5. CROSS _ _ _ _
P _ _ _ _ TY
PULL _ _ _ _

6. A _ _ _ _ NESS
IM _ _ _ _ IAL
BI _ _ _ _ ITE

ISLANDS IN THE STREAM 3

Shade some squares so that each number is inside a white island with that given number of squares. The white islands may only touch diagonally, the black 'stream' must be continuous (i.e. no shaded squares cut off on their own) and shaded areas may not form or exceed 2 x 2 squares.

						6		
							3	
		2		4				
				2		3		
	6							
		6						

DOMINOES 5

The numbers 0, 1, 2, 3 and 4 can be arranged in 15 unique pairs. Find them here to solve the puzzle.

2	0	1	1	3	2
3	2	4	3	4	4
0	1	4	0	3	2
3	3	1	0	1	2
0	0	4	2	4	1

TANGRAM 5

The seven yellow pieces have been arranged, without overlapping, to form the blue shape. Draw straight lines on the blue shape to show how they fit together.

HITORI 3

Black out some of the cells in the grid so that each row and each column contains no duplicated numbers. Blacked out cells must not touch horizontally or vertically and all white cells must form one continuous area

2	5	3	6	2	1
2	3	1	6	2	5
3	1	4	2	4	5
5	3	6	3	2	4
1	6	4	5	3	2
5	4	5	1	5	5

Coloured Dice Puzzle 4

If the blue die has a value of 234 and the red die has a value of 204, what value should you assign to the green die?

MATHS SQUARE 4

Use the numbers 1 to 9 once only to fill in the blank squares to make the equations work vertically and horizontally (perform multiplication and division before addition and subtraction).

	x		−	5	31
+		x		+	
6	x		+		55
x		/		+	
	−	2	+		2
15		16		15	

87

SLITHERLINK 4

Connect adjacent corners horizontally or vertically to form a single closed path, with no extra branches. The path cannot cross itself. A number tells you how many lines surround that square. There is one unique solution.

		1	1	2		
2			2		1	1
1	1	3		1		3
1			1			1
1		0		1	0	2
1	0		1			3
		1	2	2		

SUDOKU 5 – HARD

2	9	5	7	4	3	8	6	1
4	3	1	8	6	5	9	2	7
8	7	6	1	9	2	5	4	3
3	8	7	4	5	9	2	1	6
6	1	2	3	8	7	4	9	5
5	4	9	2	1	6	7	3	8
7	6	3	5	2	4	1	8	9
9	2	8	6	7	1	3	5	4
1	5	4	9	3	8	6	7	2

Fill in all the blank squares. Each of the nine 3 x 3 square blocks must contain all the numbers 1–9, but each number can only appear once in the same row or column.

	6			2			4	
	9			4			8	
8	4			3			6	9
				1				
		1		5		7		
			3		9			
	1	6				8	5	
	5						3	
		3		6		4		

YOUNG AT HEART

Answers

Pg 4
CRUISE SHIP LADDER PUZZLE
None, because the ship floats.

RED COAT, BLUE COAT
The liar must be wearing a blue coat. If the person with the red coat speaks first, the other person must be wearing a blue coat and lies. If the person wearing the blue coat speaks first, the other person must be wearing a red coat and tells the truth.

CLOCK THIS
50 degrees. There are 30 degrees between each hour, but the hour hand travels 10 degrees past the 2 during the twenty minutes.

Pg 5
CRAZY OLD CAT LADY 1

Pg 6
SLITHERLINK 1

Pg 7
MAGIC SQUARE 1

1	12	6	16
15	7	9	4
11	2	17	5
8	14	3	10

WORD LADDER 1

Pg 8
ARITHMAGON 1

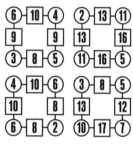

Pg 10
GRANDSON OR GRANDDAUGHTER?

There are only four possible options: BB, BG, GB, GG, each with a 1 in 4 probability.
If one is a girl, the BB option can be eliminated, leaving three options, each with a 1 in 3 probability: GG, BG, GB. So now the probability that the other grandchild is a boy is 2 in 3 or 66.666 per cent.

MINT HUMBUGS 1

Bernard can eat 1.3333 packets every minute and Gladys can eat 0.6666 packets every minute. So they eat 2 packets between them every minute. So it takes them six minutes to eat twelve packets.

SAY WHAT YOU SEE

111221 (Each number describes the previous one; in this case the previous number was 'one one, one two, two ones'.)

Pg 11
OUROBOROS 1

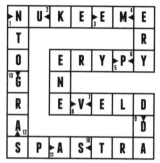

1. nuke	6. Pyrene	11. astra
2. unto	7. venery	12. argot
3. emery	8. veld	13. grasp
4. meek	9. dart	
5. pyre	10. saps	

Pg 12
SUDOKU 1

7	4	5	2	1	9	6	8	3
2	3	8	6	7	4	9	5	1
1	9	6	3	8	5	4	7	2
5	1	9	7	6	3	2	4	8
8	2	3	9	4	1	7	6	5
6	7	4	8	5	2	1	3	9
9	6	2	5	3	7	8	1	4
3	8	1	4	9	6	5	2	7
4	5	7	1	2	8	3	9	6

Pg 13
LETTER FILL 1
VETERANS

Pg 14
ISLANDS IN THE STREAM 1

Pg 15
TANGRAM 1

LOGPILE 1

Pg 16
FLOATING OR SINKING?

When the coin sinks it will displace only its volume of water. If it sits on the floating air mattress, it will displace its weight of water, which is greater, so the water level will rise slightly higher.

CHEAP HOTEL

The Lone Ranger's spare horse was called Tuesday (Silver was on holiday) and he arrived at the hotel on Thursday.

COLOURED DICE PUZZLE 1

12: the value is the sum of the faces that aren't visible, i.e. 6 + 4 + 2.

Pg 17
SKIP TO THE LOO

Pg 18
FUTOSHIKI 1

3	4	2	5	1
4	5	1	3	2
5	2	3	1	4
1	3	4	2	5
2	1	5	4	3

Pg 19
ARITHMAGON 2

7 – 10 – 3	12 – 14 – 2
16	8	20	10
9 – 14 – 5	8 – 16 – 8

1 – 7 – 6	5 – 6 – 1
6	7	7	6
5 – 6 – 1	2 – 7 – 5

Pg 20
CRAZY OLD CAT LADY 2

Pg 21
MAGIC SQUARE 2

14	7	17	2
15	4	12	9
3	18	6	13
8	11	5	16

WORD LADDER 2

C	L	E	A	N
C	L	E	A	T
C	H	E	A	T
C	H	E	A	P
C	H	E	E	P
S	H	E	E	P
S	H	E	E	T

Pg 22
MISSING INGREDIENT
Water.

DING DONG
11 seconds. There is a one second gap between each strike.

NUMBER SERIES 1
1) 41 (the sum of the previous number and the number three places behind)
2) 3263442 (the number multiplied by 1 more than itself)

Pg 23
PATH HUNTER 1

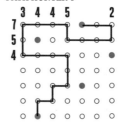

Pg 24
OUROBOROS 2

1. emir	5. wares	9. uptime
2. melanite	6. awe	10.push
3. etude	7. Sikh	11.remit
4. uteri	8. kiss	12.retina

Pg 25
DOMINOES 1

3	3	2	1	1
1	0	1	0	3
2	0	2	2	3
1	3	0	2	0

MISSING FISH
Only three people went fishing: a father, his son and his grandson – two fathers and two sons.

93

YOUNG AT HEART

Pg 26
LETTER FILL 2
PRIMEVAL

Pg 27
CIRCUIT BOARD 1

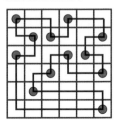

Pg 28
WEDDING PLANNER

Richard

Sandra — Jeannette

Robert — Elizabeth

Joe

NUMBER SQUARES 1

Each box displays the number of adjacent squares.

3	5	3
5	8	5
3	5	3

TWO ROPES
Light both ends of one rope and only one end of the other. The first rope will burn out in 30 minutes. At this precise moment, light the other end of the second rope. This will burn out in 15 minutes. Total time elapsed: 45 minutes.

Pg 29
OLD LADY HANDBAGS 1

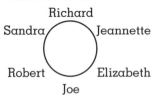

Pg 30
3D ODD ONE OUT 1

MAGIC SQUARE 3

16	13	10	3
6	7	12	17
11	18	5	8
9	4	15	14

Pg 31
OLD AGE WORDSEARCH

S	C	H	S	L	G	A	U	F	R	Y	L	I	M	A	F
J	E	I	J	W	O	Z	C	L	F	P	D	E	G	A	G
B	J	N	N	C	L	Y	V	O	S	A	V	O	J	C	D
G	M	P	I	N	F	E	L	G	B	I	E	E	L	E	S
P	A	N	G	O	N	D	G	E	R	E	M	Y	E	E	H
N	P	L	N	B	R	C	J	N	Q	H	V	O	S	U	T
S	I	T	N	R	H	T	R	A	O	L	T	S	Y	M	L
D	V	K	Q	W	S	I	R	C	C	L	A	G	X	V	A
C	F	H	Z	U	M	E	V	A	F	S	R	U	A	E
A	R	V	E	E	B	L	D	Q	G	R	T	N	F	I	H
Q	K	T	M	P	P	K	J	D	D	E	T	Q	E	Q	B
W	W	O	J	R	O	F	G	M	H	T	W	C	V	P	S
J	R	N	D	M	L	O	D	C	Z	I	C	N	K	C	Z
Y	R	Y	R	U	V	U	C	T	M	R	O	D	W	R	Q
E	F	E	T	R	A	V	E	L	R	E	T	T	H	M	A
Z	J	X	A	K	T	R	I	P	S	G	E	Q	O	F	K

94

Pg 32
WORD FILL 1
1. OLD   4. AND
2. TAR   5. RUB
3. ACE   6. DEN

Pg 33
SLITHERLINK 2

			1		1	2
1	2		1	1		1
	0	2		3		1
0		2		2		1
0		2		1	2	
1		1	1		2	2
0	2		2			

Pg 34
THE PRIEST AND THE VICAR
Thursday. The priest can only make his statement on Monday (lying about telling the truth on Sunday) or Thursday (telling the truth about lying on Wednesday). The vicar can only make his statement on Thursday (lying about telling the truth on Wednesday) or Sunday (telling the truth about lying on Saturday).

MINT HUMBUGS 2
He doesn't need any extra. The three great-grandchildren will eat 100 packets in 100 minutes (they eat one packet a minute).

COLOURED DICE PUZZLE 2
12: the value is the bottom face multiplied by the top face, i.e. 3 x 4.

Pg 35
TANGRAM 2

MATHS SQUARE 1

3	+	2	−	1	4
x		−		+	
4	x	5	−	9	11
−		+		−	
7	+	8	+	6	21
5		5		4	

Pg 36
DOMINOES 2

3	1	1	1	3
1	3	0	0	2
2	2	1	2	0
2	0	0	3	3

LOGPILE 2

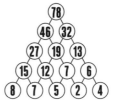

Pg 37
HITORI 1

5	6	2	4	1	
	5		1		6
6	1	4	2	3	5
	3	5		2	1
3	4	1	5		2
1		6		5	4

Pg 38
LETTER FILL 3
ENDURING

Pg 39
MEDICATION MISSION

Pg 40
PADLOCKED CHEST
Brian padlocks his chest and sends it to Derek. Derek locks the chest with his own padlock and sends the chest back to Brian (so now it has two padlocks). Brian removes his own padlock and sends the chest back to Derek, who can open it because now it is only protected by Derek's padlock.

POTTING CHALLENGE
She has 4 seeds and three pots.

NUMBER SERIES 2
1) 60¾ (each number is the previous number x 1.5)
2) 16½ (the sum of half the previous number and the number behind that one)

Pg41
SUDOKU 2

9	1	3	5	2	4	6	7	8
8	7	6	9	3	1	2	5	4
2	4	5	8	7	6	9	3	1
3	2	9	1	8	7	4	6	5
4	5	8	2	6	3	7	1	9
7	6	1	4	9	5	8	2	3
5	3	2	7	4	8	1	9	6
1	9	4	6	5	2	3	8	7
6	8	7	3	1	9	5	4	2

Pg 42
SHIKAKU 1

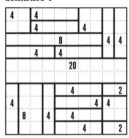

Pg 43
WORD FILL 2

1. TEN
2. RAG
3. TOE
4. JAM
5. FIR
6. LOG

Pg 44
MAGIC SQUARE 4

13	11	18	8
20	6	15	9
7	17	12	14
10	16	5	19

WORD LADDER 3

B	R	E	A	D
B	R	E	A	K
B	L	E	A	K
B	L	E	A	T
B	L	E	S	T
B	L	A	S	T
B	O	A	S	T
T	O	A	S	T

Pg 45
PATH HUNTER 2

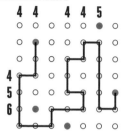

Pg 46
ARITHMAGON 3

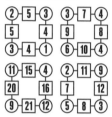

Pg 47
FIFTEEN BOTTLES
Removing two bottles with your first turn leaves 13 bottles remaining. Then make sure that the sum of your opponent's bottles plus yours always adds up to four (e.g. if he removes 1, you take 3; if he takes two, you take two). He will always end up with the last bottle.

NUMBER SQUARES 2
Each number is generated by taking the number in the same position in the previous table and adding

44	29	45
33	54	33
45	29	46

the numbers in any rows, columns or diagonals of three of which it is a part.

COCKTAILS
Violet's statement is correct because she only tells the truth. Rose can't be the woman with the green drink because she always lies (so she would have told Violet she was wrong), so Agatha must have the green drink and is telling the truth, so it's Monday.

Pg 48
TANGRAM 3

MATHS SQUARE 2

9	x	8	+	1	73
/		/		+	
3	x	2	-	7	-1
+		x		-	
5	x	6	+	4	34
8		24		4	

Pg 49
CIRCUIT BOARD 2

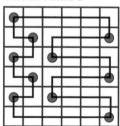

Pg 50
SHIKAKU 2

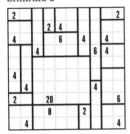

Pg 51
OUROBOROS 3

1. ace
2. cadet
3. slate
4. semi
5. time
6. gruff
7. urge
8. up
9. puff
10. medulla
11. moor
12. allude

Pg 52
POISONED QUICHES

Yes. Initially, the probability that the billionaire has the safe quiche is 1 in 3. So he is twice as likely to have a poisoned quiche (since there are two pets and only one of him). However, once it is known that the cat's quiche has been poisoned, the dog's quiche becomes the safest option.

Say you ran the scenario 99 times, then the odds are that the billionaire would be holding the safe quiche every 1 in 3 occasions and so swapping would be bad on those 33 occasions. However the odds are that the billionaire would

be holding a poisoned quiche on the other 2 in 3 occasions, and so swapping would be good on those 66 occasions. So on average, swapping is the best move in two-thirds of the scenarios, no matter how many times you repeat the experiment.

LOGPILE 3

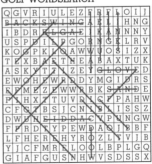

Pg 53
OLD LADY HANDBAGS 2

Pg 54
GOLF WORDSEARCH

Pg 55
FUTOSHIKI 2

1	4	2 <	3	5
3	1	4	5	2
2	3	5	4	1
4	5	1	2	3
5	2	3	1	4

Pg 56
WORD FILL 3

1. BAT   4. RAN
2. FIT   5. SET
3. GOT   6. LIP

Pg 57
DOMINOES 3

1	2	0	3	2
1	0	2	3	1
1	0	1	2	3
0	3	3	2	0

MATHS SQUARE 3

9	+	2	x	1	11
-		x		+	
5	-	8	/	4	3
-		+		x	
7	+	3	x	6	25
-3		19		25	

Pg 58
THIRTEENTH HOLE
In six months' time it would be winter and the lake would be frozen.

COLOURED DICE PUZZLE 3
8: the value is the top face multiplied by the sum of the other visible faces, i.e. 1 x (3 + 5).

Pg 59
SUDOKU 3

7	9	3	4	6	2	5	1	8
4	5	8	3	1	9	7	6	2
2	6	1	5	7	8	3	4	9
8	3	5	7	4	1	9	2	6
6	4	9	2	3	5	8	7	1
1	2	7	8	9	6	4	5	3
9	7	6	1	5	3	2	8	4
3	8	4	6	2	7	1	9	5
5	1	2	9	8	4	6	3	7

Pg 60
PATH HUNTER 3

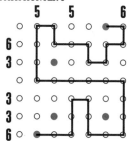

Pg 61
HITORI 2

4		2	5	1	
2	1		3		5
	5	3	2	4	1
1	2	4		3	
5	3		1	6	4
	6	5		2	

99

YOUNG AT HEART

Pg 62
SLITHERLINK 3

			1	1	2	3
1		0		1		
2	3		3		1	
			2			
	1		0		1	1
		3		0		0
2	2	1	3			

Pg 63
LOGPILE 4

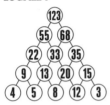

WORD LADDER 4

B	E	A	C	H
B	E	N	C	H
T	E	N	C	H
T	E	N	T	H
T	E	N	T	S
T	I	N	T	S
T	I	N	E	S
T	O	N	E	S
T	O	N	E	D
T	O	W	E	D
T	O	W	E	L

Pg 64
MINT HUMBUGS 3
No. If Bernard gives two packets and Gladys gives nothing back, she loses the bet and must give

Bernard one packet, so he has lost one packet overall. However, if Gladys wins the bet by giving Bernard three packets, he must give her one packet. So Bernard stands either to lose a packet or break even.

NUMBER SQUARES 3

45	20	20
20	120	-5
70	95	20

Each number is generated by taking the number in the same position in the previous table, subtracting 1 and then multiplying by 5.

MILLIE'S GRANDMA
Her father's mother is two years older than Millie's mother.

Pg 65
ISLANDS IN THE STREAM 2

Pg 66
LETTER FILL 4
TIMEWORN

Pg 67
SHIKAKU 3

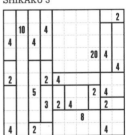

Pg 68
TANGRAM 4

3D ODD ONE OUT 2

Pg 69
CRAZY OLD CAT LADY 3

C	◆				◆	◆	C
◆	②		◆				◆
		C				◆	◆
◆	◆	◆			◆	②	C
C			◆				
	◆		C	②			◆
	◆		②	C	②		
C	◆			◆	◆	②	C

Pg 70
HOW MANY DROPS OF WHISKY?
One. After the first drop the hip flask is no longer empty.

CIRCLE OF SWEETS
There are 26 sweets. If the 8th sweet is opposite the 20th sweet, then the 14th sweet must be an equal distance from both of them, since 20 minus 14 = 6 and 14 minus 8 = 6. So the 26th sweet must be an equal distance from both of them on the other side of the circle.

DOMINOES 4

3	2	2	2	3
0	2	3	2	1
0	1	0	0	1
3	3	1	1	0

Pg 71
CIRCUIT BOARD 3

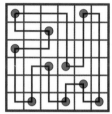

Pg 72
MONEY RUN

Pg 73
MAGIC SQUARE 5

4	18	15	11
16	10	5	17
9	13	20	6
19	7	8	14

YOUNG AT HEART

CUTTING PATTERN

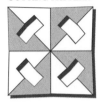

Pg 74
KNITTING WORDSEARCH

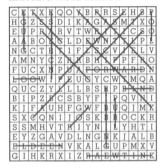

Pg 75
FUTOSHIKI 3

2 <	3 <	4	1	5
1	4	3	5	2
3	2	5 >	4 >	1
4	5	1	2	3
5	1	2	3	4

Pg 76
NUMBER SERIES 3
1) 0 (the previous number multiplied by n, where n decreases by one each time)

2) 94 (add 1 and multiply by 2)

WORD LADDER 5

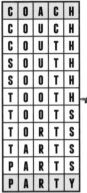

C	O	A	C	H
C	O	U	C	H
C	O	U	T	H
S	O	U	T	H
S	O	O	T	H
T	O	O	T	H
T	O	O	T	S
T	O	R	T	S
T	A	R	T	S
P	A	R	T	S
P	A	R	T	Y

Pg 77
OLD LADY HANDBAGS 3

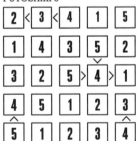

Pg 78
SUDOKU 4

3	2	4	1	7	8	5	6	9
6	7	9	2	5	3	4	1	8
8	1	5	6	4	9	2	7	3
1	6	3	4	8	5	7	9	2
9	4	2	3	6	7	8	5	1
5	8	7	9	1	2	3	4	6
7	9	8	5	2	6	1	3	4
2	3	1	7	9	4	6	8	5
4	5	6	8	3	1	9	2	7

Pg 79
3D ODD ONE OUT 3

LOGPILE 5

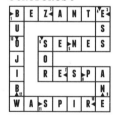

Pg 80
OUROBOROS 4

1. bezant
2. zebu
3. Etna
4. Essenes
5. Nesset
6. sores
7. Eros
8. pane
9. nap
10. ripsaw
11. spire
12. bijou
13. Ojibwa

Pg 81
ARITHMAGON 4

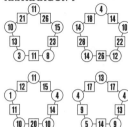

Pg 82
THE INHERITANCE RACE
He told them to swap bikes. This means they can now race to the finishing line to try to beat their own bike and inherit Bertie's money.

NUMBER SQUARES 4

152	76	228
532	380	456
684	608	304

Each number is generated by taking the number in the same position in the previous table and multiplying it by one less than the number in the centre square.

Pg83
WORD FILL 4
1. TENT
2. RACE
3. PILE
4. LANE
5. OVER
6. PART

Pg 84
ISLANDS IN THE STREAM 3

YOUNG AT HEART

Pg 85
DOMINOES 5

2	0	1	1	3	2
3	2	4	3	4	4
0	1	4	0	3	2
3	3	1	0	1	2
0	0	4	2	4	1

TANGRAM 5

Pg 86
HITORI 3

2	5	3	6		1
	3	1		2	5
3	1		2	4	
5		6	3		4
1	6	4	5	3	2
	4		1	5	

Pg 87
COLOURED DICE PUZZLE 4

204: the value is the sum of its faces that aren't visible multiplied by the sum of the visible faces of the other two dice, i.e. 12 x 17.

MATHS SQUARE 4

9	x	4	–	5	31
+		x		+	
6	x	8	+	7	55
x		/		+	
1	–	2	+	3	2
15		16		15	

Pg 88
SLITHERLINK 4

Pg 89
SUDOKU 5

3	6	7	9	2	8	1	4	5
1	9	2	5	4	6	3	8	7
8	4	5	7	3	1	2	6	9
6	7	9	8	1	4	5	2	3
4	3	1	6	5	2	7	9	8
5	2	8	3	7	9	6	1	4
7	1	6	4	9	3	8	5	2
2	5	4	1	8	7	9	3	6
9	8	3	2	6	5	4	7	1